SECRETS
OF A
SCOTTISH ISLE

Books by Erica Ruth Neubauer

MURDER AT THE MENA HOUSE

MURDER AT WEDGEFIELD MANOR

DANGER ON THE ATLANTIC

INTRIGUE IN ISTANBUL

SECRETS OF A SCOTTISH ISLE

Novellas

MURDER UNDER THE MISTLETOE

Published by Kensington Publishing Corp.

SECRETS OF A SCOTTISH ISLE

ERICA RUTH NEUBAUER

KENSINGTON
PUBLISHING CORP.

www.kensingtonbooks.com

KENSINGTON BOOKS are published by

Kensington Publishing Corp.
900 Third Ave.
New York, NY 10022

All Kensington titles, imprints and distributed lines are available at special quantity discounts for bulk purchases for sales promotion, premiums, fund-raising, educational or institutional use. Special book excerpts or customized printings can also be created to fit specific needs. For details, write or phone the office of the Kensington Special Sales Manager: Kensington Publishing Corp., 900 Third Ave., New York, NY, 10022. Attn. Special Sales Department. Phone: 1-800-221-2647.

The K with book logo Reg. US TM & Pat. Off.

Library of Congress Control Number: 2023949855

ISBN: 978-1-4967-4118-9
First Kensington Hardcover Edition: April 2024

ISBN: 978-1-4967-4120-2 (e-book)

10 9 8 7 6 5 4 3 2 1

Printed in the United States of America

For Mike B.
To the bones.

CHAPTER ONE

The black hood that had been placed over my head felt suffocating, even though I could actually breathe just fine. They had also wrapped a rope around my waist three times, which bothered me nearly as much as not being able to see anything—which was the point, of course. Both made me uncomfortable in a way that was visceral, which was likely the intended purpose. I knew where the members of the Order of the Golden Dawn were because I could hear their voices as they chanted, but I couldn't see what they were doing.

And the whole reason I was here was to keep an eye on them.

Someone came forward to fetch me, smelling strongly of incense. I thought that my other senses were probably heightened because I couldn't see, but it was also possible that the person just smelled that strongly. It wasn't a pleasant aroma. Whoever it was sprinkled my head with something; I could feel little drops hitting the black hood over my head. "Child of Earth, arise and enter the Path of Darkness."

It was a man. Not Robert Nightingale, the man I was supposed to be investigating, but one of the other "officers" of this order. I hadn't quite caught all their names before I was brought into the abbey where this ceremony was being conducted.

I got up off my knees, with some difficulty since the floor was hard stone and I couldn't see anything to balance myself. I was going to have bruises on my knees and shins, that was for certain. The man took my arm and led me forward. They all were silent, and I remembered that this was where I was supposed to recite the lines that I'd studied.

"My soul is wandering in darkness, seeking the light of occult knowledge," I said, stumbling a little over the words. I'd worked hard at memorizing them, but they simply didn't come naturally to me.

I felt my hand being placed on something that was hard and felt triangular in shape. Now it was Nightingale's voice asking a series of questions.

"Do you promise to keep secret everything in relation to the order, to maintain kind and benevolent relations with all the fraters and sorors of this order? Do you promise to neither copy nor allow to be copied any manuscript lest our secret knowledge be revealed?" Nightingale paused dramatically.

"I do." I felt uncomfortable saying the words, feeling as though I was at some kind of dark wedding and had just bound myself to something sinister.

"Do you promise to not suffer yourself to be hypnotized or mesmerized or placed in a state of passivity, to never use occult powers for any evil purpose, and to persevere through the ceremony of admission?"

"I do." I had a lot of questions about everything he'd just said, though now obviously wasn't the time to ask. I would try to find out later what all of that meant.

"Do you swear that, if you violate any of these oaths, you will voluntarily submit to a deadly and hostile stream of power set in motion by the chiefs of the order, by which you should fall slain and paralyzed without visible weapon as if slain by a lightning flash?"

This time, I was the one who paused, since I was uncomfortable agreeing to any of that, but I forced myself to do it anyway since it was what needed to be done for the job. "I do," I ground out, hoping that my voice sounded normal and that none of the members had noticed my hesitation.

But now I felt something heavy, cold, and metal at the back of my neck. It was there for only an instant and then was gone, but it was long enough that my blood ran cold. I'd been assured that there wasn't any sort of blood sacrifice or even bloodletting associated with this order, but just how certain could I be? We'd had very little time to prepare for this assignment before I dove right in, and I felt as though I was woefully unprepared.

I was bodily turned, then my hood was suddenly removed, only to find that I was staring at the point of a sword glinting in the light from a lamp held by the chief of ceremony. Then I was in darkness once more and being turned yet again. I was stopped, seemingly faced in the opposite direction, and my hood was again removed. This time, I was being threatened with a large scepter that had wings sprouting from either side at the top. I had only a moment to register what I was seeing before my hood was pulled down tight again.

I was getting quite tired of this back and forth with the hood. Not to mention being spun in circles.

Then I heard Nightingale's voice again. "I come in the power of light. I come in the light of wisdom. I come in the mercy of the light. The light hath healing in its wings."

Voices all around me joined in, as someone urged me back to my knees. It took all I had not to grumble about getting back down onto the stone floor—at least with the hood they couldn't see me grimacing. "Inheritor of a dying world, we call thee to the living beauty. Wanderer in the wild darkness, we call thee to the gentle light," the voices intoned. I noticed that someone to my left was clearly tone-deaf.

I was once again helped to my feet by someone grasping

my left arm, and my hood was removed, I hoped for the last time. I found that I was now standing under a circle of wands and swords, held by the various members gathered around me.

Nightingale stood before me, draped in a robe the color of fresh blood. "Child of earth, long hast thou dwelt in darkness. Quit the night and seek the day."

My first thought was that I had, in fact, been in darkness too long, because of the hood they'd placed on my head. But I held my tongue and tried to appear somber.

"I consecrate thee with fire." A man in a black robe stepped forward and waved incense at me. I did my best not to cough.

"I purify thee with water." A woman also wearing a black robe stepped forward and made the sign of the cross on my forehead with a wet thumb before sprinkling my head three times with more water.

Then Nightingale clapped loudly, once, making his final pronouncement. "Fortier et Recte, we receive thee into the Order of the Golden Dawn."

And with that, I was initiated.

CHAPTER TWO

"Fortier et Recte is an interesting choice for a name," Robert Nightingale said to me afterward. I didn't have anything to say in defense of my initiate name, but Dion Fortune came to my rescue, sparing me from having to make up something on the spot.

"I think it's a wonderful choice. In Latin, it means 'bravely and justly,' and aren't those qualities we should all strive for?" Dion's stance was slightly aggressive, and I got the feeling that she and Nightingale butted heads frequently.

Still wearing robes, the members of the order—myself now included—were milling around the medieval abbey church where my ceremony had taken place. It was cold—the stone building was unheated, although it had been restored in the last decade, so at least it had a roof. Much of the rest of the buildings at this ancient site were still in ruins, however, and I was grateful for what cover we had as it was March and the temperature on this remote Scottish island bordered on something just short of frigid. During the day, the perennially overcast sky didn't help much either. I was wearing heavy clothing beneath my white robe—the color for an initiate—but even with my woolens, I longed to get back to my small room with its cozy fire.

I also wished dearly that my fiancé Redvers were here with

me, but we were trying to ensure that we weren't seen together by any members of the order while on the island. The
islanders themselves would obviously need to see Redvers,
and perhaps even the two of us together, but Golden Dawn
members were best avoided so that no one reported back to
Nightingale that I wasn't here alone. I needed to get close to
Nightingale and learn everything I could about the man and
his occult activities, and that was best accomplished if I didn't
have a mysterious paramour lurking about the island.

And Nightingale knew who Redvers was. Which was the
reason why I was the clandestine operative and very much on
my own within this group.

"It's fortunate that you were able to join us on Iona and
do your initiation ceremony so close to the solstice," Nightingale was saying. "The island itself has mystical powers.
The veil is thin here, you know."

I got the feeling that this was a man who loved to explain
things to people, especially to women. Unfortunately, I was a
captive audience, so I nodded while Dion rolled her eyes and
moved away from us to join another group of members clad
in robes of various colors. I found that I was jealous of the
woman and her easy escape, but reminded myself that my
goal here was to do exactly what I was doing, so I stayed
with Nightingale and nodded some more.

"Ordinarily, we would require that you be a much higher
grade to join us for the solstice ritual, but you do come highly
recommended by Madame Blavatsky in America." Nightingale's blue eyes regarded me for a moment. Out of the corner
of my eye, I saw that the name Blavatsky had caught the attention of a few of the members nearby, but Nightingale was
on to his next question before I could wonder about it. "Why
didn't you initiate there?"

It was easy to recall the story I'd practiced over and over in
my head in case this exact question came up. "I felt it would
be more powerful to have my initiation with the original

chapter. And especially in a place that has so much power in and of itself, as you said."

Nightingale sniffed, apparently satisfied with this answer. He'd seemed to accept my letter of introduction when I'd met the group here on the island as well, even though it was entirely forged, as was my backstory. Since Blavatsky was still in America, we'd hoped I could find out all I needed to know about Nightingale before he tried to contact her, which he might decide to do if I wasn't convincing enough. With that foremost in my mind, I decided it would be smart to direct the conversation away from myself and my dubious occult connections.

"What can you tell me about the veil here? How do we know it's particularly thin in this place?" I wanted to ask how the group was able to conduct any sort of ceremony in a Christian chapel—even after hours—since it felt distinctly sacrilegious, but I kept to safer questions.

Nightingale launched into a long explanation of the island's history, including St. Columba and early Christianity, while I tuned out, watching the other members out of the corner of my eye. They weren't the object of my investigation, but I was still curious about the type of people who would join an order like this.

Dion Fortune was quite high in the group, part of the inner circle. It had come as a surprise to me that women were accepted into the order at all, let alone allowed to become high-ranking officials. She was a tall woman, broad in stature with equally broad features. She eschewed any type of ornamentation or makeup and might have been considered plain except for the intelligence in her sparkling brown eyes. They were the focal point of her face.

The only other woman present was Netta Fornario, a quiet woman in her twenties with frizzy black hair and so many large necklaces displayed on her chest that I wondered whether they hurt her neck. She had a scattered air about her, as though she was always thinking of otherworldly things, which I supposed that she was. Netta and I were staying at the same cottage and had shared a few words over breakfast that morning, but I wasn't sure any of what we'd spoken about had actually registered with her.

The rest of the individuals present were men. The order allowed women to join, even encouraged it, but the membership was still predominantly made up of men. And of the men present, the only other one that I recognized was William Butler Yeats. He'd won the Nobel Prize in Literature only a few years earlier, and I found it hard to believe the man was involved with this type of group. I hadn't spoken to him, but found my eyes repeatedly drawn to him; his gray hair was slightly long and slicked back, and his Irish lilt was easy to pick out from the crowd, as were the little round glasses perched on his nose.

I tuned back in to what Nightingale was telling me, pausing the agreeable bobbing of my head, just in time. "And it's fortunate that you've joined this faction of the order."

This caught my interest. "As opposed to?"

Nightingale pursed his lips. "Mathers's wife, Mina, has taken her group—smaller than ours, of course—in a direction that I think her late husband would find very disagreeable. I'm surprised you haven't heard about it."

I knew from my preliminary research that Mathers had started the Order of the Golden Dawn, but it sounded like there had been a great deal of infighting and that the larger order had broken into factions. It didn't have any direct effect on my investigation, so I'd only heard the barest sketch of what had happened and why.

"I heard some rumblings, but I wanted to get your expert take on it. Were you close with her late husband?"

Nightingale's chest puffed up. "Very. I was his right-hand man, you know. I moved up in the order more quickly than anyone ever has before. Only took me a matter of months to move through the ranks and become a chief. I found the skills easy to master, but I'm a special case. You shouldn't expect to advance so quickly."

"That's quite impressive," I said. Not because it was, but because that was what he wanted to hear. "I can certainly learn quite a lot from you, which is why I just knew that this was the order I should join."

Nightingale looked like a bird preening his feathers at this compliment. He really was predictable, which was exactly what I would report back to Redvers and his people. If Nightingale succumbed this easily to flattery, I didn't think he would be very useful in the field. It made him entirely too easy to manipulate.

CHAPTER THREE

The cold broke up the gathering not long after my initiation ceremony. I walked alongside Netta back to the McCrary cottage, following the windswept dirt path bordered on either side by low stone fences. We didn't speak much along the short walk, both of us instead concentrating on our footing on the uneven path. There were a few other members going our way, but most had split off for their various lodgings. The island had only two hotels, which had filled quickly, so a handful of the two hundred inhabitants of Iona let out rooms in their homes for travelers such as ourselves. It meant that, as a group, we were scattered around the small village of Baile Mòr and the surrounding area.

When we arrived at the cottage, our hosts had already retired for the evening, so I went straight to my room, waited a few beats to ensure that Netta was in for the night, and then very quietly ventured back out again. I had a date to keep, despite the cold and the late hour.

I'd initially suggested meeting Redvers at a little stone chapel called St. Oran's set a bit apart from the abbey, but he'd pointed out that it was entirely too close to one of the hotels in town and we might be seen by other members of the order. We'd agreed to meet at yet another stone chapel instead, St. Ronan's, on the other side of town near the ruins of the nunnery. I managed to avoid running into anyone who might recognize me and pushed open the heavy wooden door to the chapel, leaving it open while I lurked just inside. I was grateful that the roof here had been restored; if it hadn't, I might have insisted on meeting at St. Oran's Chapel, despite the danger of being seen there. A roof might close out the light, but it offered just enough extra protection from the cold and wind.

Moonlight, cold and pure, streamed through the open doorway. I had a flashlight, but I turned it off to preserve the battery—it was rare that I was able to see on the island without its aid, and I was grateful that the cloud cover had cleared up, at least for now. I was listening carefully, but heard nothing approach and was startled when a man in a black cloak swept through the doorway. He tipped his hood back and gave me a grin.

"How did it go, darling?" Redvers asked.

"Don't you think the cloak is a bit dramatic?" I asked, but stepped forward for a kiss.

Redvers held me close, and my senses tingled the way they always did when he was near. "I don't want you to be the only one having fun with cloaks and robes," Redvers said. He loosened his hold on me just enough that he could see me in the moonlight streaming through the open door. "How was the ceremony?" he asked again.

"It was strange. I was blindfolded, and I think I'm going to have permanent bruises on my knees."

"Suffering for the cause," Redvers said. "Very noble. Have you learned anything?"

"Yes," I said. "Robert Nightingale is insufferable."

Redvers chuckled. "We already knew that."

I nodded. We did already know that. "I genuinely think his arrogance is a drawback. He is much too easily manipulated by a little flattery."

"I think the same could be said of a lot of men," Redvers said.

"But not you, of course," I teased.

"Of course not." Redvers smiled, then became serious for a moment. "That's a good observation, although not enough to completely disqualify him. Plenty of men out in the field have outsized egos."

Nightingale kept volunteering his services to the British crown as an agent, claiming that his various "contacts" abroad would make him a valuable asset. But the crown, and Redvers' employers, were decidedly skeptical, especially given his high ranking within the Golden Dawn. Which was what brought me to this island—I needed to learn what I could about the man and his "contacts."

I'd learned some time ago not to bother asking too many specific questions about Redvers' employers. I had my own conclusions about them, and that sufficed. For now, anyway.

"Are you certain Nightingale knows who you are?" I asked, already knowing the answer, but somehow hopeful it would change from the last time we'd covered this ground. This case would be entirely more palatable if I could be seen with my fiancé.

Redvers chuckled. "He does. I'm afraid we have a mutual acquaintance in London that outed me."

"One of his 'contacts'?" I frowned. "I hope that person was given a talking to."

Redvers' face became quite serious. "That person won't be a problem in the future."

I studied him for a moment. "He won't be . . . eliminated, will he?" I could hear that my voice had gone up ever so slightly.

Now Redvers tipped his head back and laughed. "We're not in that business. Well, not necessarily. No, he was just spoken with and relocated to a place where communication is more difficult."

"Banished to a tiny island then, I assume. Why can't we just do that with Nightingale?" I said wistfully. I was sure the man had some redeeming qualities, but I'd yet to see any.

"Not that simple, I'm afraid. We'll need to learn his contacts and just what this group is all about. You'll have to spend some more time with him, I'm afraid."

I sighed. "I know."

He tugged me back into him. "I'll make it up to you."

"Oh, I know you will."

The next morning, I awoke alone in my bed and sighed. The sooner this assignment was over the better—I'd gotten quite spoiled over the last several months, sharing a bed with Redvers. It had become more comfortable than sleeping alone, something that I never thought I would say after my disastrous first marriage. Life was ever surprising.

I washed up in the small bathroom in the hallway and dressed in a knit sweater and a wool skirt, adding a pair of thick tights and my flat-soled, leather T-strap shoes. I headed downstairs to the dining room for breakfast and found Michael McCrary, the owner of the cottage, just sitting down to eat. This was unusual; the family had normally eaten and were cleared out by the time the guests came down for their meals.

"You'll excuse me, lass," McCrary said as his wife Fiona bustled in with a bowl of piping-hot porridge for her husband as well as a plate of eggs and sausage. "Had to see to some trouble with the sheep this mornin' and didnae get to my breakfast."

"No trouble at all," I said. "It's your home." I was doing a better job of understanding the McCrarys after a few days of staying with them. The thick Scottish accent had given me quite a bit of trouble when I arrived, and even now, it took me a moment to untangle the words in my head before I could respond.

Fiona returned, a plump woman with thick brown hair pulled into a bun on top of her head and nearly always wearing an apron. "Here's your dram," she told her husband, setting a little glass before him.

Michael grunted his thanks, then took the glass and dumped it into his porridge. He caught me looking at him, openly wondering what the liquid was he'd added. Syrup?

"A wee dram of whiskey in the porridge warms the insides," McCrary said, nodding once and then setting into his meal.

I'd never heard of adding booze to breakfast cereals, but who was I to say what a farmer should or shouldn't add to his morning meal? I took a moment to study the man. He was what one would expect of a Scottish sheep farmer, dressed quite practically in a wool sweater and thick trousers. His hair had long since gone gray, and his face was quite ruddy, evidence of many years spent outdoors in the wind and sun. Despite this, I estimated him to be only in his early fifties.

Fiona hurried back into the room carrying a plate for me with two fried eggs, some "tattie scones," fried mushrooms, and one sausage link. It wasn't a full Scottish breakfast, but Fiona had quickly caught on to the fact that I was not going to partake in some elements of the full breakfast. I couldn't quite stomach haggis or black pudding, and I wasn't a fan of baked beans at any meal, let alone first thing in the morning.

Fiona also brought me a small pot of coffee, and I thanked the woman with enthusiasm. She smiled, giving her head a little shake.

Michael McCrary eyed my cup of coffee. "You're certain you dinnae want a dram in that?"

I smiled over the top of my cup, happy now that I was pouring the dark brew into myself. It was the only way to start a day, as far as I was concerned. "Oh, I'm quite fine without. But perhaps this afternoon I'll give that a try."

He shrugged. "Suit yourself."

I'd tucked into my own breakfast when Fiona reappeared in the room with a frown. "Have you spoken with Netta this morning?" she asked me.

I shook my head. "It was quiet up there when I was getting ready."

"I knocked on her door just now, and she refused to come out."

"Do you mean she didn't respond, or she said she wouldn't come out of her room?"

Fiona's hands were on her waist, and she frowned. "She willnae come out."

I sat back a bit in my seat. That was certainly strange, although from everything I'd learned about the girl so far, she was a bit strange all around. Eccentric was probably the best word to describe her.

"I didn't talk to her this morning, but once I'm finished here, I'll go see if she'll talk to me."

Fiona looked relieved. "I would appreciate that, Miss Jane. I need to get on with the rest of my chores and cannae be waiting on her for breakfast."

I nodded and hurried to finish my breakfast, although I did make certain to drain every last drop of the coffee in the pot Fiona had provided me. Once I'd managed that task, I pushed up from the table and made my way to the stairs at the front of the cottage. They were simple wooden stairs, narrow, with a sturdy wooden railing running alongside the landing above. There were numerous family portraits hanging on the white beadboard wall, photos and paintings that made the cottage feel like a home.

I climbed the creaky stairs, noting which ones made the most noise, as had become my habit, and knocked on Netta's door. "Netta? It's Jane."

I heard a mumbled response that sounded a lot like "morning," but I couldn't swear to it. "Will you be coming out?"

"No." Netta's voice was quite clear. There was no mistaking that answer.

"May I ask why not? Mrs. McCrary needs to finish making breakfast so that she can get on with her day."

"I don't need food. I'm fine without."

I paused. If that was true, at least it wouldn't put Fiona out, and the woman could get on with her chores. But it was still strange that the girl was refusing to come out, and I felt a nagging sense of concern. "Is there a reason you won't come out? Did something happen?"

Netta was quiet for a moment. "There's a disturbance in the astral plane, and it's best if I don't come out until it's resolved."

I didn't have the slightest idea what that meant, but I probably needed to act as though I did. I didn't want her reporting back to any of the other members that I wasn't familiar with their terms. "Is there anything I can do to help?" I didn't think there was, but it seemed the safest response.

"No, thank you. I've got it under control for now." Netta's voice sounded as though it was just on the other side of the door now. I was thinking about how strange it was to be talking to someone so close-by yet with a wooden barrier between us when an envelope slid beneath the door at my feet. "But could you give this to Dion for me?" Netta asked.

I bent down and picked up the envelope. It was sealed and had "Dion Fortune" written on the front of it. I shrugged to myself, weighing it in my hand. It wasn't terribly heavy, so it held probably only one piece of paper. "Of course. I'll deliver it to her now."

"Thank you, Jane." Netta's voice was already drifting away from the door deeper into the room.

Well, that was strange. But, so was the young woman, from everything I had observed so far. However, it was no trouble to do as she asked, especially since it gave me an excuse to spend some time with Dion Fortune. It was the perfect opportunity to ask some questions about Dion's relationship with Robert Nightingale.

CHAPTER FOUR

After assuring Mrs. McCrary that she didn't need to wait on Netta for breakfast, I pulled on my thick wool coat and cloche, adding a plaid woolen scarf around my neck, and left the cottage to head to Dion's lodgings. As I walked down the front path, I felt a prickling at my back and turned to look back at the McCrary cottage, with its stone fence and tidy garden. Nothing seemed amiss, but looking up, I could see that Netta was standing in the window of her room watching me. I gave her a little wave, but she didn't respond—not a wave, not a smile or a nod, nothing. She stood still as a statue, and I couldn't decide whether the girl even saw me. After a beat, I turned and continued on my way, shaking my head.

Our cottage was just a bit outside the village of Baile Mòr, which was simply called "the village" by the locals. It was a several-minutes walk into town across windswept fields bordered by stone fences, but the location worked for me since I needed to be able to sneak out without being seen in order to meet up with Redvers. He was staying on the other side of the tiny island in an attempt to stay hidden from Nightingale and the other members of the occult group. It was an aggravating but necessary arrangement.

The village itself was little more than a single street lined with small shops and homes, with a few offshoots reaching toward the rocky hills. Dion Fortune was staying in a cottage on this main drag, close to the post office, which I found ironic since I was delivering a letter to her.

The owner of the cottage informed me that Dion wasn't in, and when I asked if she knew where Dion had gone, I was told that she'd gone to Sìthean Mòr. I could feel my face frowning, as I had no idea what that was, and the elderly woman tsked at my ignorance before informing me that Sìthean Mòr was the Angel's Hill from St. Columba's time, and she sketched out some general directions for me.

With a sigh, I huddled back into my charcoal gray jacket, grateful for its warmth against the biting wind, resettled my wool cloche on my head, and set out. I wandered down the meandering main street, including where it went uphill and away from the water. The buildings eventually thinned and then ended. Here I went right, following a path across the middle of the island that cut through the green fields stretched between the rockier hills on either side of Iona.

I saw Dion long before I reached her, seated on the small, elevated hill that her landlady had described, a blanket spread on the ground—she'd clearly come prepared. The grass was already green, but the ground still had to be quite cold to sit on, and I shivered in my coat just looking at her. She seemed completely unbothered by the cold or the wind, however.

Dion's eyes were closed when I approached, but she seemed to sense my presence before I'd come within ten yards of her, and she raised one hand in greeting, eyes still shut tight. I wasn't sure what I should do in return—she couldn't see me with her eyes clamped shut—so I simply trudged upward until I stood before her.

"I'm sorry to bother you," I said. "But I have a message from Netta."

At this, Dion finally opened her eyes. "Hmm." Dion looked

thoughtful and gestured for me to join her on the blanket, and I paused for a moment before lowering myself onto the thick plaid cloth. I'd been correct—the ground was cold, seeping quickly and easily into my legs despite the heavy fabric. This conversation would have to be shorter than I'd initially hoped if I was to be able to feel my extremities later.

I pulled Netta's letter from my pocket and passed it over to Dion, who was wearing trousers and sitting comfortably cross-legged, as though it were twenty degrees warmer. She held the envelope for a long moment, and I wondered exactly what she was doing, but didn't ask in case I should already know.

Finally, Dion shook her head again and opened the envelope, quickly scanning the short note before sighing and sliding it back into the envelope, but saying nothing. She stared off into the distance, even though there was nothing to be seen other than rocky hills and the choppy Atlantic Ocean, which was admittedly quite beautiful when the sun was out, as it was now.

"Bad news?" I finally ventured to ask.

Dion looked at me, her eyes focusing quickly and sharply on me. I knew I would have to tread most carefully with this woman if I was going to maintain my cover in their occult group. "Netta has always been a bit . . . troubled. She's saying that she can no longer be a member of our order."

"That seems abrupt. Will she join another?" I asked.

"No, we're the second faction of the Golden Dawn that she's belonged to." Dion paused, obviously considering how much to tell me. "Netta had some trouble with the other faction as well."

"Perhaps it's just not a good fit for her." I knew there were numerous other occult groups operating, all of them as secretive as the next. I couldn't even begin to say whether they believed the same things or had any similarities beyond their secretive natures.

"She's a lost soul," Dion said sadly. "We will see what to-morrow will bring."

That could mean any number of things, but I decided to point the conversation in another direction before I could no longer feel my legs. How long had Dion Fortune been sitting here? I was already freezing cold. The month of March was not warm in Scotland, despite the sun currently shining on my face.

"Is it possible that she doesn't get along with Robert? Or that something happened between them? He seems . . ." I chose my words carefully in case she did like the man after all. "He seems to have a large personality."

Dion laughed at this, her eyes crinkling appealingly. "You could say that again." She cocked her head, actually considering my question. "I don't think Netta has anything particularly for or against Nightingale. They coexist without interacting a great deal, so I don't imagine anything happened between them either."

"But you have to interact with him more regularly. Since you're higher up in the order."

Dion's eyes were bright. "I don't have to, but I choose to. Men like that need a little challenge, don't you think?"

I smiled. I did think that to be true, and I rather enjoyed that Dion liked to give the man a difficult time. I couldn't, since I was there to investigate Nightingale, but Dion certainly could. And I could enjoy the show.

Then she shrugged. "Nightingale is actually quite powerful. Gifted, really. The trouble is that he knows it. He moved up very quickly within the order."

"Yes, he told me," I said dryly.

Dion laughed. "I'll bet he did. He'll bring it up any opportunity he's given."

This exchange made it seem that the tension I'd noticed between Dion and Nightingale was nothing more than this— Dion trying to take the man down a few pegs.

I had one more question before I hauled myself off the cold ground and headed somewhere to warm up again. "What is an angel ring?" If I was supposed to know, I didn't. And in this case, I didn't think asking the question would reflect too poorly on me, since it appeared to be specific to the island we were on.

"Ah, you've spoken to my landlady, I see," Dion said. "This is also known as a fairy ring."

This was not helpful since I didn't know what either of those things was.

Dion must have realized this because she launched into an explanation. "Saint Columba was an early founder of Christianity on the island of Iona, and Scotland in general, centuries ago. Came over from Ireland, around the year 560 BC, I think. In any event, this hill was where Columba liked to pray, and one evening a monk saw him at dusk during his evening ritual. The monk swore there were angels all around Columba—thus the name Angel's Hill. Since then—or likely even before—it's believed to be an especially significant place for reaching beyond the veil."

I nodded as though this all made perfect sense. "Why don't we conduct ceremonies here then?"

"That's an excellent question." She smiled. "I think it has to do with the cold; at least the church has a roof, and it's a powerful site within its own right." She shifted on the ground, rearranging her crossed legs, her only acknowledgment that she might be uncomfortable on the cold ground.

"And where do fairies come in?" I asked.

Dion paused, looking at me for a beat too long, and I rushed to explain my lack of knowledge on this subject in case it had made her suspicious. "We don't have fairy mythology in America."

Dion nodded, then answered. "Fairy folk are part of ancient mythology. The Celts regarded this as a fairy hill, although there is a much more famous one on the Isle of Skye.

Legend holds that if you come upon a fairy hill at the right time, mortals will hear strains of music from a fairy revel, where they play music and dance beneath the earth. A soul can venture inside, but the danger is that the fairies may keep you. Some say that an iron dagger can open the portal but still allow you to leave." Dion paused, thinking. "The fairy folk—or little people—can be mischievous and play tricks on people, according to myth. Many blamed their bad luck on angering the fairies."

I didn't have a reasonable response to any of that, but I thought I at least was picking up on a main theme here. "So, regardless of their specific beliefs, various groups find this hill to be an especially powerful site."

Dion nodded.

It appeared that there was a great deal of mysticism related to this little island. Who would have guessed such a small, windswept place would have so much mythology associated with it?

Back at the McCrary cottage, I knocked on Netta's door again, but this time there was no answer. I couldn't tell if she was still inside or not, and putting my ear to the door didn't tell me anything about its occupant either. With a shrug, I went downstairs into the parlor and stood in front of the fire for a bit, my back to the flames to warm the parts of my body that had withstood contact with the cold ground for so long. I thought that Dion Fortune must be either made of steel or insane since the woman was still sitting in the same position on her blanket when I left her.

Dion hadn't given me much about Nightingale that was new or useful, which was understandable since I was a relative stranger. I decided that Netta might actually be my best bet, since her flighty nature might lend itself to sharing her thoughts more readily, but she obviously wasn't interested in a chat today. I hoped that by tomorrow she would be feeling more social and would come out of her room so I could engage her in conversation—calling questions through a wooden door wasn't the way to go about this. I was curious not only about her thoughts about Nightingale, but also why she'd suddenly decided to leave the order. Did it have anything to do with its chief? Had something happened that Dion wasn't aware of? Or was it something else entirely?

I needed to go upstairs and do some studying, but I was more than reluctant to do so. I'd been given "secret materials" to read so that I could progress to the next stage in the order, and while I'd glanced at them, I couldn't yet convince myself to study them with any enthusiasm. This was both because I was hoping this assignment would end before I really needed the knowledge, and because I thought it was utter nonsense. There was a lot of talk about "magic" and "magical power," but I hadn't seen anything to lead me to believe it was anything but a lot of hot air.

I was surprised that W.B. Yeats had been taken in by it all, though. The man was a famous poet, a Nobel Prize–winning one, and a senator in the Irish government as well. What was he doing associating with this sort of group?

Perhaps that was the next question I should be asking.

Chapter Five

It took a bit of asking around, but I finally learned that Yeats was staying at one of the hotels in town. Even calling it a hotel was a bit of a reach; it looked like a slightly larger home along the stretch of buildings on the main street facing the ocean. It had two stories, was built of stone like most of the rest of the buildings on the street, and had a sign above the door reading HOTEL ARGYLL. I found the man seated in front of the fire in the lounge, a pad of paper and a pen at the ready while he stared into the flames. I was a little hesitant to interrupt him, but took a seat across from him all the same.

"Mr. Yeats?" I asked quietly.

The man flicked his dark eyes over to me and cocked his head. "You look familiar." Yeats spoke slowly and ponderously.

"I just joined the order."

"Aye, the ceremony last night." Yeats's Irish accent was as lovely as the local Scots accent and equally difficult to understand. "What can I do for you, lass?"

"I was wondering how you came to be involved in the order."

The poet regarded me for a long moment, looking down his hawkish nose at me. I squirmed a bit under his scrutiny. "I overheard you mention Madame Blavatsky last night."

I froze in my seat. Blavatsky was part of my cover, but I'd never considered that someone might actually know the woman. I'd never once met Blavatsky, nor would she have any idea who I was—my letter of introduction was entirely forged, as was my history with the occult.

Yeats nodded. "I know Madame Blavatsky quite well, now. I've known her since I was a young lad in London."

I bravely gave a smile. "She's lovely, isn't she?"

W.B. gave a humorless bark of laughter. "She's not, in truth. You've never met the woman, have you now?"

I stared at him, trying to decide what the best move here would be. Was my cover about to be blown? Could I trust this man?

"If you had, you might know that she's dead. Has been for quite some time."

I'm afraid my mouth fell open at this point.

Yeats nodded slowly. "It's true, although not many people know it. I'm quite certain Nightingale isn't aware of that fact."

My mind was racing. How had we not known this important detail about the woman? Of course, it meant that Nightingale wouldn't hear anything back if he did try to contact her about me. Unless, of course, someone decided to let him in on the secret about Blavatsky's status among the living. My blood ran cold—we needed to wrap this up before Nightingale heard the news and realized that my introduction was entirely invented.

Yeats had been quiet, watching me absorb the news. "You don't have to worry on my account, lass. I won't tell himself about you," Yeats indicated upstairs with a tilt of his head and a roll of his eyes, clearly referring to Robert Nightingale. I got the distinct impression that he didn't much care for the man.

"Why would you do that?" I asked.

"It's amusing to me that Nightingale believes your letter of introduction," he said with a shrug. "He really thinks himself infallible, and it's nice to see him taken down a peg, even if he doesn't know it."

I thanked him for keeping my confidence, and then thought for a moment, trying to decide if I really could trust this man.

"Back to your original question. I think you were wondering what someone like me is doing with someone like Nightingale, since I don't care for the man," he finally said. Yeats was nothing if not perceptive.

I allowed myself a small smile. "I suppose so, yes."

He put his pen down and nodded, dark eyes bright behind the little wire-rimmed spectacles he wore. "He is an arse, Nightingale, and a bit of an eejit, despite his talents with magic. And I'm not technically in the order any longer—I left several years ago now, when the infighting began." He considered for a moment. "But I've always been curious about attending a solstice ceremony, and Nightingale is trying to woo me back into the fold. When he invited me to attend the ceremony here, I decided to accept."

I opened my mouth to ask again how he'd joined the order in the first place, but he beat me to it.

"I've always been interested in the occult. Have you read any of my poetry?"

My face flamed. I hadn't—poetry wasn't even remotely an interest of mine—but it was an awkward thing to admit to the man's face. I opened my mouth to say something, invent some sort of excuse, but he held up a hand.

"It's alright, lass, I imagine you've been busy with . . . other pursuits. But there's quite a bit of the mystical in what I write about. The Irish, we have our own beliefs, passed down from the ancient Celts."

I nodded, not really knowing any of this. If I'd had any idea I would be confronted with the prize-winning poet, I would have done some research on the man. As it was, I'd done only the barest amount of research on the Golden

Dawn—enough that I could pass as someone wanting to join—but I hadn't read much on its early history or historical influences. And clearly, I wasn't the only one, since Redvers' employers hadn't been aware that Madame Blavatsky was dead before forging a letter of introduction from the woman.

Unfortunately, today was not the day that I was going to get a history lesson on the group either, because Robert Nightingale came down the hall and joined us. I heard Yeats's small sigh when he noticed Nightingale coming through the doorway, and I hid a smile. He was just as thrilled as I was at the man's appearance.

"W.B., I was just knocking on your door upstairs. I wanted to see if you would join me for lunch."

Yeats mumbled something that sounded like an excuse, but Nightingale took it as agreement. "Excellent." Nightingale cast his eyes over at me. "I'd ask you to join us, Miss Wunderly, but I'm afraid we have inner-circle matters to discuss. You understand, of course. And it gives you something to look forward to—advancing high enough in the ranks that you might be included in such discussions."

I wanted to point out that Yeats wasn't even a part of the group any longer, let alone a member of the inner circle, but I kept this to myself. "Yes, of course," I said instead, with as much sincerity as I had available to me. Which admittedly wasn't a lot, but it seemed to be enough for Robert Nightingale.

Yeats wasn't fooled, though, quickly arching an eyebrow at me, before his serious mask was back in place. I'd yet to see the man crack a smile. He seemed awfully serious as a whole, which somehow felt at odds with such an encompassing interest in the occult and all things mystical. I found myself curious about him and disappointed that we'd been interrupted. Perhaps I would look into finding a volume of his poetry after all.

Nightingale was still standing a little behind our chairs,

and my neck was craning at an awkward angle to include him in the discussion I'd been having with Yeats. Nightingale was entirely oblivious to my discomfort, and I would guess to anyone else's comfort, as a general rule.

"I've been enjoying getting to know the other members. They've been very helpful," I told Nightingale, hoping to redirect the conversation.

"Speaking of other members, you're staying at the same place as Netta, are you not?" Nightingale asked. "Have you seen her this morning?"

I paused, unsure how much to disclose to the man. A quick glance at Yeats told me that he'd gone back to his notepad, ignoring Nightingale—and now me—entirely. I wondered if Yeats would end up having lunch with the man or if he would simply ignore Nightingale until he gave up.

"I haven't seen her." I said. "She's in her room."

"Let me guess," Nightingale said, disgust evident in his voice. "She won't come out."

I gave a small shrug of the shoulders, feeling a little protective of the young woman against this pompous man. It made me wonder whether something *had* happened between the two of them that made Netta want to withdraw from the order.

But it also raised the question of whether something like this had happened with Netta before. When I returned to the cottage, I would have to ask Fiona whether Netta had a history of sequestering herself in her room. I'd only been at the cottage for a few days, but Netta had been staying there for nearly a month already, so Fiona would know.

"So dramatic, that girl." Nightingale shook his head and blew out a sigh that was dramatic in its own right. "She's very troubled. Always needs to draw attention to herself."

I couldn't exactly argue with Nightingale since I didn't know Netta well at all, but I did have to bite my tongue in order to stop myself from doing precisely that. Especially since Nightingale had more than a little flare for the dramatic himself. "She sent a note to Dion," I offered.

"Hmm. I suppose I'll talk with Dion then, to see what the silly girl has to say for herself. Mark my words, that one will come to a bad end."

Nightingale looked as though he was expecting some sort of congratulations for being so perceptive, or perhaps a question about what he meant, but I refused to give him the satisfaction. I could, however, tell that my brows had pulled together at his ominous pronouncement—I simply couldn't keep my face from reacting. His eyes sharpened on me, and I was afraid he would question me, but a beat later, Nightingale glanced at his watch, then clapped his hand on Yeats's shoulder. "Ready?"

"You know, I'm not terribly hungry," Yeats was saying, a devilish gleam in his eyes. Perhaps the man wasn't entirely serious after all.

I decided it was time to take my leave before I did something else to rouse Nightingale's suspicion. I hadn't learned much from Yeats, but I would follow up with the poet later about Robert Nightingale since Yeats clearly wasn't a fan of the occult leader. Hopefully, I could learn something useful for our investigation. Something else was troubling me, though. Yeats had said he was on the island because he was curious about the ritual, but why would he accept an invitation from Nightingale if he disliked the man so much? Was there something I was missing?

At least I'd learned quite a bit about how Nightingale felt about Netta Fornario, as well as my own dubious introduction to the occult. It felt like enough information gathering for one morning.

"Excuse me, gentlemen." I stood and walked away as Nightingale began arguing with the Irishman over the lunch that Nightingale apparently felt quite strongly about. I didn't want to stick around to see how it ended up. I had a date to keep.

Redvers and I had arranged to meet every afternoon on a remote beach, tucked away from everything and out of view of anyone who might be wandering the fields. When I arrived on Iona, I'd made a bit of a spectacle about my love of walking in order to explain my daily hikes across the island, even in the cold and wind and rain. I got a few raised eyebrows, but no one ever questioned my apparent dedication to exercise. I was ever so grateful that I'd brought my most comfortable walking shoes, and I tugged my coat tighter around my neck as I set out, doing my best to pin my cloche to my hair. I didn't have as much information to report to my fiancé since the night before as I might have liked, but I was missing Redvers and looking forward to seeing him.

What they said was true—absence really did make the heart grow fonder.

I took the same route out of town toward the fairy hill where I'd seen Dion sitting, but this time I kept walking, keeping my eyes on my footing and only occasionally glancing up to take in the rugged beauty of the island. The grass was already a startling green, especially against the gray stone that jutted up out of the earth everywhere, making it quite apparent that we were resting on a small piece of rock in a large ocean. I followed the narrow path up and down the sloping hills, and when I neared the ocean, I turned right and followed the coastline to the north. We'd tried to meet on the Back of the Ocean Beach, but it was entirely too rocky to be comfortable. Instead, we'd moved our meeting point to the Port Ban Beach, and I was nearly there. Finally. I could feel how red my cheeks were from the wind.

Port Ban Beach opened up between large rock formations, hulking gray stone covered in orange lichen and even grass in places. But the sand here was fine and white, visually striking against the startlingly clear blue ocean waters that lapped up, and the large rocks offered a reprieve from the wind. I didn't need to put any part of myself into the water to know that it was freezing cold, however appealing it might look. When the sun was out, the colors were nothing short of stunning, in various shades of blue and turquoise, a striped quilt of sea.

I found Redvers tucked into a little cove, a thick plaid blanket spread on the white sand. I flopped onto the blanket beside him, kissed him briefly in greeting, then glanced around above us. It was a good location that Redvers had chosen—hard to spot from the rocky hills around us, and we would see anyone coming along the beach long before they got to us. The ground was cold, and I knew it would not be long before the chill seeped through. I'd learned that the hard way only a few hours earlier on Dion's blanket.

Redvers wasn't satisfied with my brief kiss, and we took several moments to get reacquainted before getting down to business.

"I'll be glad when this is over," I said, as I did every time I laid eyes on him.

Redvers looked amused. "Yes, you've said."

The fact remained that things were simply more . . . well, fun when Redvers was with me.

"Did you learn anything interesting?" Redvers was casually stroking my hair, and I could tell he didn't expect a response with any substance.

"Netta refuses to come out of her room. And she sent me with a note to give to Dion Fortune claiming that Netta is leaving the group."

"That's interesting," Redvers said. But I could tell I didn't have his full interest—that is, my *words* weren't catching his interest. So I told him that Yeats knew Madame Blavatsky, and worse yet, he had called me on the carpet about my letter of introduction since the woman was dead.

That finally got his full attention.

"She's dead?" Redvers' voice was incredulous.

"That's what the man said. Has been for some time, apparently."

Redvers was quiet for a moment. "Do you think he'll out you?"

I considered that, much as I had done during my walk across the island. "I don't think so, since he clearly doesn't seem to care for Nightingale. But he also didn't ask why I'd bothered with the deception."

Redvers made a noise, obviously thinking over the implications.

"I know. I'll keep an eye on it, of course. And I'll try to feel him out again, make sure he really will keep my confidence about this. Do you think Nightingale will try to reach out to Blavatsky?" If he did, someone would likely inform him about the woman's demise and the ruse would be over immediately.

"I certainly hope not. The outgoing mail and any telegraphs will be monitored, of course."

"Of course," I said, unsurprised.

"So we can intercept that sort of message and respond appropriately. But if he attempts to make an overseas phone call—"

"I didn't think that was even possible," I interrupted.

Redvers shrugged. "It became possible only a few months ago. Of course, it isn't likely to be accomplished from somewhere as remote as this island, so we probably don't need to worry about that."

We were both quiet for a moment, thinking over how this news complicated things for us. Then I told Redvers about Nightingale's ominous prediction about Netta coming to a "bad end."

"It doesn't necessarily mean anything bad will happen, but it is strange," Redvers said.

"Very true. It's likely that he was simply being dramatic,

but it's worth noting all the same." I frowned a little. "Dion didn't seem terribly surprised about Netta's antics either. Perhaps they're correct that Netta is simply troubled." I would check in on Netta when I returned all the same, though. Perhaps I needed to be a little more forceful about getting the girl to speak with me so that I could make sure she was alright.

"It seems likely. And while vague threats against the girl don't make Nightingale look good, it's still not enough to report back to the office that we shouldn't utilize him and his supposed contacts."

"Is someone else looking into the 'contacts'?" I asked.

Redvers nodded. "Of course."

I was disappointed we hadn't been assigned to that task instead of our current one.

Redvers opened his mouth to say something, and I put a finger over his lips. "My instincts say that you shouldn't utilize Nightingale or even believe that he *has* contacts, but you're right. We need something substantial to back that up, more than just a feeling."

"How did you know that's what I was going to say?"

"Since my induction to the group, I'm now a mind reader," I said with a smile.

"Is that so? What am I thinking about right now?" He asked.

I kissed him soundly, which distracted us both for a moment. Eventually, I pulled away, and I sighed, thinking of my cold and lonely bed, and I said so aloud.

Redvers grinned. "Maybe there's a way around that."

"You'll need a ladder to get to the second floor," I warned, but my heart felt light at the idea of a late-night visit. Necking on a blanket out in the elements wasn't the same as sharing a bed, and it would be worth the trouble even if he couldn't stay the entire night.

Redvers winked. "I have my ways."

I certainly hoped that he did.

CHAPTER SIX

An hour or so later, I made the trek back to the McCrary cottage, my heart and feet a little lighter after my visit with Redvers, even if I was physically no warmer. When I arrived, I was surprised to find a small pile of trunks and luggage outside the front door. Michael McCrary was standing beside it, hands on hips, shaking his head.

"What's going on?" I asked.

"Och! That lass thinks she can leave the island today. I told her there isnae a ferry until tomorrow, but she widnae listen to me. Or to anyone else—my Fiona tried as well."

I felt my brows pull together in a frown. "Where is she now?"

"She dragged her things out here and then went to the ferry landing. I'm supposed to get these down there, as well as the rest in her room, but there isnae any use to it."

It was common knowledge that there wasn't ferry service that day, and I wondered what Netta could be thinking, dragging her things outside and going to the launch. I was also curious about how she went from locking herself in her room to needing to get off the island with such urgency.

"I'll go talk to her," I said. I'd been looking forward to warming myself up by the fire after my long walk in the wind, but it sounded like Netta was struggling with something, and it looked more and more like that something was in her own mind. I didn't know what I could do to help, but at least I could talk to the young woman, perhaps convince her to wait until the following morning before making any rash decisions.

"Thank you, Miss Jane. I think all this is a load of rubbish, what that girl is involved in. Seems to be making her crazy," McCrary rubbed a hand down his face in frustration, then realized who he was speaking to. "No offense, miss."

"None taken." I would have loved to tell him that I felt exactly the same, but I managed to hold my tongue. I had a cover to maintain, after all.

I turned and headed back toward town in search of Netta, turning toward the ocean once I'd walked past the Hotel Argyll in the direction of the ferry launch. There wasn't a ferry at the dock, and I assumed that it had moored at Mull until its return the following day. Standing here, gazing across the water, I could understand Netta's frustration—you could see Mull from where I stood, and it felt as though it should be nothing at all to get across this tiny stretch of water separating Iona from its neighbor.

I looked all around me, but it was obvious that Netta wasn't at the dock; it was an open area, with few places to shelter oneself. A gust of wind bit through my coat, and I guessed that Netta must have gotten tired of the wind and cold and headed back to the cottage, although I couldn't begin to guess how she'd passed me without my seeing her—there weren't many paths to choose from.

With a shrug, I headed back to the cottage myself. I'd see if Netta had returned, and if not, I would check the most likely spots in town for her. If I still couldn't find her, I decided that I would spend the rest of the afternoon studying my Golden Dawn materials while I waited for her to come back for her things. I wasn't excited in the slightest about the prospect of my afternoon reading, but I did need to be a little more conversant in their rituals and ideas if I was going to keep this ruse going for even a little while longer and keep Nightingale from asking Madame Blavatsky about me. Studying my manual would be a good use of my time spent otherwise waiting for Netta.

I just hoped the readings didn't put me right to sleep, as they had in the past.

Several hours later found me dozing in front of the small fire in my room. After searching the village for Netta and coming up empty, I'd returned to my room and curled up in the upholstered armchair and started looking at the manual I'd been given—and promptly fallen asleep. I set the little booklet aside with a sigh, then stood and stretched my stiff limbs. I didn't know how on earth I was going to learn any of this—perhaps I could convince Redvers to read it to me. Of course, spending time with that man came with its own distractions, and none of them led to falling asleep quickly.

A knock at my door startled me, and I crossed the room to open it, rather hoping to find Netta on the other side. Instead, I found Fiona McCrary, one hand twisted in the flour-dusted apron she wore.

"Have you spoken with Netta?" Fiona asked when I opened the door.

I shook my head. "I couldn't find her earlier."

"She's back in her room now, but widnae talk to me. I was hopin' you could get some sense from the girl."

I cocked my head. "I'll try."

Fiona shook her head, opened her mouth, then shut it again. When she didn't say anything, I prompted her.

"What is it?"

Fiona pressed her lips together, looking to one side and then the other quickly before dropping her voice and leaning toward me. "I read the leaves this morning. Wisnae good, what I saw." Her eyes sparked with something I couldn't quite decipher. "You willnae tell Mr. McCrary that I said anything."

I promised the woman that I would keep it to myself, although I was a little curious why she didn't want her husband to know that she read tea leaves. It probably had something to do with the attitude I'd seen from the man earlier—he likely thought it was nonsense.

I wasn't sure how I felt about the ritual myself. I'd never done any research into the reading of tea leaves or tarot cards or anything of that ilk. I hated to make snap judgments about things I knew nothing about, although it all struck me as superstition more than anything else. Much like the fairy ring Dion had told me about earlier.

But Fiona seemed genuinely troubled, and even more important, it sounded as though Netta was back and not making sense. I left Fiona scurrying back downstairs and crossed the hallway to Netta's room, knocking softly on the door. "Netta? Are you in?"

I heard a rustling noise behind the door, although I couldn't quite decide what it was. Shuffling papers? She didn't respond, so I knocked again. "Netta? It's Jane."

"Oh, Jane." Netta's voice sounded relieved, and I wondered who she'd thought I was. Fiona? But why would our landlady make her nervous? "I'm fine."

What I wanted to say was that she didn't seem fine. Not in the slightest. But instead I asked, "Are you certain?"

"Yes. I've closed the curtains, since I could see faces in the clouds. And that has helped."

That set me right back on my heels. What on earth was she talking about? "Faces?" I asked.

"Of my clients." Her voice got quieter as she moved across the room and then louder as she crossed closer to the door again. Was she pacing? And what clients was she referring to?

"What kind of clients do you have?" I finally asked. I didn't think any answer she gave would make more sense to me, but I was curious enough to ask.

"I do spiritual healing. I've been taking a break because it takes such a toll on me, so I came here to rest and rebuild, using the energy of the island." Netta's voice continued to get quieter and then louder as she spoke. I decided that the woman was indeed pacing her room.

She was silent for a few beats, and I reached down to quietly try the doorknob, but found that it was locked. I carefully released it while I considered what to say, hoping it wasn't obvious that I'd tried to open her door.

"I can understand needing a rest," I finally said. "Is there anything I can do for you right now? The McCrarys are worried about you." She didn't respond, so I added, "And so am I."

Her voice came from across the room again. "I'll leave in the morning. And if you're wise, you will too."

Chapter Seven

I couldn't get Netta to respond to me any further after that pronouncement, so I returned to my room to puzzle over what the woman had said. I hadn't the slightest idea how one went about doing "spiritual healing" or what seeing faces in the clouds might mean. Could she be having some sort of episode? It certainly seemed as though that was the case. It was altogether unsettling, but short of breaking through her door, I didn't think there was anything else I could do for Netta tonight. I hoped that, if she was going to leave in the morning, she might be able to get some help. Perhaps I could gently suggest seeking the help of a doctor once she was back on the mainland.

The rest of the evening passed without event. Fiona was happy to bring a plate of stew with some hearty bread to my room for dinner instead of serving me downstairs by myself. I could tell from the looks she cast at Netta's door that the woman was still worried about her other tenant, but all either of us could do was shake our heads at each other over Netta's behavior. We agreed that, hopefully, things would look better in the morning.

Once I'd finished my dinner and returned the dishes, I found myself glancing out my window quite often, despite my inability to see very far through the inky darkness, hoping that Redvers could indeed find a way to my room. And my bed. But my eyelids grew heavy, and there was no sign of my fiancé, so I tucked myself beneath the cheerful handmade quilts and fell fast asleep.

The fire was nothing but embers when a noise woke me up. I blinked my eyes open and sat up, trying to figure out whether the noise was real or from the strange dream I'd been having. There was no further sound, but I got out of bed, shivering as the cold hit my bare arms, and I crossed to the window to look out. Could Redvers have come this late? I pulled aside the curtain and peered outside, but saw nothing other than moonlight peeking through the ever-present cloud cover, caressing the green fields that stretched out into the sea of night. Nothing within my view was moving except a few sheep, which led me to believe that whatever I had heard had been a dream. With another shiver, I crawled back into my warm bed.

The following morning, I awoke from another strange dream in which my Aunt Millie ran the ferry service from Mull to Iona. Her captain's hat made me giggle, but she was very serious about her duty, much as she was in real life. It was then that I recalled that I'd woken up in the middle of the night as well. It probably had to do with the strange group I'd been initiated into—the weird symbols and rituals were affecting my imagination, which was running wild and giving me intense dreams. It was hardly surprising that my sleep wasn't restful.

I dressed for the day in a practical knit dress and my comfortable shoes, already anticipating my hike across the island to see Redvers. I'd been disappointed that he hadn't visited me during the night, as he'd suggested he would, but perhaps he'd decided against it. As much as I wanted him to follow through with a late-night visit, it probably wasn't worth the risk of getting caught and having our cover blown.

I was about to head straight down to breakfast, but before I took the first stair, I turned and went back down the hall to knock on Netta's door instead. I rapped several times, and when there was no answer, I tried again. There was no sound coming from behind the door; it was the kind of silence that felt absolute, as though there were no one in the room at all. I tried the knob as I had the day before, gently twisting it, and this time it turned easily in my hand. It was unlocked.

I knocked again, calling Netta's name, but I knew in my gut that there was no one in the room. I pushed open the door, and a quick glance around told me that I was correct.

Netta had come prepared to stay for quite some time, judging by the trunks and luggage piled near the door. It appeared her things were still packed, although it was difficult to say whether the bed had been slept in or not—it looked as though it hadn't been made up in several days. I thought that was strange; even though I made my bed every morning, Fiona came in and straightened it for me, as well as the rest of the room. Had Netta asked Fiona not to do the same for her? Or had Fiona simply not been able to get into Netta's room?

I glanced around, not wanting to intrude on the woman's personal space, but also curious. There was no fire banked in her fireplace, but there were scraps of paper in the ashes. I paused, wanting to see what they might be, but not wanting to get caught openly going through the young woman's things. After looking around a moment longer, I closed the door again and headed down to breakfast.

As I took my seat, Fiona brought me a little pot of coffee. I thanked the woman enthusiastically, filling my cup and adding a bit of fresh cream.

"Has Netta been down this morning?" I asked Fiona.

She paused a moment to shake her head, face troubled. "I havnae seen her, miss. She didnae come down." Fiona paused a moment longer, then bustled back into the kitchen.

I enjoyed my coffee and the wafting smells of freshly baked bread while I thought about Netta. I hadn't heard any noise from her end of the hallway this morning, but I had heard that strange noise in the middle of the night. Could that have been her? I hadn't seen anything when I looked out the window, but, of course, my bedroom only had a view of the back of the house. If Netta had left out the front door and traveled the path to the village, I wouldn't have seen her. But where would she have been going in the middle of the night?

After I finished my breakfast, I decided to look for Netta. She wasn't anywhere to be found in the house, and I was becoming concerned, especially after her erratic behavior the day before. She'd clearly been troubled, and I hoped that nothing had happened to her. I also hoped that she hadn't done anything to herself. It was a notion that hadn't occurred to me before, but now I was worried this might be the case.

Robert Nightingale's warning about Netta coming to a "bad end" also replayed in the back of my mind, hurrying my footsteps.

The first place I checked was the ferry launch, since Netta had seemed so adamant about getting off the island the day before. Her luggage had been moved back to her room at some point the day before, but perhaps she'd decided to leave without it, especially since there was so much of it. When I arrived at the launch, the few small fishing boats moored there had already set out for the morning, and there was no sign of either Netta or the ferry—the first scheduled arrival from Fionnphort wasn't for another hour yet. A pair of noisy gulls greeted me, but there wasn't another living soul in sight.

I turned on my heels and trekked into the village, my plaid wool scarf wound around my neck and my coat pulled tight against the wind whistling past my ears. I headed to where Dion was staying, in the hope that Netta might have gone there. My only bit of luck so far this morning was that Dion was there, finishing up her breakfast. When I explained that I was looking for Netta and why, she frowned.

"I'll join you. Just let me grab my coat."

I waited in the foyer, ignoring the dirty look her elderly landlady was shooting me from her post in the doorway of the breakfast room. Luckily, Dion was fast, and we were soon back out on the stoop.

"Your landlady didn't look thrilled at my interruption," I said.

Dion chuckled. "Mrs. O'Leary believes you need to sit and let your food digest for an hour before doing anything. It's nothing personal." Her face became serious. "I have to admit that I'm worried about Netta. This isn't a big island, and she couldn't have got off of it yesterday."

I agreed. Netta had to be on the island somewhere. I rather wished I'd gone to Redvers first thing to enlist his help, but it was too late now that I had Dion with me. It would have been helpful to have Redvers' keen eyes combing the island, but I would make do with the help I had.

Dion and I split up to cover the village and agreed to meet in front of the pub after an hour. Between the two of us, we managed to speak to all of the Golden Dawn members who were staying on the island, but no one had seen Netta.

Not that they would admit to, anyway.

I was glad that Dion was the one who'd spoken to Nightingale; I could only imagine what his reaction to her inquiry had been. Dion didn't elaborate, but I could tell that Nightingale had made it clear he thought we were wasting our time looking for Netta. And yet I was beginning to fear that this wasn't time wasted at all. Instead, I was beginning to fear quite the worst for the young woman.

After combing the village, the abbey, and the ruins of the nunnery with no sign of her, Dion and I decided to enlist help in our search. I spoke to the McCrarys, and Fiona begged off the actual search, volunteering to provide provisions instead, but Michael McCrary grudgingly agreed to look.

"She's staying at my cottage; I suppose I'm partially responsible for the girl," Michael said.

All I could offer in reply was a small shrug. I couldn't say whether anyone was responsible for Netta, but I did think we needed to look for her.

McCrary whistled for his dog, a furry gray mutt that lived among the sheep, and tugged at his wool cap. "I'll ask MacGregor as well. He has a knack for finding things. Sheep mostly, but it should apply to people too."

I thanked the man and set out again. Dion and I had agreed to split the island—I would travel up the west coast, and she would take the eastern side. If things went according to plan, in a few hours we would meet on the other side of Iona, near where Redvers was staying. I hadn't seen the cottage where he'd taken a room, but his description had led me to believe it was little more than a hut, with barely enough room for a guest—even a paying one. I sighed, looking at my watch. Unless Netta miraculously turned up, I would not be making it to our afternoon meeting, and for a moment, I considered leaving a message at the cottage where Redvers was staying, but immediately nixed the idea. It would link me to him, and our overall investigation couldn't afford that yet.

I normally walked with purpose on my treks across the island, quickly and head down, keeping an eye on my footing and only occasionally glancing up to take in my environs. But this time, I had to search the surrounding fields and stone, venturing off the path here and there to ensure I wasn't missing any sign of Netta. Nearly an hour later, my face hurt from the cold wind, so I paused for a moment, back to the gusts, letting my body enjoy the feeling of not being in motion as I scanned the landscape. There was a wild beauty to this island that I appreciated, although I couldn't imagine living so remotely on a full-time basis. But for short-term stays, it had a lot of appeal. Especially if one enjoyed hiking, as I claimed to.

I would be perfectly fine not participating in any outdoor pursuits for a while after this trip, however, if my aching feet had anything to say about it.

I set off again, down a gentle green slope and back up another incline, coming close to the fairy hill where I'd met Dion the day before, when a movement on that hill caught my eye. What I saw was close to the ground and still at quite a distance, but my heart sped up at the same rate that my feet did. I was nearly running by the time I came upon what I'd seen, which was the flapping of a black cloak.

Unfortunately, it was Netta's body that was wearing it.

CHAPTER EIGHT

I hurried to Netta and checked her pulse, but it was immediately obvious to me that she was long past any help. Her body had gone cold, and her lips were a disturbing shade of blue. I was far from an expert, but I would guess that she'd already been dead several hours.

I looked around, searching for a pile of clothing, but found none. This was strange because Netta was entirely naked except for the black cloak she was lying on, with only her arms tucked inside. Why would she be out here in the cold without any clothes or shoes on? The wind might have picked up her clothes and scattered them, but shoes were heavy enough to have stayed put. And there was no sign of anything—neither shoes nor scattered clothes. I did my best to tuck the cloak around Netta's body to cover her up, even though she was long past caring, but I would have to summon others here, and I wanted to give her some dignity. It crossed my mind that this might, in fact, be the scene of a crime, especially given Netta's lack of clothing, but this small action wasn't going to change anything substantially. If anything, protecting her body from the wind might preserve some bit of evidence I couldn't see.

While I covered her with the black cloak, I noticed that her skin was liberally covered with tiny scratches, the type you might get from a cat's claws, although I hadn't seen a single cat since I'd been on the island. I assumed there were some, I just hadn't seen any during my stay. It was strange that she was covered with these marks instead of having a scratch or two in one isolated area, which would be the case if a cat had done them. I looked at the scratches for a few moments, try-ing to determine what else they might be from, but didn't come to any sound conclusions before I had to look away.

I stepped back and surveyed the area. As I'd tucked the cloak around her, I'd also noticed that something seemed to be carved into the ground beneath her body, although I wouldn't be able to tell what it was until she'd been moved. If I had to guess, I would say that it had been made with the small dagger Netta clutched in her hand. Upon closer inspec-tion, I found that it was clean of blood, but there was a bit of dirt on the tip of it.

Next, I studied the ground around us. It was too hard to take footprints, so I walked all the way around the body, searching. As I did so, I noticed that the bottoms of Netta's feet were dark with mud and dirt and also scratched, even showing signs of dried blood in a few places. Which meant she'd been walking without shoes as well, perhaps all the way across the island, barefoot and nearly naked.

But besides the strange scratches on her body and the dam-age to her feet, there were no obvious signs of injury, and she had a weapon in her hand to defend herself with. So how had Netta died out here? And why?

With a heavy heart, I walked back toward the village; it was nearly twenty minutes before I came across a pair of lo-cals who had joined the search for Netta. I informed them that I'd found her body and asked them to call off the search and alert the authorities. Then I turned on my heel and headed back in the direction I'd just come from. I was chilled to the bone and wanted nothing more than to head back to the McCrary cottage and warm myself by a fire, but I couldn't leave Netta's body lying alone on that hill. Instead, I trudged back to stand guard over her until the proper authorities could be summoned.

It was a long wait, and I paced back and forth in order to keep warm—at a reasonable distance, of course. My feet were displeased, but it gave me an opportunity to think and to observe the area around the body. There weren't any foot-prints that I could see, and I wasn't leaving any either since the ground was still hard. Other than Netta herself, there was no sign that any other person had been in the vicinity. That didn't mean there hadn't been, of course, just that I couldn't see anything. I widened the circle of my search and still came up with no sign of clothing, nothing scattered on the wind or caught on a rock—nothing to indicate that Netta had come out here with anything but the black cloak.

I was still genuinely confused as to why she would be out here without any clothes on besides the cloak. As cold as it had been, even the cloak was close to wearing nothing at all, especially at night, and leaving the cottage in such a state of undress would have been incredibly cold and uncomfortable. But if she'd had clothes on and taken them off once here— and again, why would she?—her things certainly weren't here now. Could someone else have been with Netta and taken the clothes away with them? Which led me to the next question—was someone else responsible for her death?

I didn't know how long it took, but eventually a small cadre of people arrived, including Michael McCrary, and while I didn't know where he'd left his dog, I didn't bother to ask. The island and its regular population were so small that they didn't have a police force on the island, but McCrary told me that someone from Mull had already been summoned.

"It will still take a bit of time, wi' the ferry going there and back," Michael said, never taking his eyes from the body.

Now that Netta was surrounded by this small group of

men, I was glad I'd taken the time to tuck her cloak around her, hiding her from these prying eyes.

The men began making a plan to remove Netta's body so that an autopsy could be performed, and I decided that was sufficient for me to take my leave. I checked my watch, hoping I had time to warm myself by the fire before my appointed meeting with Redvers, but no such luck. With a sigh, I reminded myself that I was fortunate to even make it to our meeting today, which was only possible because I was already on this side of the island. No one was paying me any mind as I left the gathering and trudged toward the ocean, taking the familiar turn north toward our meeting spot and comforting myself with the knowledge that I was already more than halfway there.

On my walk, I recalled again what Robert Nightingale had said about Netta coming to a bad end, and I cringed. I hated that he'd been correct, and I certainly didn't want to see what his reaction to such news would be. The last thing I wanted was to hear him crowing that he'd been right while Netta lay in a morgue somewhere. Of course, I couldn't be positive that would be the man's reaction, but I could certainly picture it well enough that I wanted to avoid Nightingale for the near future.

I would dearly love to avoid him forever, but because of our investigation, that wasn't in the cards. Or in the leaves, as Fiona McCrary might prefer.

Which sparked another thought. Fiona had seemed overly concerned about Netta and "what she'd seen in the leaves" when I'd spoken to her the previous day. Could she know more than she'd been telling? Or had she simply had a feeling in her gut, much like I'd had, that Netta was not in a good state of mind? I would speak with the woman later, apart from her husband.

I made it to the meeting place, where Redvers was waiting for me. Without a word, I stepped into him, wrapping my arms around him while he did the same with me, both for comfort and for the warmth. I'd moved past shivering into numbness and couldn't quite feel my face anymore.

"You're frozen through," Redvers said.

"I had to stay with the body," I told him.

I could feel him go still.

"What body?"

"Netta's. I found her on the fairy hill." I went on to describe how I'd found her—naked except for the cloak, with a dagger in her fist.

If I'd had a free hand, I might have given my forehead a smack. I'd forgotten that there had been something carved beneath her, which wouldn't be revealed until after the body was moved. I probably should have waited until the men moved her, but I would have to pass the hill on my way back to the McCrary cottage anyway, so I could take a detour to the top of the hill to see what the carving was.

Yet another walk. I was already dreading it.

CHAPTER NINE

"Let's go back to my room. We need to get you warmed up." Redvers' voice was quite concerned.

"Are you sure that's a good idea?" I asked. There weren't any Golden Dawn members staying on his side of the island, but it still felt risky to have him sneak me into his quarters, if only because we were unmarried. His landlady was sure to have objections.

He gave a shrug as his answer, but was already moving me in that direction, his arm still wrapped around me so that I was tucked into his body. I decided not to argue any further—I really was quite cold. With that thought, I started shivering.

"It doesn't take much to die of exposure, especially in a damp place like this, with the wind blowing as it does."

"Do you think that's what happened to Netta?" I asked.

"Do you think it is? You're the one who saw the body."

I thought about it for a moment. "There were no obvious signs of injury that would lead to death. But I can't imagine what would make someone head out into the cold wearing nothing but a cloak, and then lie down on the cold ground to die after carving something into it." I told him about the dirt on the dagger and then shook my head. "I also can't explain the strange scratches all over her body or the fact that she was also barefoot, and her clothes and shoes were nowhere to be seen."

Redvers thought that over. "Could she have made the scratches herself?"

"The ones I saw, sure. It's possible that she did. The real question will be if they were on her back as well, where she couldn't reach. But I didn't move the body to find out."

"That's for the best. I'll find out where the autopsy is being performed."

He didn't need to say that he would be in attendance—I'd already assumed that he would be. Or, if not present during the autopsy itself, Redvers would get all the information we needed afterward. His sources really were quite useful.

The walk from our meeting place on the beach to where Redvers was staying was mercifully a short one. Contrary to what he'd claimed, this was hardly a hut in the middle of nowhere—it was a lovely white-washed two-story cottage with a slate roof and a typical stone fence surrounding it. The front door was painted a cheerful green, and we stood outside while Redvers poked his head through the door and, seeing no one in the foyer, ushered me quickly inside.

The owner of the cottage was in the kitchen, and we made it past the downstairs hall and up the stairs into Redvers' quarters without being seen. I moved immediately to the fire, which was burning in the fireplace, standing as close as physically possible without standing in the fire itself. Redvers took my coat off, slinging it onto a nearby chair.

"I was using that," I said mildly.

"You'll warm up faster without it," he said, moving around me to add another log to the banked fire, then stoking the flames higher with the iron poker.

"How do you figure that?" I asked, still concentrating on the flames before me. I hadn't realized just how cold I was until I started to thaw. I found that sometimes it was best not to think about how uncomfortable you were until it was over. And I'd had plenty to occupy my mind.

Redvers turned me toward him, which made me feel a bit like I was roasting on a spit, a sensation I was fine with since I was now thawing my backside. He stepped into me and pulled me into his arms.

And then I was quite warm for a while.

Despite pleasant distractions from the weighty events of the day, it came time to turn our minds back to the issues at hand. We got dressed again and each took a seat in the upholstered chairs that we pulled close to the fire. Redvers added yet another log, and I nodded my approval.

"Even though it's unlikely that Nightingale was involved, I would still like to look into Netta's death." I didn't want to call it a murder, since we really had no idea what had happened to her, but I felt an obligation to look into things all the same.

"I agree. I'll find out what I can about where she's being taken and then what they learn at the autopsy."

"Thank you. In the meantime, I'll talk with the McCrarys and with Dion Fortune. Dion seemed to know Netta fairly well. It sounds as though they've known each other for some time. And Netta sent her that note about leaving the order." I frowned. "I'm sorry I didn't get a look at it."

Redvers arched an eyebrow at me. "That's rather surprising, knowing you."

I wrinkled my nose at him. "I wasn't about to steam the envelope open, and holding it up to the light didn't tell me anything."

He looked even more amused, if that was possible.

I looked around his room, which was spacious, considering it was on the second floor. Whereas my room was made small by the sloping eaves of the roof, this room was barely touched by such an architectural detail. And the owner's taste ran to cozy, with a thick, handmade quilt on the bed and a wool rug with a generous pile covering the wood floor. Even the chairs we were sitting in were quite comfortable. "I was given the impression—by you, I might add—that you were staying in something just short of a shed out here on this side of the island. I think this cottage might be nicer than the one I'm staying in."

Redvers winked at me. "I didn't want to make you feel bad that you'd chosen so poorly."

I looked around for a pillow to toss at him but came up empty. With a sigh, I sat back in my seat. "I feel terrible that Netta left the cottage in the middle of the night and died and I didn't do anything to stop her."

"You couldn't have known something like this would happen. And I'm not certain you could have stopped her, even if you'd heard her leaving and tried."

I shrugged. "Of course, I couldn't have known, but she was acting so strangely yesterday." I explained how she'd insisted on trying to get off of the island and that I should leave too. "And I did hear strange noises in the middle of the night—I thought they were a dream, but now I think they were probably Netta leaving. I got up and looked out my window, but I didn't see anything. Even still, I should have gone and checked on her."

Redvers was quiet for a moment, then reached over and took my hand, the one with the engagement ring on it shining brightly. I still wasn't quite used to wearing a ring again, but I loved this one, not only because it was beautiful, but also because it had been in his family for generations. It made it all the more meaningful.

"I hope you can find a way to stop blaming yourself," Redvers said. "I don't think you have a bit of culpability here." He gave my hand a squeeze. "And we'll figure out what happened to her."

I squeezed his hand back. I knew we would.

CHAPTER TEN

The walk back was equally as cold as the trip there, but more pleasant now that I'd been properly warmed up. I appreciated the fact that Redvers was always willing to dive into a new investigation with me, even if it wasn't connected to our current one. I also appreciated the fact that he trusted I would be able to juggle both issues.

The sun was sinking low in the sky—I'd spent longer with Redvers than I'd thought, and I hoped no one would ask where I'd spent the afternoon. I didn't have a good excuse at the ready, and I didn't think anyone would believe I'd spent that many hours in the cold.

To get out of the cottage, Redvers snuck me back down the stairs and right out the front door, after first checking to see where the farmer and his wife were in the house. I conceded that there were, in fact, quite a lot of sheep around the property, but I scoffed openly again at his earlier claim of staying in a hut.

I walked back the same way I'd come, climbing back up the fairy hill where I'd found Netta. The body and all the onlookers were now gone, and I hoped that they had treated her with care when they removed her.

I paused at the spot where her body had been, taking a large step back to get the full picture of what had been carved into the ground beneath her. It appeared to be two intersecting triangles, one upside down and laid over the top of the other in the shape of a pentagram. It felt ominous, although I had no real knowledge of what it actually meant. The only thing I knew for certain was that it was strange, and I had some research to do on the meaning behind it.

My own cottage was quiet when I arrived, and I saw that the mirrors in both the hall and the sitting room had been covered with black cloth. It was an old superstition to cover the mirrors when someone passed away, but I wasn't terribly surprised that Fiona kept it. There were a lot of old traditions and superstitions that seemed to be alive and well here on the island, even ones including fairies and tea leaves. Which reminded me yet again that I needed to speak with the lady of the house.

I found Fiona McCrary in the kitchen, stirring what looked like another stew. I was glad I didn't have to contend with a haggis—once I had learned what was in it, I hadn't been too keen on eating one, but I also wasn't keen on being impolite to my hosts by turning up my nose at what they served.

"Lamb stew tonight," Fiona said, eyeing me up. "I'm sorry it's another stew, but since you and the mister have been spending so much time outside, I thought you could stand something warm and hearty."

"Where is Mr. McCrary?" I asked.

"Out with the others. They got Netta to the ferry, poor mite. Mike thought we should send her things as well, so he was here for a spell this afternoon, told me to get them ready."

That explained how she knew what was happening, but I was surprised that Michael McCrary would be so quick to get rid of her things. Netta had died only hours before. Was he really that anxious to get the room rented to someone new?

"But the police sent word not to disturb anything, to leave everything where it be."

"The police were here?"

Fiona shook her head, still not looking at me. "The doctor came and took a look at 'er, and then called the police. They haven't been by yet, but they sent a message. The ferry has never made so many trips to and fro." The woman finally stole a look at me, and her voice dropped to a whisper, even though there was no one about to hear us. "I heard she was naked as the day she were born."

"That much is true." I was pleased that the police had come to the island—I hadn't been sure they would make the trip since there were no obvious signs of foul play. I wondered if it was the little scratches on Netta's body that made the doctor call the police; it was the only outwardly suspicious sign I'd seen. Other than the fact that she'd been naked, with no clothes in sight.

Fiona glanced at me again quickly before rummaging around in her cupboard for some spices. "I also heard that a man in a black cloak was seen on the island. They're sayin' if anything evil happened to her, 'twas probably him."

I was glad that Fiona wasn't looking at me because I couldn't say for certain that I was able to keep my face from reacting to this news. I knew for a fact that the man in the black cloak wasn't involved, because that man was Redvers. I would have to tell my fiancé that he needed a less dramatic piece of outerwear for the remainder of his stay on the island if he didn't want to be arrested for Netta's death. Or hunted down by the locals.

Fiona took a quick taste from her large iron pot. "You should head on upstairs, lass. This will still be a bit of time."

"I will in just a moment, but I had another question. You said you saw something in the leaves."

Now Fiona looked a bit panicked. "I shouldnae have said anything," she muttered.

"I promise I won't tell Mr. McCrary," I said. "But what did you see?" I didn't believe that some sludge in the bottom of her cup could tell the future, but I did believe that her subconscious might have known something she hadn't thought of before she studied the bottom of her cup.

Fiona shook her head. "Not now."

I watched her for a moment, then decided to retreat for the time being. I would readdress this later, although I wasn't sure what had her spooked now. "Okay. Whenever you're ready to talk about it."

Fiona nodded, never taking her eyes from what she was doing, and I left the kitchen, heading for the front stairs.

Where I nearly walked right into Michael McCrary.

"Whoa there, lass. You'll knock a soul over," Michael said, hands coming up quickly to steady me.

"Sorry." I took a step back, then cocked my head at the man. He looked weary and cold. "Has everything been taken care of?"

He rubbed an ear, then nodded. "Aye. The body is off to Mull, where she will be seen to. Do you know if she has any people that we should notify?"

I shook my head. "She never mentioned anyone, although Dion Fortune might know."

With a dismissive shrug, McCrary started toward the kitchen. "I suppose we'll let the police handle things from here out, then."

I watched him go, wondering how on earth Fiona McCrary had known that her husband was in the house. I hadn't heard a single noise.

Chapter Eleven

I went upstairs, but instead of heading straight to my room, I went directly to Netta's. Since the police had been called, I wanted to take a look at her things before they did, and I imagined they would be here soon, now that the body was off to Mull. In fact, I was surprised that they weren't here already, but I hadn't seen anyone on the hill or on my walk back, although perhaps they were occupied with speaking to the other members of the order first.

My first item of business was to see if I could tell what Netta had burned in her fireplace. I hadn't taken a closer look earlier, but given everything that had happened, I dearly wanted to see if I could figure out what it was.

Opening the door to her room, I found Netta's trunk and various other pieces of luggage just inside the door, still packed from when she had decided to flee the island. I felt a moment of regret that the ferry hadn't been running that day—perhaps if she had been able to leave, she would still be alive.

I moved past her luggage and went to the fireplace, grateful that Fiona hadn't been in here to clean anything yet. Even still, there was very little left in the fireplace. Most of whatever Netta had burned had long since turned to ash or was charred beyond use, but I took the metal poker and sifted through the detritus, finding a few scraps of paper that the fire had missed. I blew them off and squinted at the writing. One tiny scrap had some cramped handwriting, although it was impossible to make out more than a few letters. Another piece had part of a symbol on it, but I couldn't quite tell what it had been part of. The final piece was a little larger, and I could just make out the word "Golden" on it.

If I had to guess, these were parts of a pamphlet or manual relating to the Golden Dawn. But why would Netta burn them? She'd left the group, but why bother burning the materials instead of giving them to someone like Dion? Unless these were materials that Netta didn't want anyone to see. But what could those possibly be?

Next, I searched the small bureau, finding nothing but a few pieces of blackened jewelry that had clearly once been silver laid on top. It was strange, since Netta was always bedecked with quite a lot of jewelry, but perhaps these pieces hadn't been worn in some time and simply needed to be cleaned. There was nothing else, however. Netta had been thorough in packing up her things.

Which left her luggage. There were quite a lot of pieces, and I sighed but got to work, starting with the smallest and leaving the largest for last. There was a lot of clothing, which was quick enough to sort through, and I was able to put aside a few cases quickly. I finally came to a suitcase that was heavier than the rest. Putting it on the bed, I opened it to find a stack of books related to mysticism and the occult, with titles like *The Occult Sciences* and *The Book of Forbidden Knowledge*. None of them seemed particularly out of the ordinary, though, especially given Netta's interests and membership in Nightingale's group. Putting them aside, I uncovered a few Golden Dawn manuals at the very bottom of the suitcase, similar to the one I'd been provided with for studying. If these were still intact, though, what materials had Netta burned?

With that question simmering in the back of my mind, I sifted through the rest of her things, finding nothing else of real interest. No love letters, nothing to indicate that she'd been involved with anything other than the occult. And it was quite obvious that she had a lot of interest there, especially based on the stack of books she'd brought with her, but I'd already known that, so it was no great revelation.

I tidied up her things and left the room, closing the door quietly behind me just as I heard someone coming up the stairs. I stealthily moved down the hall to make it appear I was coming from either the bathroom or my own room when I saw Fiona appear at the top of the landing.

"Dinner is ready, lass."

I smiled and thanked her before following her downstairs.

After dinner, I decided to make the most of my time, so I bundled up in my coat and cloche and headed down the path and into the village to the pub located in the lobby of the St. Columba Hotel. If I had any luck, there would be at least one or two people there that I needed to talk with, and running into them at the pub would have a more casual feel than seeking them out to interview them about Netta's death.

I reminded myself that I couldn't lose sight of the fact that I was still gathering information on Robert Nightingale. If I could connect him with Netta's death, I could kill two birds with one stone, since the crown couldn't use an inmate as an agent, although it was unlikely to be that simple. I couldn't see Nightingale having a motive to murder the poor girl, despite his ominous predictions about her "coming to a bad end." And I still wasn't certain Netta had even been murdered—there wasn't much to indicate that she had been, other than the strange scratches on her body and the lack of clothes and shoes. I was hoping we'd have more answers after the autopsy.

The St. Columba Hotel was a long, white two-story building with blue-trimmed windows and doors, set apart from the village but near St. Oran's Chapel and the abbey. I could hear the roar of the surf, even if I couldn't see it in the darkness that had descended—the hotel faced the ocean directly, offering stunning views to its guests during the day, as well as a short walk to the abbey and its ruins.

I entered the lobby and walked through to the pub area. I saw that I was in luck since a few members of the Golden Dawn had assembled over a pint, including Dion and Robert Nightingale. I headed for Dion, who was waiting at the dark wooden bar for the bartender to bring her drink.

"Jane, you made it."

That made it sound as though I'd been invited in the first place, instead of just taking a chance that folks would be at the local pub. "Was I supposed to be here?"

Dion cocked her head. "I left word at your cottage that we were meeting here tonight. A few of us want to discuss . . . things . . . surrounding Netta's unfortunate passing."

I frowned since no one at the cottage had told me as much. But perhaps Fiona had simply forgotten to relay the message. It had to be the case, given the day's events—I couldn't imagine what the McCrarys would have to gain by keeping me from this meeting.

I snuck a glance at the other members, and it was quite apparent to me that not everyone was present, so I wondered at being included in this small gathering. Had that been Dion's idea or Robert Nightingale's?

The bartender brought a glass of something brown for Dion. She picked it up and took a small sip. "Whisky, neat," she explained to my inquiring gaze. "I don't like a bitter taste."

I nodded and ordered the same from the bartender. I didn't care much for beer myself and decided I may as well try the local spirits. While the man was pouring another glass, I asked Dion the question foremost in my mind.

"What exactly did the note say that Netta gave you?"

Dion sighed and took another sip of her scotch whisky. "She told me that she was leaving the group, that's all. I wasn't surprised; she'd been rather unhappy with Nightingale for a while." This was said while glancing in the man's direction to ensure we wouldn't be overheard. There was no concern there, since he was pontificating about heaven only knew what to the group gathered around him.

"In what way? I thought you said they didn't interact much." It wasn't exactly different from what Dion had told me before, but it was different enough that I was curious as to why her story would have changed regarding Netta and Nightingale.

"He's taken us in a different direction since we broke off from Mina Mathers's group."

"Who is Mina Mathers?" The question was out before I could question whether or not I should already know the answer.

Dion gave me a strange look. "She and her husband founded the Golden Dawn."

"Of course, of course. That was a silly question." Sloppy backpedaling on my part—I needed to be much more careful in the future. The bartender brought me my snifter of scotch, and I took an experimental sip, the peaty taste burning a path down my throat, and I coughed while both the bartender and Dion looked amused. "It's good," I said through another fit of coughs.

I had more questions for Dion, but she tilted her head, indicating that we should join the others, and I reluctantly followed her to the little group. Nightingale and Yeats had taken seats nearest the fire, with John Bychowski and another member seated next to them. Dion and I were the only women present, and the only female members of the group now that Netta was gone. We took our seats in the only chairs left, farthest from the warmth. I left my coat on.

Nightingale looked at me critically. "Glad you could join us, Miss Wunderly."

I smiled at him, feigning ignorance of his pointed tone, and took another sip of scotch, managing not to cough up my lungs this time. It was starting to warm my insides instead of burning them, and I found that warmth in my belly also made Nightingale slightly more tolerable. "My pleasure," I said.

He frowned slightly, obviously expecting an apology from me and confused at not getting one, but after blinking a few times, he continued on with what he'd been talking about before we arrived. "With Netta gone, we'll have to see if we can get someone to fill her role for the ceremony. We only have two days to do that. Does anyone have a suggestion for a member who might be able to make the trip at such short notice?"

I did my best not to physically recoil at the insensitivity. Netta was dead; it wasn't as if she had taken a trip. And she hadn't died simply to inconvenience the man and his upcoming ritual, which is how he made it sound.

Nightingale looked around the group, his face serious. "I am sorry that Netta passed away. She was a valuable member of our group, and her loss will be felt. Does anyone know if she has family that needs to be contacted?"

This was the first sensitive thing I'd heard from Robert Nightingale, and I hoped my face didn't show my surprise at the sincerity in his voice. No one volunteered any information about Netta's family, instead whispering among themselves, so I finally spoke up. "I think the police will take care of notifying her next of kin."

I looked around at a lot of shocked faces in the group.

"The police have been involved?" Yeats asked. He turned to Nightingale. "I cannae be involved with this if the police be asking questions. I'm a senator now, I cannae have my name associated with this."

Nightingale had also looked surprised at my announcement, but he recovered quickly to reassure Yeats. "W.B., I'm sure it's just a formality. And there is no need to worry—I'll make sure that your name is kept out of everything."

Yeats said nothing more, but he looked as though he didn't believe this reassurance in the slightest. I wondered if the poet would leave the island before the ritual in order to avoid publicity. If he did, I could hardly blame him.

"Do we know how she died?" Bychowski asked, the firelight glinting off his glasses as he looked around the little group. "All I've heard is that she was found." Nearly everyone in the order was British, but from his accent, it sounded as though Bychowski was a fellow American. I would need to avoid him as much as possible to avoid questions that I couldn't answer, starting with how I knew Madame Blavatsky and how a dead woman could have recommended me to the group. I was starting to think we should have chosen an occult figure who was not as well known for that letter of introduction, as well as one who was still alive.

The other members of the Golden Dawn looked around at each other with little shrugs, either not knowing anything about Netta's death or unwilling to share what they had heard.

"I found the body," I heard myself say, causing a chorus of gasps.

CHAPTER TWELVE

I sighed inwardly as soon as the words were out and mentally blamed the scotch for my loose tongue, although it was likely that word would have gotten around soon enough, since quite a few locals, including Michael McCrary, were well aware that it had been me who'd found Netta. Numerous people had also seen the body, and while I didn't think McCrary was a gossip, I couldn't speak to any of the rest of the men who'd been there, especially since things like this tended to be foremost on everyone's mind and thus popular topics of discussion. Even McCrary, closed-mouthed as he seemed to be, was likely to be asked prying questions since folks knew he'd been at the site.

No one said a word for a long moment after my sudden pronouncement. Even Robert Nightingale appeared to have been startled into silence, which I hadn't thought possible.

I peered into my glass, which was now nearly empty. I decided that I should stay away from liquor and stick to beer. Or maybe I could try to finally develop a taste for tea. "There will be an autopsy," I said into the heavy silence. "It wasn't . . . immediately apparent what killed her."

"Well." Nightingale was still having trouble finding his tongue. "Well." He took another sip of his drink, and then changed the subject entirely. I assumed it was because he was uncomfortable not knowing more than someone else about any given topic, but perhaps I was wrong.

"I think we should all retire for the evening, but please come up with someone who might be able to assist us with our solstice ritual," Nightingale finally said. "The clock is ticking." With that he stood, put his half-full pint glass on the fireplace mantel, and swept out of the room.

I was left slightly startled by the man's abrupt departure, but the others seemed nonplussed by this behavior. Bychowski and his companion drained what was left in their glasses and prepared to leave as well, although Bychowski grabbed Nightingale's glass from the mantel and took it back to the bar along with his own.

Which left me alone with Yeats and Dion. I was finished with my scotch and knew with certainty that I wasn't going to drink another one, but I wasn't finished asking questions for the evening.

Nor was I finished answering them, it would seem.

Dion was frowning. "You couldn't tell what had happened to her?"

I shook my head. "There were no obvious signs of what might have killed her." I paused, then decided to forge ahead. "There were a few things that were strange, though."

Dion and Yeats looked at me expectantly.

"She was lying on a pentagram that had been carved into the ground. I don't know if she did it or if someone else did." She'd had the dagger in her hand, but it could have been put there by someone else, although there was no sign that there'd been anyone else out there with her.

Dion looked thoughtful. "Netta probably did that herself. The pentagram is a symbol of protection; she probably carved it to protect herself."

"From what?" I asked.

Dion shook her head. "Hard to say."

That was interesting, and it fit with Netta's strange behavior and insistence that she get off the island. Maybe she thought she was under attack from something and carved the pentagram to protect herself. Although it didn't explain why she was on the fairy hill, naked except for the cloak. I decided to leave that part out. "She also seemed to be covered in tiny scratches."

At this, Dion looked shocked, and the glass in her hand shook slightly. She didn't say anything for a long moment, finally muttering, "It couldn't be."

"It couldn't be what?" I asked.

Dion finally looked at me, then glanced at Yeats, who was sitting quietly and taking everything in. She shook her head again, tipping back what was left in her snifter, but not saying anything else. Yeats took the hint and excused himself.

"I'll see ye tomorrow, then. Off to bed wi' me now."

I said goodnight to the man, and Dion mumbled something that also sounded like "goodnight." Once he'd exited the pub and Dion and I were alone, she glanced around again. "I shouldn't say anything."

I sat quietly, hoping she would continue without any encouragement. I'd found, at times, that people were more willing to talk when you didn't ask them to do so.

Dion pulled up her long shirtsleeve, revealing tiny scratches on her arm. I was shocked and, for a moment, didn't know what to say.

"Those are just like the scratches that Netta had on her body," I said.

Dion nodded, letting her sleeve drop back into place. "I have them all over. Three days ago, I was accessing the astral plane, and I was blocked."

I wasn't entirely certain what this meant, but it was obvious that Dion believed that the astral plane was not only a real thing, but something that she could be stopped from accessing. "Do you know who blocked you?" This was the best question I could come up with without asking her to explain things I should probably know about.

"I do know. It was Mina Mathers."

I dearly wanted to ask more questions about Mina Mathers—and I had many—but now was clearly not the time. Especially since I'd nearly blown my cover once that evening by not recognizing the name of a founder of the occult group I'd been initiated to. I clearly should be familiar with all things Mina Mathers, which was research I would conduct later. Or perhaps Redvers could do it for me. "How do you know she was the person blocking you?"

"I think I'm going to need another whisky to tell this story." Dion held up her empty glass, then indicated my own with a nod of her head. "Can I get you one?"

I paused, not wanting any more scotch whisky, but also not wanting Dion to feel as though she was drinking alone and spilling her secrets while I simply sat there taking it all in.

I reasoned that, even if she got me one, I didn't need to drink it.

"Certainly," I said.

Dion went to the bar, carrying our empty glasses, and returned shortly with our refills. I pretended to take a sip, but managed to keep any of the scorching liquid from passing between my lips. I hoped Dion wouldn't notice that my glass stayed full.

"Where was I?"

"Mina blocked you from the astral plane."

"She did. I went into my trance and could feel that my energy was being blocked. And then she was there, telling me that I was banned from the plane because . . ." Here she paused, and I could tell that she had been about to say something else and changed her mind. "Because I left the group and went with Nightingale's faction instead of her own."

I considered pressing her on what she had been about to

say, and I decided to do it gently instead of accusing her outright. "Is that the only reason?"

She nodded, but wouldn't look at me. "Mina values loyalty, and she was very angry when I decided to leave with the others."

"Why did you? It seems like there's no love lost between you and Nightingale."

Dion grimaced. "You're right; he's not my favorite person. In fact, he might be one of my least favorite. But he is very talented and quite powerful." I hadn't seen any evidence of that at all, so I supposed I would have to take her word for it. "But I felt that I had more to learn from him than I did from Mina at this point." Dion sighed, sipping at her scotch, and I followed suit, although I wasn't actually drinking it, just letting it bounce off my closed lips. "Mina is . . . well, rather limited in her thinking. Especially since her husband died. She . . ." Dion trailed off, thinking. "I think 'lost' is the best word to describe her now."

"I understand why she would be upset to lose you," I said. That much was true; I did understand why someone would want Dion in their group. "But why would she have attacked Netta as well?"

Dion shrugged. "The same reason. She was angry that Netta left her group."

I was certain that an astral attack could not kill a person, but I was curious about whether Dion believed it was possible. "Do you think Mina could have killed Netta? Through an astral attack?"

Dion seriously considered my question before answering. "I do, actually. She was angry enough that she sent black cats to torment us. It was before coming to Iona, when Netta and I were staying together on Mull."

I couldn't stop my eyebrows from popping up. Someone sending attack cats to harass another person might be the most outlandish thing I'd ever heard anyone claim. I couldn't even formulate a question, which was just as well because Dion continued on quite seriously.

"Day and night, black cats everywhere, and they smelled terribly." Dion wrinkled her nose at the memory. "But Netta and I did a powerful cleansing ceremony together, and they disappeared—we didn't have problems with them after that. But when we didn't come crawling back to Mina for help, she must have decided to try a different approach and took things to the astral plane."

I thought this sounded like a case of overactive imaginations and a lot of foolishness, but Dion clearly believed that what she was saying was true. It was hard to reconcile—Dion seemed so practical, and much like my thinking about Yeats, I couldn't understand how someone who appeared to have two feet on the ground otherwise could buy into this occult business.

As far as Netta was concerned, it was clear that she had bought into all this entirely. I'd assumed, when she was talking about seeing faces in the clouds and experiencing trouble with the astral plane, that she was having some kind of mental problem requiring a doctor's care, but perhaps that hadn't been the case after all. I still didn't believe any of these things were true, but they seemed to fit in with this overall belief system that both Netta and Dion adhered to. I wasn't certain what all this meant, but it had given me a lot to think about.

Of course, this still didn't answer the question of what actually had killed Netta.

CHAPTER THIRTEEN

"You're drinking slowly," Dion observed. She was almost done with her scotch, and it had become quite clear that I wasn't drinking mine.

I smiled and took a real sip. It burned less now, although I still wasn't sure whether I actually liked it or not. I would have preferred to stick to my gin, but I hadn't seen any behind the bar. "Too much thinking, I guess." I cocked my head. "Why would Netta burn Golden Dawn materials?"

Dion stopped toying with the glass in her hand to look at me. "Why do you ask that?"

I didn't want to admit that I'd been poking through her things after she died, so I hedged a bit. "When I went looking for her, I checked her room, and I just happened to see some scraps in her fireplace. Before . . . well, before we knew where she was. Anyway, I thought it was strange."

Dion nodded, but she was now studying the flames in the fireplace and wouldn't meet my eyes. "I don't know why she would, but Netta was an odd one. It was probably because she was leaving the group. A way of cleansing herself perhaps."

I thought it would be easier to take a bath, but I held my tongue. "That's probably it." Dion nodded, but was still avoiding eye contact, making it obvious that she knew something she wasn't telling me. Quite a few somethings, if my instincts were correct.

"I'm done in. You'll be fine getting back to your lodgings?" Dion asked, already standing up and looking a little bit unsteady on her legs.

I nodded, knowing full well what answer Dion was hoping for. "I'll be fine. I have a flashlight, and I'd like to finish my drink." Dion's face relaxed in relief, confirming what I'd thought. I wondered if she was anxious to put some distance between us because she felt she'd shared too much. Scotch apparently had that effect.

I watched as she left the pub, waiting until the door was closed before I stood and made my way to the bar, where I deposited the rest of my drink. The bartender raised a gray eyebrow at me, and I smiled sheepishly, then went out myself.

It was dark now, the moon hidden behind the clouds once again, and I flicked on the small flashlight I'd taken to carrying around in my pocket. I was nearly to the path leading toward the McCrary cottage when I heard a whispered voice call "Jane," somewhere to my left, and I shrieked. I was torn between running off into the night or grabbing a rock to defend myself when a man in a black cloak stepped out of the shadows.

"Dammit, Redvers, you scared the life out of me." One hand to my rapidly beating heart, I shined the flashlight toward him and could see his grin glinting. A quick flick of my light to the left showed an opening in the stone fence I'd been walking along where it was bordered by two pillars—that was where he'd concealed himself.

I kept talking to cover how scared I'd been, although I was certain I wasn't fooling Redvers. "You really need to find a coat instead of wearing that cloak. The locals are already talking—they think 'the man in the black cloak' is involved in Netta's death."

He chuckled, then stepped forward, pushing back his hood and wrapping me in his arms for a moment. After a too-short embrace, he released me, except for my hand, which he took in his, pulling me back in the direction I'd come from.

"Where are we headed?" I asked in a hissed whisper. Going back toward the hotel seemed a sure way to be seen, and the last time we'd spoken, we'd agreed that we still needed to maintain our cover. The streets were deserted this time of night, but even still.

"Just here," Redvers said, leading me down a short path and through the arched doorway into St. Oran's Chapel, a tiny medieval stone chapel with whitewashed walls inside. It had been renovated recently, so at least there was a roof between us and the mist that had begun saturating the air. It was said that around fifty Scottish kings were buried in the graveyard adjacent to the chapel. I'd tried to look at the gravestones earlier in the week, but they were so worn by the elements that they were unreadable.

"Aren't you afraid of being seen by someone?" I asked once we were safely inside the chapel.

Redvers looked mildly offended. "I'm very good at getting around without being seen."

I raised a skeptical eyebrow since plenty of locals were talking about the man in the cloak.

"I'm not hiding from the locals," he said. "Just the Golden Dawn members. And they aren't the most observant crowd. Now, I heard most of the conversation in the bar, but I couldn't hear what you and Dion were discussing. She was speaking very quietly."

"How exactly did you manage that? Were you hiding in the fireplace?"

"That's silly. No, I was hiding in the back."

"And the bartender didn't see you skulking around the back of his bar?"

"Of course he did. But I know the fellow."

I sighed. "Of course you do."

Even in the dark, I caught the glint of amusement in his eyes. "I didn't know you liked scotch."

I wrinkled my nose at him. "I'm fairly certain that I do not." Although it was going a long way toward keeping me warm, even now. I could still feel the heat radiating upward from my stomach.

Or perhaps that was from being near to Redvers.

I corralled my straying thoughts. "Dion thinks that Mina Mathers attacked her on the astral plane and might have done the same to Netta."

Redvers just looked at me for a long moment.

"I know. I thought the same thing. But she believes that it's true, which is the important thing." I giggled at the continued look on his face. "I won't tell you about the cats."

He grimaced. "Please don't."

"What's interesting, though, is that Dion also had little scratches on her arm. Like the ones on Netta's body." I looked at him intently. "Has the autopsy been scheduled?"

He nodded in the dim light of my flashlight. "Tomorrow. I'll go over on the first ferry."

"Hopefully we'll have some answers after that." My mind returned to the scratches. "I don't believe that Dion got her scratches on the astral plane."

"No," Redvers said firmly. "Could she have done them to herself?"

"And done the same to Netta?" I thought that over. "It's a strange way to try to throw suspicion off of yourself—claiming mysterious scratches. It would be far easier to just establish an alibi. And I can't think of a reason why Dion would have wanted to hurt Netta."

"You only saw the scratches on her arm?"

I nodded. "I wasn't about to ask her to take her clothes off in the pub." Or anywhere else, for that matter.

Redvers was quiet for a moment. "It's strange, I'll say that."

I nodded. It was very strange. But then I took a step closer to my fiancé, flicking off the flashlight and putting the case out of my mind for a few moments.

I was chilled again by the time I made it back to my room, but it had been worth the extra time spent in the cold with Redvers. I wanted to figure out what happened to Netta, but I was even more eager to put this entire case behind me so that I could go back to spending time in public—and private—with my fiancé.

I'd finally become accustomed to calling Redvers my fiancé, especially since I had a ring on my finger as a constant reminder. But we hadn't discussed the wedding at all. All I knew for certain was that I didn't want a big to-do this time, as angry as that would make my Aunt Millie, who had made her own ideas about what I should be planning quite clear. I had no intention of giving in to her on this, though. In fact, it would be ideal if Redvers and I could simply do it alone, with no one but the officiant. I would talk to him about that at some point in the near future.

But for now, it was time to sleep. The fire was already banked, and I put myself to bed, hoping things would have more clarity in the morning, especially after learning what we could from Netta's autopsy.

Unfortunately, I had a restless night's sleep, which I blamed on the slight headache I had from the scotch and the evening's strange topics of conversation. Bizarre dreams plagued me, although the only one I could remember involved my being hunted by black cats the size of wolves. It didn't take Freud to figure out where my subconscious had pulled that from, but it had felt real enough that I sat straight up in bed as I was about to be attacked. I had a hard time falling back asleep after that, and I dozed in and out until it was finally time to get up.

Downstairs, I ate a quiet breakfast and lingered over my little pot of coffee, not sure where I should head next. Redvers had canceled our afternoon meeting since he would be on Mull for the autopsy, and I found myself at loose ends for the day. I had briefly considered accompanying him, but I'd seen Netta's body—in fact, I could still see it when I closed my eyes—and I didn't need another look at her, especially not during the procedure. For once, I was fine with Redvers simply reporting back.

A knock at the front door interrupted my musings, and I heard Fiona answer it. A man's loud voice rang clearly through the first floor. "My daughter stays here. Where are her things?"

It would appear that Netta's father had arrived.

I couldn't hear Fiona's response, but the voices got nearer as she ushered the man into the dining room, where I sat. Fiona looked frazzled at this man's arrival and indicated for him to take a seat. "Let me get you a cup of tea first. Then we can talk."

He was a large man with dark hair and dark eyes and a thick accent that I guessed was Italian in nature, although I couldn't be sure. He grumbled but took a seat at the other end of the table, spearing me with his eyes. "Who are you? Did you know my Netta?"

Definitely Italian. "I did, but not very well. I only met her because we were staying here together." I watched as his large hands repeatedly smoothed the white tablecloth in front of him. "You must be Netta's father. I'm so sorry for your loss."

He must have sensed my sincerity, which was very real. "Thank you." His eyes filled with tears, and for some reason, I was reminded that a crocodile could produce tears as well. Perhaps it was his toothy grin. "She was everything to me, and this is, how you say, devastating."

I had no doubt that was true, but I did wonder how he had managed to get here so quickly. Had he been staying nearby? Surely, he hadn't been all the way in Italy—there was no way he could have gotten word of her death and then been here in one day. Could we even be certain that this was Netta's father? It was entirely possible that someone had heard of the young woman's demise and decided to make the most of an opportunity.

Fiona came back with a cup of tea for the man and then hovered nearby, hands working at her apron.

I glanced at her and back at the man before us, trying to keep all suspicion from my face. "And what is your name?"

He slapped his head with his hand dramatically. "I am so sorry! I never say. It is Giuseppe Fornario." Giuseppe took a sip of his tea and grimaced. "The English, I never understand how you drink this." He looked at me, gesturing to his cup. "You drink?"

I shook my head, hiding a small smile. I had to agree with the man—English tea wasn't my cup of tea, as it were. "I have coffee." I lifted the pot, testing the amount left. "There's still a bit left, if you'd like some."

Giuseppe looked as though he was about to agree, but then shook his head. "I would like to see her things. I should not waste more time."

I glanced at Fiona, who was looking a little disgruntled, probably because of this man's reaction to her tea, which I was certain was quite good for what it was. I cocked my head at her, and she made a face, so I volunteered to take the man upstairs. I didn't mind—it was a good opportunity to see if I could discover whether he was actually related to Netta.

"Thank you. That is very kind. Just show me the way, and I will be fine."

I led Giuseppe upstairs and showed him into Netta's room. As soon as he was inside, he thanked me with another toothy smile and firmly shut the door, which I found even more suspicious. I hadn't expected to be invited inside to look at her things with him, but his abrupt dismissal was definitely strange. He'd shed tears downstairs, but as he shut the door he'd seemed . . . I sought the right word to describe him in that moment, and it came to me a few moments later.

Determined. Giuseppe had seemed determined.

I made a point of walking down the hall to my own room, then crept back so that I could put my ear to the door. It was clear that Giuseppe was going through Netta's luggage, muttering to himself in Italian while he did so. I dearly wanted to demand some proof that Giuseppe was truly Netta's father, but that was a job for the police, not me. Even if I were to ask, he was unlikely to produce any since I had no official standing.

After a few moments, I went back to my room for real, closing myself inside. Regardless of whether Giuseppe was a fraud, it was clear that he was searching for something in particular, but what could that be? Her occult manuals? Whatever it was that she had burned? Or was it something else entirely?

And who exactly was Giuseppe Fornario?

CHAPTER FOURTEEN

I was restless for answers and, after an hour of pacing my room, hadn't come up with a way to prove Giuseppe's identity, so I decided to go for a walk, even though Redvers was on the Isle of Mull attending to Netta as her autopsy was performed. I certainly didn't want to be in attendance for that, but I was anxious to hear what the results were, hoping that whatever we learned would help fit together pieces of this puzzle. Since my mind wouldn't stop turning things over, I decided that perhaps some exercise in the brisk Scottish air would help me think.

On my way out of the cottage, I saw Fiona, who informed me that Giuseppe would be staying with us, taking Netta's room.

"It was not my idea," Fiona muttered as she went back into the kitchen.

Which meant that it was Michael McCrary's idea. I was a little surprised that Michael would agree to let the room to Giuseppe against his wife's wishes, but the inner workings of their marriage weren't my business, even if they did make me curious about their relationship. I did agree with Fiona, however—I wasn't thrilled about sharing the small cottage with the man claiming to be Netta's father. Even if he was who he claimed to be, something about him was distinctly off-putting.

Stepping outside, I found that it was a typical Scottish spring day—cloudy with a brisk wind that bit through my heavy wool coat. Without the promise of a warming embrace at the other end of this walk, I almost rethought my decision to be out in the elements, but it felt good to get my legs moving and let my mind wander.

It wasn't long before I found myself approaching the fairy circle where I'd found Netta's body. I hadn't intended to come here, but apparently my subconscious felt that I needed another look. Once again, I found Dion Fortune on the hill, although this time she was sitting directly on the pentagram that had been carved beneath Netta's body.

I made my way toward her, unable to keep the look of repulsion from my face.

"I know what you're thinking, but I wanted to see if I could get any readings from her pentagram," Dion called to me when I was about halfway through my climb.

I did my best to wipe my face of any further reaction before I responded and thought I'd been pretty successful by the time I was standing before her. "And have you . . . felt anything?"

I was close enough now that I could hear Dion sigh. "Nothing useful." Her eyes were fixed on something behind me, and I turned to look at what she saw. In the distance, I could see Giuseppe Fornario coming toward us. "Did he follow me?" I muttered.

"Most likely," Dion said.

I didn't like the idea that Giuseppe had followed me here nor the fact that I hadn't noticed I was being followed. I clearly needed to be much more aware of my surroundings. "Have you ever met Mr. Fornario before?"

Dion shook her head. "But I've seen a photograph of Netta with her parents when she was a child. It looked a great deal like him." She gestured with her chin toward the man steadily making his way toward us.

It wasn't definitive proof, but Giuseppe did have a distinctive look about him, so it was entirely possible that Dion could recall the man from an old photograph. And I had no reason to doubt that Dion would lie to me about this, so perhaps I could lay my suspicions of Giuseppe's true identity aside. Although if Giuseppe was Netta's father, how did he arrive on the island so quickly? We were quiet as we watched Fornario's approach up the hill, although I moved to stand next to Dion, who made no attempt to get off the ground.

Giuseppe was puffing for air when he finally reached us. He glanced around, then between the two of us. "Is this where it happened?" he asked.

I considered not answering the man's question for a moment, but decided he had a right to know, regardless of my distaste for the question. "It is," I said.

Fornario shook his head. "I do not understand these crazy symbols." He gestured where Dion was sitting. "I see them sometimes in things Netta was reading at home. But I know, I felt that something bad was going to happen. I felt a, how do you say, psychic feeling."

Dion's broad features had arranged themselves in a way that led me to believe she already didn't like this man. I knew the feeling. "Is that how you managed to arrive here so quickly? Your psychic feeling?" Disdain dripped from her words, which I found rather ironic, given her own interests.

But I appreciated that she had asked the very thing I'd been wondering. I would have gotten around to inquiring, but she went straight to the heart of things. I wasn't surprised at her direct manner—I'd seen her go head-to-head with Nightingale, after all. But Fornario was certainly surprised.

He sputtered for a moment. "I was on my way to see her, because of this feeling. It came to me in a dream one night. So I was already nearby when I got the word that my precious Netta had passed away."

Dion's lips pursed at this. "The same precious daughter

you hadn't bothered to see in over a year? Except to ask for money, of course."

Giuseppe drew in some air. "That is an outrageous thing to claim. How could you even know such a thing? And to say this to me," he put his hand on his heart, "a grieving father. You should feel ashamed." He drew himself up to his full height, which honestly wasn't much. He couldn't have been more than an inch taller than myself.

Nor did it have the desired effect, because Dion looked far from ashamed. In fact, it looked very much like she was ready to go in for the kill, an impressive feat from her seat on the ground. It was clear that Giuseppe was hoping to intimidate us, towering over Dion, but she was not having any part of it. I crossed my arms over my chest and sat back on my heels, enjoying the show.

But before Dion could open her mouth, Giuseppe's mood changed like the weather, from outraged to pandering. "I am sorry; my Italian temper gets the best of me." He smiled his toothy smile, which was white against his five o'clock shadow, looking between the two of us. "I do not want to be enemies, here among Netta's friends." He spread his hands at us. "And you must have known my Netta well." This was said as a statement, but it felt exploratory.

Dion cocked her head and leaned back on her forearms, reclining on the ground like she hadn't a care in the world. "We were friendly." Her voice was casual, but her eyes were sharp, dissecting the man before us.

I was surprised Dion had even answered the question, frankly. But she seemed to want to keep this interaction going.

Giuseppe didn't even look at me. He must have decided, after our brief conversation back at the cottage, that I didn't know Netta well enough to have any answers for him. He shifted on his feet, and it looked as though he was trying to decide on his next question. I fully expected him to ask for more details about what had happened to her or what her mind-set had been in the days leading up to her death, but I was wrong.

"Did she leave any papers with you?" Giuseppe asked. "It seems like some of her papers might be missing."

My eyebrows shot up, but a glance at Dion told me that she was far from surprised.

"What papers would you be looking for, Mr. Fornario?" Dion asked, venom dripping from every word, which led me to believe she knew exactly what he was referring to, had even anticipated this question. "Perhaps she burned them." She tipped her head at me, and I grimaced at being brought into things. "Jane saw pieces of paper in Netta's fireplace. Maybe she burned whatever it is you're looking for."

Giuseppe stiffened, his eyes going back and forth between us. "I do not believe this."

I shrugged, following Dion's lead. "You'll have to tell us what it is you're looking for. Otherwise, we can't tell you if it's what she burned." I was surprised that Dion had brought this up, since she'd had such a strange reaction when I'd initially told her about it, but I was pleased at the strong reaction it was getting from Giuseppe. We were obviously onto something here.

His face reddened, and without another word, he turned on his heel and stalked back in the direction he had come from. My guess was he was headed back to the cottage to look through the ashes in Netta's fireplace. It was too bad that he wouldn't find anything—I'd taken all the scraps there were to be found.

Dion and I watched the man for a while in silence, the wind whistling by us. I glanced at her once he was completely out of earshot. "What do you think he's looking for?" I asked.

Dion sighed once more. "Probably her will."

CHAPTER FIFTEEN

"Why would Giuseppe be so interested in finding his daughter's will?" I asked.

Dion's face was troubled. "Netta was quite wealthy. What I said was true—her father made bad investments. Seemed to make a habit of it, really, and the only time Netta heard from the man was when he was asking her for money."

"How did Netta have money when her father didn't?" I asked.

"Someone on her mother's side of the family left it to her."

I nodded. That made sense, as did the accusations Dion had leveled at the man.

"You knew her well then?" If Dion knew this much about Netta's family, it was likely that they were more than casual acquaintances, which is what I had assumed the two women were. I'd only known Netta for a few days, but casting my mind back, I hadn't seen Netta interact with Dion much other than the letter Netta had asked me to deliver.

She shrugged. "Well enough." Dion stood and dusted off the back of her flowing pants, her numerous necklaces clanking together despite her heavy overcoat. She seemed to dress in an eclectic style, like Netta. I reflected that the occult, in general, likely attracted a more eclectic personality, so it made sense.

"I'm not getting any vibrations from the earth here. I'll try again another time," Dion said.

I was pretty sure she wasn't referring to an earthquake, but once again I didn't ask any questions about what she meant. It was becoming frustrating not knowing what members were referring to, and I thought that perhaps I should take another crack at my manuals. But first I had more questions. "I keep thinking about what you said about Mina Mathers and her attack on the two of you. Have you spoken to Mina recently? Other than on the astral plane."

Dion shook her head, shifting from foot to foot and obviously anxious to end this conversation. "I haven't. But I did hear that she and some of her followers are staying on Mull."

"For the same reason we are staying here?"

"I would assume so. The solstice ritual is very powerful, and as you know, this island is one of the best places to fully tap into its power."

"Of course. Though, why wouldn't she stay here on Iona?"

"If I were Mina, I wouldn't stay on the same island as Nightingale either." Dion glanced at her watch. "I'll see you later, Jane. I think we're meeting in the pub again tonight."

I nodded and watched her go before starting off again in my own direction, toward the hills. Dion had raised nearly as many questions as she'd answered, starting with what had happened between Mina Mathers and Robert Nightingale, making it that Mina wouldn't stay on the same island as the man.

By the time I returned to the McCrary cottage, I had resolved to take a closer look at the ferry schedule. I hadn't paid it much mind, although I knew it didn't run on Sundays, something I still regretted, for Netta's sake. But I needed to speak with Mina Mathers for a variety of reasons, and it looked like those reasons necessitated my taking a trip to Mull. I just hoped I could make it there and back in one day.

The cottage was quiet, and I was hoping to avoid seeing

anyone, so I slipped up the stairs, avoiding the creakiest treads. The second floor seemed just as quiet as the first, but that didn't mean Giuseppe wasn't in Netta's room—well, his room now—so I made my way down the hallway as quietly as possible.

I was glancing behind me when I opened my door and almost shrieked when I turned to step inside my room. Redvers was reclining on my bed.

With a great deal of effort, I managed to hold in my noise of surprise and closed the door behind me, leaning back against it. "You scared the daylights out of me."

"I seem to keep doing that. You should practice better awareness."

I looked him dead in the eyes for so long that he laughed. "I'm teasing. You couldn't have known I'd be here."

I finally cracked a smile and crossed the room to join him on the bed. "Why are you here? Not that I'm not delighted to see you, of course."

"Of course," Redvers said, kissing the top of my head. Then he sobered. "I just got back from Mull."

"And the autopsy."

"And the autopsy," he agreed. "You're not going to like it."

I couldn't imagine what I wouldn't like about an autopsy besides everything, and I told him as much.

"It was inconclusive."

"You're right, I don't like it," I said. I gave it a moment's thought before posing my next question. "What does that mean exactly?"

"The physician couldn't rule out foul play, even though it's likely she died of exposure. But the manner in which she died—completely naked and covered in scratches—well, it's inconclusive."

"You can keep saying the word, but it doesn't really clear anything up."

Redvers chuckled. "You make a good point." But he didn't

explain, just continuing with his report instead. "There also appeared to be faint marks on her wrists. Again, they were inconclusive. It was impossible to tell if she'd been tied down at any point or not."

I gave him a gentle sock to the shoulder at the word "inconclusive," but I was taking it all in. "The marks weren't enough to know whether she had been tied up for certain. Were there any on her ankles?"

"There were not. And the ones on her wrists could be from something else, like a bracelet that was too tight or was pushed into her skin."

I thought about the discolored jewelry that had been on top of her dresser and mentioned it to Redvers. He looked thoughtful.

"That's interesting, but the marks still could have been from something else. It's hard to say. I'm not sure that discolored jewelry would leave marks on the skin, but it's worth looking into." He shook his head. "And there's still the matter of why she was nearly naked out on the hill. With cuts all over her body—and her feet as well."

I'd noticed the condition of her feet when I found her. "Her feet made it look as though she'd left the cottage without shoes on, which is a terrible idea this time of year. I think it's likely she left without clothes on as well, since there were none to be found out there."

"But why would she do any of that? You said she'd been acting strangely, so perhaps she was simply having some kind of mental break."

"It's possible. But I still think there's more here."

"And I have learned to trust your instincts."

I smiled up at him, and we paused our conversation for a long moment in other pursuits. But even his nearness couldn't distract me from our purpose forever. We finally pulled apart, and I filled him in on what I'd learned about Giuseppe, Dion, and Mina Mathers. It was quite a lot, and he listened intently while I talked. When I'd finished, we were both quiet for a moment.

"Dion obviously knows more than she's telling."

I nodded. "Clearly." I already knew what was coming next.

"I'll see if I can search her lodgings."

I didn't bother to argue that I should come along. "Tonight might be a good time. We're meeting at the local pub again."

He nodded. "Excellent."

"And I need to get over to Mull to speak with Mina Mathers. I would like to know what happened between her and Robert Nightingale—maybe it's enough to conclude our investigation against him," I said hopefully. I saw Redvers' skeptical expression and sighed, then continued on. "I'd also like to know what Mina has against Dion and Netta, since Dion thinks the two of them were attacked by Mina."

"I wish there were a way that I could come with you," he said.

"I do too, but it's not worth the risk. Too many members out and about during the day. It's bad enough that you're here now." I didn't think anyone in the house would report directly to Robert Nightingale that I had been seen with a man or that a man had come out of my room, but things had a way of getting around quickly, especially on an island as small as this one. I had no doubt that a full description would be circulated before nightfall if anyone were to see Redvers anywhere near here.

He gave a sly wink. "Oh, I have my ways of getting around."

"I hope you're not relying on that cloak to do it. It's going to cause you more trouble than it's worth at this point. You're a suspect among the locals, remember."

He looked mock offended. "I like the mystery of it."

I thought it was more likely that he hadn't thought to bring anything else with him and said as much.

He looked a little chagrined. "You may have me there." Then he grew thoughtful. "I hate being the one on the outside of the investigation."

"You attended the autopsy," I said.

"And you were the one who found the body. And then told me about it. And you'll be at the meeting tonight, and the one talking to Mina Mathers." He caught my eyes with his own. "I suppose I have some idea of how you feel when I run around investigating without you."

I arched an eyebrow in amusement. "Is that so?"

Redvers smiled. "I'll try not to leave you out in the future."

I just hoped he would actually remember to do that.

CHAPTER SIXTEEN

We passed the time until dinner together, and when it was time for Redvers to make his escape, I went out of the room first, checking for other occupants of the cottage with the intention of distracting them while Redvers slipped out. No one seemed to be about, though, and Redvers slid out into the growing darkness and deepening cold with no trouble at all. He was planning to be in the back of the pub during our meeting again so that he could listen in, and I mentally braced myself for him to come popping out of the darkness afterward.

He really did have a terrible habit of startling me with his stealth. But I assumed that stealth was how he was able to get around the island without being seen by members of the Golden Dawn.

I watched Redvers go, scanning the area for anyone who might potentially see him; seeing no one, I wandered about the house for a moment. My stomach growled loudly, so I popped my head into the kitchen in the hope that Fiona was hard at work fixing our evening meal. But the kitchen was as deserted as the rest of the house, so, with a shrug, I bundled up and headed to the St. Columba Hotel. I would be there well before the meeting started and could order a plate of food to quiet my stomach's protests.

When I got to the hotel, I heard voices even before I opened the door. Loud, angry voices. I pulled the heavy wooden door open and stepped inside to find Giuseppe Fornario and Robert Nightingale shouting at one another on the other side of the lobby, just inside the pub. Fiona and Michael McCrary stood nearby, still at a distance from the scene, but they and everyone else in the place were openly watching the two men argue.

"That isn't her will, and you know it," Nightingale was shouting. "It's not even close to her handwriting. I'll see you in court, you scheming bastard."

Giuseppe was giving as good as he got. "Who is the scheming bastard, eh? You just want her money. How would you know her handwriting? Unless you were having an affair with my Netta." He was waving a piece of paper around. If it really was Netta's will, I wondered where he had found it. I moved to stand next to Fiona; she and Michael both gave me a nod of acknowledgment.

"Where did he find the will?" I whispered.

"In one of the books in her room. Or maybe a manual? It's not very clear," Fiona whispered back.

"Hmm." I hadn't shaken out the books or manuals I'd found, so it was possible that Netta had stowed a will in one of them. I just didn't feel that it was a terribly likely scenario. And even if it was, it was simply too convenient that Giuseppe had suddenly found a will when he'd gone through her things thoroughly that morning, then approached Dion and me on the hill to ask if we had any of Netta's papers. I thought it was extremely unlikely that he would suddenly go back through her books and find it.

I was irritated with myself for not having searched each book and manual, but I'd been pressed for time when I'd done my search of her room. Even still, I should have done it, because then I would know definitively whether or not the will Giuseppe was holding was real.

"I'm done with this," Nightingale shouted, then pointed a threatening finger at Netta's father. "But this is far from over." He stomped to the door of the hotel, passing by the three of us. He opened the door, then paused before he left. "Tonight's meeting is canceled, but we're still doing the ritual in two days' time," Nightingale called over his shoulder before letting the door slam behind him.

I assumed this was meant for the two or three Golden Dawn members scattered about the lobby, but I couldn't help but feel that this announcement sounded threatening.

What was most interesting, however, was that Nightingale had shut down and walked out once Giuseppe had suggested that Robert had had an affair with Netta. Not to mention that he'd left without so much as acknowledging the charge. Was it possible that Netta and Nightingale had been involved somehow? I thought about the interactions I had seen between the two—they'd seemed cordial, but that was all. And Nightingale had been dismissive of the odd woman in a way that led me to believe he didn't respect her in the slightest. Not only that, but he'd also made that ominous prediction about Netta coming to a "bad end."

Of course, that didn't necessarily mean anything, especially not with a man like Robert Nightingale. And he had been downright respectful about contacting her family, although if he'd known about Netta's father, there was no doubt he would have been singing a different tune.

Fiona's mind had obviously traveled a similar path as mine because I heard her mutter, "I cannae believe it's true about Netta and that man. And Robert Nightingale was never in my house, that's for certain. I would have known about it."

I grimaced inside, hoping that she wouldn't "know" about Redvers being in her house.

"Och, he's full of hot air," Michael said before turning to

the barkeep. "A pint for myself and a half for the missus. Miss Jane? Would you like somethin'?"

"Uh, I'll have the same as Mrs. McCrary." I doubted it would be an improvement over the scotch from the night before, but I figured it was worth a try.

I took my first sip of the slightly warm, bitter beer, and I decided that I would go back to the burning scotch for the rest of my time in the country, unless I could find some gin.

Michael laughed at the look on my face. "It takes some gettin' used to, eh?"

I did my best to smile and nod, taking another sip in the hope that it would get better. It did not, but I would finish the thing all the same since there were no plants in this place for me to water with it. Perhaps it would be somewhat tolerable with food.

Michael and Fiona went to sit with some neighbors, and I sat down at the bar by myself, wondering how I could get a look at the supposed will that Giuseppe had been waving about.

I didn't have long to wonder, because the man came and took the stool next to mine, ordering himself a pint as well.

"I am surprised that you associate with such a man as that Nightingale," Giuseppe said to me, plenty of judgment in his tone.

I bit my tongue before it could spit out, "You don't know me." Instead, I responded with, "He's difficult, to be sure."

Giuseppe snorted and took a long drink of his beer, but said nothing else. I didn't mind the quiet since I certainly didn't want to have any further conversation with the man. I'd accepted that he was most likely Netta's father, but he couldn't have been on the island when Netta died, so it was unlikely that he had any information that I needed or wanted. I did, however, want a look at the will he had stuffed into his jacket pocket.

"Where did you find the will?" I asked. "When I saw you this morning, you were still looking for it."

"In her books." Giuseppe didn't elaborate, nor did he deny that the will was what he'd been searching for.

"And what does it say?"

He looked at me for a long moment, as though trying to decide if he should bother showing it to me. But he reached into his pocket and pulled it out, passing it over to me, although he never took his eyes off of it. It was a simple piece of stationery, dated only the week before. I quickly read through the short missive; essentially, Netta was leaving everything to her father, Giuseppe. It was rather convenient for the man, but he also was her father, so perhaps her wishes weren't that unusual. Although it did renew my suspicions about whether or not this man was actually who he claimed to be.

I also found it unusual that Netta had written it only the week before. There was too much about this entire scenario that was convenient, falling in favor of Giuseppe Fornario. Could this man be some kind of imposter, here to collect Netta's fortune? Of course, how had he—or anyone—heard about Netta's death in so short a time after it happened?

I didn't know what Netta's handwriting looked like, but I would be searching for a sample soon—not in Netta's room, since Giuseppe had taken it over. But as soon as I saw Dion, I would ask if she had anything with Netta's handwriting on it so that I could compare it with this. Something like the note Netta had sent Dion only days before. Truth be told, I would love to get a look at that note anyway, to make sure it said what Dion had told me it said.

Of course, getting Giuseppe to show this to me again would be tricky. I did my best to commit a picture of it to memory before I passed it back to him, and he ran a hand down the paper to smooth it, as if I had wrinkled it by simply looking at it.

"Maybe you can convince that man," Giuseppe said.

"Convince whom of what?" I asked, knowing full well what he meant, but wanting him to say it aloud.

"That I am telling the truth. Who else would my Netta leave her money to besides her own family? Now that her mother is gone, rest her soul."

I took a sip of my beer and considered the man for a moment. I knew as well as anyone that family could be difficult and that sometimes people chose a family instead of remaining a part of the one they'd been born into. If I had to wager a guess, I would say that Netta had felt closer to her occult family than this man and whatever it was that he offered. Or asked for, if Dion was to be believed.

Assuming, of course, that he was Netta's real father. I would have to come up with a way to verify that.

Giuseppe nodded once, even though I had offered no response, and stood up, draining the rest of his pint. "Thank you for your help. I will see you later."

I murmured something noncommittal and watched the man leave. He seemed to think I was on his side, which was simply arrogance on his part. I hadn't agreed to anything, nor would I have.

I did have a feeling this wouldn't be the last we heard about Netta Fornario's will, however.

Chapter Seventeen

The rest of the evening passed quietly. I ate dinner in the pub, which was apparently quite shocking—a woman sitting alone in a bar—based on the looks I received from the other patrons, but it let me keep an eye on Dion, who was drinking a scotch in the corner with John Bychowski. I hoped that Redvers had left the pub once he realized we weren't having a meeting in order to search Dion's room while she was occupied here.

Once I finished with my meal, I went back to my room, where I read some of the Golden Dawn manuals until I fell asleep, which admittedly happened rather quickly whenever I picked them up. Much like the last time I had read the occult writings before bed, I had strange dreams. Nothing that I could remember this time, but it left me feeling vaguely unsettled when I woke up the next morning.

According to Nightingale's terse announcement, the ritual was still scheduled to go ahead the following day, so I decided to make the most of this one and head to Mull in the hope of talking with Mina Mathers. I hurried through my breakfast and was at the dock in time to catch the early ferry.

I boarded the small ferry and stood at the rail toward the back, hoping to be protected from some of the wind by the bulk of the ferry in the center, where I assumed the captain stood to pilot the craft. We pulled away from the dock, passing small fishing boats as the abbey slowly became smaller, as did the large rocky hill hulking just behind it. The sky was overcast again today, and the sea nearly matched its gray color, nothing of the gorgeous blues I'd seen a few days prior when the sun was out.

It was the work of only a handful of minutes for the ferry to cross the Sound of Iona and pull up to the dock at Fionnphort on Mull, the landscape looking much the same as what we'd just left, with a rocky shore broken up by swaths of creamy sand. It probably took more time to unload the ferry than it did to actually make the crossing, and I stood with the rest of the passengers waiting for the go-ahead to disembark.

Mull was a much larger island, with a matching population to boot, so I was a little concerned about finding where Mina was staying. I couldn't ask Dion because I didn't have a reasonable explanation for why I wanted to find the woman, especially since Dion felt that Mina had attacked her and Netta. And I didn't feel as though I could tell Dion that I was looking into Netta's death, either. I didn't believe Dion had anything to do with it, but she was definitely hiding something, and I didn't want to make her suspicious of me in any way. Or, *more* suspicious of me—I'd already stepped on a few verbal land mines with my ignorance, and I wasn't sure I'd recovered from those.

It turned out that I didn't have much to worry about, however, since Fionnphort was hardly bigger than Baile Mòr, although it didn't have the dramatic backdrop behind it that Baile Mòr did. There were the same rocky hills of Iona, but here they were grouped closer to the beach or farther out in the distant fields. I'd passed through this village on my journey out to Iona, but I hadn't remembered that Fionnphort was so small, although I supposed that I had been too caught up in the upcoming investigation to really take note of the small village, especially since it wasn't where I was staying.

I headed to the nearest guesthouse and asked at the front desk if I could speak with Mina Mathers. The woman shook her head. "No one here by that name." She pointed farther up the road. "Try the Staffa, though, and you might have mair luck."

I thanked her and trekked down the road, grateful that this village was at least fairly flat. The next guesthouse was much like the first—two stories, built of stone, with white-trimmed windows. I was quite surprised that Fionnphort didn't boast an actual hotel, but the clerk had assured me that guesthouses were all I would find here.

I did have more luck at the Staffa guesthouse, although the clerk politely informed me that the woman in question had just headed in to breakfast.

"I'll wait for her then," I said, and started to make my way toward a chair that was pulled close to the fire. I'd become quite fond of finding the most comfortable chair near a fire since my arrival in Scotland.

"She was alone, so I'm sure she wouldn't mind if you joined her." The young man was trying to be helpful, but the problem was that I didn't have the faintest idea what Mina Mathers looked like. It would be much easier to simply have a room number to knock on rather than admit that I didn't know the woman I had just asked after. I smiled and thanked him, while cursing my good fortune at the same time. I'd found her lodgings—and Mina—on only my second try, but this part could be a challenge.

I walked into the cheerful breakfast room as I was directed, scanning the few tables. There weren't many, and I could immediately rule out any that had more than one person at them, since the clerk had said Mina was alone. That left two tables. I gave a small sigh and headed for the first, where a woman in her fifties sat drinking tea and noisily attacking a bowl of porridge.

"Mrs. Mathers?" I asked.

The woman, her mouth full, shook her head, but gave me a decidedly strange look. I smiled and ducked my head apologetically before heading over to the other single woman.

She was younger than I thought she would be, or perhaps she only looked young. I guessed her to be only a handful of years older than myself, perhaps in her late thirties. Either way, it seemed awfully young to have cofounded an occult group that had already been operating for several years. She had hooded eyes beneath dark eyebrows and a straight roman nose. Her features were altogether quite striking.

"Mrs. Mathers?" I asked.

She looked up from the piece of toast she was buttering, spearing me with her intense dark eyes. "Do I know you?"

I shook my head, but gestured at the chair across from her. "You do not, but may I join you?"

She considered me for a moment, then inclined her head. I took the seat just as a member of the staff hurried over. "Can I get you anything?"

I didn't bother looking to see what Mina's reaction might be—I planned to stay for a minute and ask my questions, whether she liked it or not. "I'll have a cup of coffee. Thank you."

I looked back to Mina, whose lips had tipped up slightly in amusement. "You're American," she said.

"I am." All morning, I had considered what the best approach with Mina would be without breaking my own cover. In the end, I had decided to play it by ear, letting Mina dictate what I revealed. "I'm interested in the islands, especially at this time of year."

"The thinning of the veil for solstice," Mina said. "Understandable. But what brings you to me?"

"I happened to be staying in the same cottage as Netta Fornario." I watched Mina's reaction carefully, and I saw a veil of sadness fall over her face.

"It's tragic what happened to that poor girl." Mina sighed and took a sip of her tea, which had been going cold in front of her. She grimaced and put the cup back in its saucer. "We used to be close, but her behavior became erratic. And she had some strange beliefs that weren't in keeping with our teachings." Her eyes sharpened on me before I could ask about Netta's "erratic behavior." The teachings of this group were strange enough that I wondered what someone had to do in order to be considered erratic themselves. Unless it was simply behavior similar to what I'd already seen from Netta before her death.

"Are you with Nightingale and his group?" Mina asked. The word "Nightingale" was said with a surprising amount of venom.

"I've been speaking with them, but I'm not entirely convinced of either him or his leadership." It was a purposely evasive answer, but it held enough of a grain of truth that it must have been convincing.

"You should come to my ceremony this afternoon," Mina said firmly. "I head the original Golden Dawn group, and I think you would be far better served in your spiritual journey by joining our group. We hold to the original principles that my late husband believed in."

I nodded. "I would like that." It wouldn't help in my investigation of Robert Nightingale, but I was quite curious about what sort of ceremony she would be leading.

Mina nodded in satisfaction. "Excellent." She looked as though she were about to get up from the table, but I stopped her with another question.

"What happened between you and Robert Nightingale?" I asked. "It would be very helpful in my decision about joining if I knew more about him. I've heard some things, but I'm sure you know more about him than most people do."

Mina's lips thinned. "That man. My husband thought highly of him, believed he was gifted, and inducted him into the order himself. But after my husband passed, Nightingale believed that he should take over the order." She looked as though she wanted to growl at the very thought. "But Samuel was very clear that I was to carry on as head of the Golden Dawn. I was his priestess Isis, after all." She shook her head sadly, and I got the feeling that she still mourned her husband's loss even though it had been many years ago, from what I understood. Then she sniffed. "I decided that Nightingale and I should part ways."

I was quite certain that Nightingale would tell it differently, but I supposed that, in the long run, it didn't really matter who had broken with whom. Nightingale had started his own faction, and Mina had held on to a portion of hers. Although, from Mina's telling, it didn't sound as though anything significant had happened to warrant the amount of venom in her tone. There had to be something more here.

"When did Netta decide to leave the group?" I asked.

"Not long after the split. I was surprised that Netta went with him, though. She had never much cared for Robert." Mina shrugged. "But that girl was as changeable as the wind. She floated from group to group, place to place."

"You mentioned that Netta's behavior was erratic. How so?"

Mina looked at me for a long moment, and I hurried to explain my interest. "She'd been acting rather strangely in the days before her death," I said.

My companion nodded. "She did some spiritual work with clients, trying to shepherd them in their own spiritual journeys. I think it affected her mind, though, and she had to take frequent breaks."

That didn't answer my question in the slightest, but I didn't dare push the issue. "Were you upset when she left your group?" I asked.

Mina frowned. "Of course not. People are free to come and go as they wish."

This was a very different story than Dion had presented. Of course, it was unlikely that Mina would openly admit to a stranger that she'd tried attacking someone—astral plane or not. I considered bringing up Dion's name, but I still had a few questions about Netta first.

"I heard that Netta and Robert were having an affair. Do you think that might be true?"

For the first time, Mina's face showed surprise. "I hadn't heard anything about that. And I sincerely doubt that it's true." Mina shook her head. "As I said, Netta wasn't fond of Robert, and vice versa. That certainly wasn't an act."

I nodded and moved on to the next mystery surrounding Netta. "Netta's father showed up on Iona," I said. "It appears as though he found Netta's will—it leaves everything to him."

Mina shrugged, unsurprised. "She wasn't close with her father, but it makes sense that she would leave her money to her kin."

"Do you know how she came to have money? I never got the impression that she was wealthy."

Mina thought for a second. "I believe the money was a trust from her mother's side of the family. Which is why Giuseppe didn't have access to it."

This was the same story that Dion had told, so at least these stories matched. "Mr. Nightingale seemed to think the will was fake," I said.

Mina tilted her head, considering. "That's odd. But, then, nothing he does would surprise me."

The venom was back in her voice; that much was a constant whenever she referred to Robert Nightingale. But it was hard to tell if Mina really didn't know why Nightingale would make such a claim or if she simply wasn't willing to share any further information with me.

Mina chose that moment of quiet to push away from the table. "If you'll excuse me, I have to prepare. Meet our group in my hotel room in about two hours." She gave me the room number and then left.

I sat at the table for a moment longer to finish my coffee, then ordered another one. It had been an interesting conversation, but I hadn't learned much besides getting an initial sense of the woman.

Perhaps the ceremony would be more enlightening.

Chapter Eighteen

I finished my coffee and considered how I should fill the time until the ceremony Mina had invited me to. I hadn't brought any reading material with me, so I decided to venture back out into the cold and explore Mull a little bit.

I walked back toward the ferry dock, then turned right toward the beach instead of going to the end of the pier. Even on a cloudy day, the beaches on these islands were lovely and surprising; the beautiful sand seemed like a discovered treasure between the lichen-covered rocks jutting out of the earth. I was watching my footing and was quite surprised when I looked up to see that the beach was already inhabited—by large Highland cattle. I blinked a few times at them, worried they might charge me, but they seemed entirely unbothered by my presence. There were six or seven of the enormous hairy brown animals, some of them lying on the sand, others poking their noses through the detritus that had washed onto shore. Shaggy fur covered their eyes, and I wondered how they could possibly see—not to mention hold up their heads, with the intimidating set of horns sprouting from them.

"That was unexpected," I muttered to myself as I quickly headed back toward the main road. I wanted to be back on solid footing before any of the beasts could change their minds about me.

I still had some time to fill, so I walked through Fionn-phort town and a little way toward the green fields stretching out before me, before deciding that I'd done enough hiking lately for several lifetimes. Instead, I returned to the guest-house and settled myself into a chair before the fire, where I watched the flames and let my mind wander instead of my feet.

I went over the two cases several times in my head, but all I had were questions. I was still disappointed that the au-topsy hadn't told us anything besides the fact that Netta may have been tied down at some point. I tried to recall if the girl had worn bracelets that could make the types of marks they'd seen on her wrists, but I couldn't recall the exact de-tails of her jewelry except that there had been a lot of it. I sighed. I might have to ask Giuseppe to see her things. Or I could go through the room again when I was sure he was out, which was a far more appealing prospect. An added benefit was that I might be able to find something in Giu-seppe's things to confirm his identity one way or another. I still wasn't convinced that the man wasn't simply an oppor-tunist who'd seen a chance to swoop in and claim Netta's money.

Checking my watch, I realized that it was time to find Mina's room. It was on the first floor and toward the back of the building. I knocked on the door, and it was opened al-most immediately by a young woman with thick brown hair and bright blue eyes who I assumed was one of Mina's acolytes. She beckoned me to enter, and I did, finding several people already in the room besides Mina herself, an older man and woman who appeared to be married, and W.B. Yeats. I was surprised to see Yeats and opened my mouth to say hello to him, but W.B. gave a discreet shake of his head, so I of-fered the group a general greeting instead.

What on earth was he doing here? He hadn't been on my morning ferry—there was no way I would have missed seeing him on the small craft, so he must have taken a later trip across. I was surprised to see him at all; I'd rather expected him to go back home to Ireland after Netta's unfortunate demise. He'd seemed very concerned about having his name attached to any sort of scandal, yet here he was, in attendance at this strange ceremony.

Mina clapped her hands once. "This is everyone then." She gestured at the empty chairs that had been pulled into a circle in her sitting room. I took a seat, looking around at the others, who looked relaxed, if not excited, for what was coming next. I had assumed this ceremony would be something similar to my initiation, but no one was wearing robes; instead, they were sitting around in their everyday clothing. Mina and the woman who had answered the door took their seats as well. "Join hands," Mina instructed, which prompted everyone in the circle to reach for the hands of their neighbors. I slowly followed suit, taking the hand of Mina's acolyte on my right and the hand of the older gentleman on my left. The young woman's hand was small and dry, but his was a little sweaty, and I resisted the urge to take my hand back and wipe my palm on my skirt.

"Let us begin," Mina said. "Everyone close your eyes." I looked around me as everyone did as instructed and reluctantly followed suit. "We will now scry in the spirit vision." Mina began chanting words that were strange and clearly not in a language that I understood. But the intonation of her voice eventually lulled me into what felt like a dreamlike state.

I heard Mina's voice describing a group of people in white robes standing on a hill and realized that that was exactly what I was seeing in my mind. It was odd but clearly had to be the power of suggestion. My imagination continued playing out the scene, as one figure from the group stepped forward and took a sword from the ground. Something gave me the impression that I was seeing Netta, but since I couldn't see her face clearly, I wasn't sure what had made me think that it was her.

"She who has passed shall put down the sword," Mina's voice intoned, and I jolted in my seat, since that was exactly what I had seen. And from Mina's words I could assume that the figure was, in fact, Netta, since she'd so recently passed.

The woman in my imagination did put down the sword, and then the vision swayed and changed. Now I was seeing a man in chain mail walking down the hallway of a castle.

"William, we are now seeing a past life belonging to yourself."

For a moment, I wasn't certain who Mina was speaking to, but then W.B. spoke up. "I expected that a castle would be more ornately decorated," Yeats said.

In my own imagination, I was surprised to realize that the castle I was seeing was indeed very plain. Or was it plain now that he'd said that? Before I could figure out the answer, the man passed through a door into what appeared to be a small chapel where a ceremony was taking place. Six girls in white were taking something yellow from the altar.

"Flowers. Yellow flowers," I heard the young woman to my right breathe out. Was she right? I supposed she could be. I couldn't quite tell if they were flowers or not, but one of the girls put them into the hands of the man in chain mail. Then the vision changed again, and we were moved into the future. Here a group of laborers were working with large stones.

"They are building a masonic house," Mina said. "Your ancestors were always building structures for the good of the unknown and the exploration thereof."

Yeats murmured something, and we watched the men labor for a few more minutes, but instead of changing to something new, the vision darkened and then was gone. I sat still for a moment before blinking my eyes open and seeing that the others were doing the same, one by one. It took me a moment to orient myself to the time and where I was—I felt as though I was fighting my way up from a deep sleep.

Until now, I had dismissed everything related to the occult as superstition or simply nonsense. The only part of it that I'd found interesting was that the Golden Dawn based some of their beliefs on ancient Egyptian texts. Otherwise, I'd agreed with Redvers that it was largely foolishness.

But now I had to stop and examine that, because I couldn't deny that I'd seen things in my mind's eye before Mina Mathers had described them. Could some of this be real and not simply an elaborate hoax? How had we all seen the same things at the same time? Mina hadn't painted elaborate pictures in our mind, but it was clear that we'd been seeing at least some details that were the same.

How was that possible?

CHAPTER NINETEEN

After the ceremony, the older couple immediately approached Mina and enthusiastically thanked her for the invitation to join in the ceremony, the husband waving his sweaty hands about in his excitement. Yeats stood right behind them, waiting for his own opportunity to speak with Mina, so I decided to speak with the young woman who had answered the door. She seemed to be Mina's right hand, at least in this.

"Does Mina do these spirit ceremonies often?" I asked. "It was very impressive." That much was true at least.

"She does them only when she has the energy to do so. They take a lot out of her. Her followers are always asking her to do more, but she often has to say no."

I nodded. "I'm sorry, I didn't catch your name."

"Colleen," she replied, glancing at Mina quickly before turning her attention back to me.

"How long have you been with her?"

The young woman, who couldn't have been much older than twenty, smiled beatifically. "Nearly a year now. Mina relies on me for quite a lot."

"I'm sure she does," I said. I had one eye on Yeats, and even though he'd finally been given his opportunity to speak with Mina, it looked like he was about to take his leave already. I had further questions for Mina, but at the moment, I wanted to speak with Yeats about what had just taken place. He was the only one here from whom I might be able to get a sensible answer.

I thanked Colleen for her time and quickly crossed the room to Mina. "Thank you so much for including me. This was a very . . . powerful . . . demonstration."

"I'm so glad you could join us," Mina said. Her eyes looked tired, and I wondered what such a ceremony took out of her. I had no idea what had really happened, but it was obvious that whatever had occurred had taken a physical toll of some sort on the woman. "I hope you'll reconsider your alliances."

"I certainly will. I hope we can talk again soon," I said. Mina gave another wan smile and nodded. I barely waited for her acknowledgment before I escaped the room, hoping that it didn't look as though I was rushing away, but wanting to catch Yeats before he got too far.

I needn't have worried since I found the man standing near the front door of the guesthouse by the time I hurried downstairs. Yeats held the door open for me, and the two of us found ourselves back in the brisk Scottish air. He had a small black walking stick in one hand, and I moved to his other side out of its path.

"I was surprised to see you at Mina's ceremony," I said.

Yeats looked amused. "I could say the same."

"I was actually surprised to see you here at all," I said slowly. "I thought perhaps you would head home after Netta's death."

W.B.'s face became pensive. "I thought about it a great deal, and even telegraphed my wife to let her know that I might return home early, but I did change my mind in the end. The girl's death was tragic, but Nightingale assured me that he could keep my name out of it." The man spoke so slowly and ponderously that I thought we would be at the ferry before he'd finished.

"And you believe him?" I asked.

W.B. must have heard the skepticism in my voice. "It's true that not much coming from that man can be trusted, but on this matter I do believe him."

I inclined my head in acknowledgment. I wanted to ask if he'd kept my confidence about my forged letter of introduction, but once again W.B. anticipated my question before I could ask it.

"I haven't said anything to Nightingale about your dubious origins," Yeats said. "Even if I am intrigued by what brings you here."

"I certainly appreciate that," I replied sincerely. I wondered what Yeats might know about Nightingale's supposed contacts, and whether it was worth asking. I decided it was. One of the few things I did know about Yeats was that he had been elected as a senator back in Ireland within the last few years. I assumed it was why he didn't want publicity about his current activities, but it also meant that he might have some inside knowledge that could be useful. "Do you happen to know if Nightingale has important contacts abroad?"

Yeats raised an eyebrow but didn't ask any of the obvious questions—for that, I was glad. Instead, he considered the question, his walking stick tapping out a rhythmic beat as we walked along. "It's possible, now—anything is possible—but I've never seen any evidence of it. His name has come up once or twice in government circles, but always with derision. He's not taken seriously." Yeats was quiet for a few steps. "Even his occult contacts are dubious. Much as with Madame Blavatsky, anyone he claims to know well is probably only a passing acquaintance."

I nodded. That was much as I suspected, although I couldn't

help wondering why Yeats would accept Nightingale's invitation if that was the case. "Why accept his invitation then?"

Yeats shrugged his thin shoulders. "Curiosity."

No further explanation seemed forthcoming, so I changed the subject. "Is this the first time you've attended one of Mina's sessions?"

Yeats was unbothered by my abrupt shift in topics and shook his head. "No, although this is the first time that the vision has been directed at myself."

"Did it mean anything to you?"

We were walking slowly, but he paused on the path to consider this and me. "I'm not certain. There was some indication of the Masons, and one of my forebears was rumored to be a Freemason. So it's difficult to say, although I do find her abilities to be remarkable."

I couldn't disagree. Regardless of the meaning of the dream vision, I hadn't the slightest idea how we all had seen the same things between us. "Do you have any idea how she does it?"

He shook his head and started moving again without saying anything else. I realized we were heading toward the ferry and decided this was a good idea. I wanted to get back to Iona and talk to Redvers as soon as I could.

"I left the order when it started splitting off into factions," Yeats said. He was repeating what he'd already told me, but I let him talk. "Such foolishness for these people to be fighting among themselves instead of finding common ground." He smiled to himself. "I suppose that's the politician in me talking now."

"Does Nightingale know you're seeing Mina today?"

Yeats chuckled at that. "Hardly. Those two are the heart of the infighting. The reason so many temples split off from the original."

I'd already heard most of this, so I decided to redirect the man's mental musings when he finally said something of interest. "I'd always wondered if there was something going on between the two of them, though. Mina and Nightingale."

"What made you think that?"

He gave a casual shrug. "Just a feeling. Mina was quite devoted to her husband Samuel, but I had also heard that their relationship was of a, shall we say, platonic nature. Even though they were married."

That was interesting, but also none of my business. I felt my face flush a bit, but took the opportunity to bring up a related question. "What about the rumor that Nightingale and Netta were having an affair?"

Yeats glanced at me out of the corner of his eye. "Some men are more . . . prolific than others. I wouldn't put it past him."

I mulled that over for a moment while we waited at the end of the dock for the ferry to begin accepting passengers. Once we boarded, Yeats went off to contemplate the sea, and I stayed on the bottom deck to contemplate other mysteries.

As soon as I stepped off the ferry, I started the trek across the island to my meeting place with Redvers. I hoped he would still be there—it had gotten late, but he knew that I was taking the ferry over to Mull today, so I hoped that he had adjusted his time expectations accordingly.

I drew close and was relieved to see that he was waiting for me. As soon as I caught sight of his figure on the beach, my face broke into a smile, and I hurried the rest of the way, nearly turning my ankle on a rock, but catching myself just in time. It didn't slow my pace, though, and I nearly knocked him over when I reached him. After some breathless moments of catching up, we broke apart and took a seat on the blanket he'd brought, tucked back into our cove and protected from the wind.

"How was your talk with Mina Mathers?" Redvers asked.

"Very strange. I ended up attending a ceremony with her."

His eyebrows asked the question, and I filled him in on exactly what I had experienced. By the time I'd finished speaking, his brows had furrowed into a deep frown.

"Are you certain you weren't hypnotized?" he asked.

It was an angle that I had briefly considered but didn't have enough information about. "I'm not certain of anything. It's possible, of course, but I'm not sure if that would be sufficient to create a shared vision. And I was seeing the things before she described them—that much I'm certain of."

"I'm not sure if hypnotism is the answer either, but it seems to be the only reasonable explanation."

"But you believe me." It was a statement, not a question.

"I believe that you experienced something, certainly. But I find it hard to believe that a group of people could all be seeing the same thing in their mind's eye without some form of hypnotism." Redvers was still frowning. "It has to be that, combined with the power of suggestion. Nothing else makes sense."

I smiled since it was no surprise that Redvers was dismissing anything even remotely mystical out of hand. Ordinarily, I was inclined to do the same, but it had been such a strange experience, and I wasn't certain that hypnotism could entirely explain it. I couldn't even be sure that we had been hypnotized. I then recalled that there had been something about hypnotism in the Golden Dawn's initiation ceremony.

"When you take the oath to join the Golden Dawn, they make you promise not to engage in hypnotism or anything that gives someone else control over your mind. Something to that effect; I can't remember precisely how it was worded."

"That's interesting," Redvers said. "Perhaps because they're using that very technique and don't want their followers to catch on to it."

I considered that for a moment and decided it was a reasonable guess. "That's entirely possible. Of course, I don't know what hypnotizing someone looks like, so I can't say for certain."

"I'll do my best to research the subject, although that is admittedly difficult to do from such a remote location." Redvers pulled me into him. "Did you learn anything else?"

The nibble on my ear was distracting, but I managed an answer all the same. "Yeats was there, which was a little surprising. I walked to the ferry with him afterward, and he told me that he'd once been suspicious that Nightingale and Mina Mathers were involved with one another."

Redvers paused in what he was doing. "Did he say why?"

I shook my head. "Yeats said it was just a feeling. But those two also appear to be the reason that the Golden Dawn has split off into so many different factions."

"It sounds like a love affair gone wrong," Redvers mused.

"That would make sense." I told him about how bitterly Mina had spoken about Nightingale. "There doesn't seem to be another reason why she would be so hostile. But a broken heart would explain the acrimony between the two." I filled Redvers in on the rest of my chat with Yeats. "He doesn't think Nightingale has any genuine contacts."

Redvers nodded. "That tracks with what my counterparts are learning. There's no evidence that he has 'useful contacts abroad,' as he claims."

I was curious about how his counterparts were going about that part of the investigation, but there were more pressing concerns. Such as what Redvers was supposed to have gotten up to the night before. "Did you manage to search Dion's room?"

"I certainly did." Redvers didn't elaborate on how he'd managed to get past Dion's landlady, and I didn't bother asking. The man had his ways.

"And?"

"And I have a feeling that I know what Netta burned in her fireplace."

CHAPTER TWENTY

I pulled away and stared at him for a long moment, then gave his arm a light punch because he was enjoying my suspense entirely too much.

He chuckled. "It's too easy."

"To torment me?" I put on my most threatening face, although both of us were far from serious. "You had best start talking, if you know what's good for you."

Redvers laughed. "Very well. I found numerous tracts written under the name Violet Firth. They were hidden under her mattress, which is a terrible hiding place. She should know better."

I was impatient with the espionage lesson. "And?"

"And it looks as though Dion Fortune is the one writing them. From the looks of the various articles and tracts that I flipped through, I would guess that she's sharing things that only insiders have knowledge of."

"Oh." I took a moment to process that. "None of the Golden Dawn leaders would be happy to know that someone was sharing their secrets. Another part of the oath is that they won't share secrets with outsiders."

"An article was recently published in the *Occult Review* under that pen name. It talked about the Golden Dawn and how it has splintered. I didn't get a chance to read further."

"It would explain why Dion is still in the group if she's exposing them, and even why she went with Nightingale's faction, since she obviously doesn't care for the man."

"It makes a lot of sense, actually."

"And you think that is what Netta burned?"

"I do," Redvers said. "And let's take that a step further. What if Netta learned that Dion was writing under this name?"

"And sharing the secrets of the order? She might have confronted Dion about it."

"Exactly. And what if that confrontation went poorly?"

I had a very difficult time imagining Dion killing Netta, but I realized that we couldn't rule it out. If someone had, in fact, murdered Netta, Dion Fortune was officially now a suspect.

On my way back to the McCrary cottage, I pondered everything Redvers and I had discussed. I was still struggling to see Dion Fortune as a killer, but I also knew that we needed to keep an open mind. Speaking of which, I was grateful that, while Redvers believed there was a scientific explanation for what I'd experienced at Mina's ceremony, he had clearly believed that I'd experienced something strange. Frankly, I hoped there was a scientific explanation. I wasn't sure what came after this life, but I knew that I didn't want this group to be right about whatever it was. Their beliefs were entirely too much for me to swallow.

I made it to the village and decided to change course from my intended destination—I was feeling restless and wanted to gather more information. Going back to the cottage and falling asleep while studying my occult materials wouldn't be helpful right now, even if a warm fire was most appealing. I needed to figure out what happened to Netta and why, not to mention gather some useful information about Robert Nightingale so that I could stop pretending to be a member of this group. Keeping up the charade was exhausting.

I paused for a second near where the path to the abbey met the path to the ferry landing to look up at MacLean's Cross, a finely carved stone cross that had been erected at the intersection sometime in the 1400s. It was tall, reaching silently toward the gray sky, the intricate Celtic carvings partially obscured by moss and lichen that painted the ancient stone in pale greens and yellow. It was incredible to me that anything could withstand the elements here for hundreds of years, but the proof rose before me. A small parish church stood not far from the cross, tucked behind the low stone wall bordering the path.

A gust of wind interrupted my reverie, and I hurried on my way. My first stop was at the hotel pub, but no one was about except a few old men enjoying a late-afternoon pint. I decided to head over to Nightingale's hotel in the hope that he would be available. I had quite a lot of questions for him, and I'd decided to use the equinox ritual as an excuse to see him. Perhaps if I could get him talking about the ritual, I might be able to sneak in some other questions without seeming suspicious.

It turned out that no excuse was necessary. I found Nightingale and Michael McCrary seated in the lobby of the Hotel Argyll in the upholstered chairs near the fire. They both looked up when I approached, and it occurred to me that both men looked awfully pleased about something. I immediately had a feeling in the pit of my stomach that I wasn't going to like what it was.

"Mr. McCrary just brought wonderful news, Miss Wunderly," Nightingale said in greeting, not bothering to temper the wide smile on his face. "He had Netta's most recent will in his possession."

"Is that so?" I hoped that my voice was curious instead of accusing.

"Aye. The lass gave it to me for safekeeping just before her unfortunate death. I brought it to Mr. Nightingale here," McCrary leaned back in his chair, hands folded over his stomach, looking very much like the cat that ate the canary.

"Why didn't you say anything at the pub yesterday?" I asked. I was also wondering why he hadn't mentioned a will at any point from the time we'd found Netta on the fairy hill until now. If Netta really had given McCrary her will, it seemed strange that neither he nor Fiona had said anything, if not to me, then at least to the police. And if the police had heard anything about it, Redvers would have also.

McCrary gave me a slightly suspicious look, but answered all the same. "Ach, I didnae want to make an argument worse. Thought it was best to hand it over in private."

I made sure to smile and nod as though I thought his explanation made perfect sense. Which it did not. It was entirely too convenient that a second will had suddenly turned up in the hands of someone Netta rarely interacted with, and I was certain that she and Michael McCrary had rarely spoken to one another. It was possible that Netta had given it to Fiona, but even that was suspicious. Furthermore, it was entirely too convenient that this will was dated more recently than the one that Giuseppe Fornario had "uncovered," and both within the last week.

It was also interesting that McCrary would bring the will to Nightingale instead of turning it over to the authorities. It made me wonder whether McCrary was receiving some sort of reward for his little "find."

"I'm hoping there won't be a lengthy court battle, especially since this version is clearly dated more recently, and it's in Netta's own hand." Nightingale patted the breast of his jacket, where I assumed he'd stowed the will. "And she wanted the majority of her funds left to the Golden Dawn. It's not surprising, really, since our order meant so much to her. There was a token amount included for her father, of course."

I tried to look pleased for Nightingale's sudden good fortune, but inside I was seething. I had no reason to believe that Netta would leave her money to either the Golden Dawn or her father—there was too much evidence that she was unhappy with both of those parties. Netta had just announced that she was leaving the Golden Dawn, so why would she write a will leaving them her money? Which meant that the will Giuseppe Fornario had "found" was more likely to be legitimate, but if what Dion had said was true—and I believed that it was—Netta hadn't been happy with her father's constant requests for handouts. If Giuseppe was even her real father, which was another issue entirely. I needed to search the man's things to see if I could find evidence of who he actually was.

All things considered, I thought it highly unlikely that Netta would have written a will leaving her fortune to either of the two men. Not to mention how unlikely it seemed that the young woman would write out two different wills just before her death.

All this begged the question of whether either of the wills was authentic.

CHAPTER TWENTY-ONE

Until now, I'd had no reason to look into Michael Mc-Crary, since his only connection to Netta was hosting her in his home. But with the sudden appearance of a will and McCrary's claims that Netta had given it to him, Redvers and I needed to look into my host's background. I briefly considered asking his wife, but decided I was unlikely to get anything from Fiona. The woman might be hiding her superstitions from Michael, but he was still her husband, and that loyalty seemed to run deep. Besides, for all I knew, Fiona was in on this scheme. I would ask Redvers to look into both of the McCrarys.

This unexpected development meant that I would save the questions I'd wanted to ask Nightingale for later. I made my excuses to the men and went back outside, pausing for a moment while I considered who might know something about Michael and Fiona McCrary and, better yet, would actually talk to me about them. Redvers had mentioned that he knew the bartender at the hotel pub, and if there was anyone in a small town that heard everything, it was the man working behind the bar.

The same few locals were still scattered about the place, mostly sitting alone, eyes focused somewhere into an unseen distance. I approached the bar, taking a seat at one of the wooden stools, and cast a glance behind me, but no one paid me any mind. The folks here were clearly content to keep to themselves and their drinking. The bartender put down the glass he'd been drying and approached me, bracing his hands against the wooden bar.

"A whisky, lass?" He seemed amused at his own question, having seen my reaction to the last scotch whisky I'd had, and I had to smile.

"A gin rickey is more my style." I looked doubtfully at the bottles behind him. "If you have it," I added.

He glanced behind him, then looked into a cabinet and nodded once. "I can do one of those."

"Thank heavens," I muttered, and his smile changed into an all-out grin.

The bartender set about pulling the ingredients together and mixing my drink for me. Once he'd set it in front of me, I stopped him with a quiet question. "You know Redvers?"

He looked at me for a long moment, then gave me a wink. "Aye. We worked together once. Long ago."

I was very curious about that story, but something told me it was yet another tale I wasn't going to hear. "I'm sorry, I never caught your name."

"James McPherson," he said with a nod, then moved down the bar to pull a pint for the old man who'd stood and come toward us while we talked. James passed the pint to the patron without a word, and with a sip and a nod, the man went back to his seat near the fireplace.

"Now you look like you have a question on your mind, lass. Let's have it," James said.

"What do you know about Michael McCrary?" I kept my voice low, but I didn't bother beating around the bush. He knew that I was here for something other than a drink.

"Ahh, Michael. Good man, although I recall hearin' that he had some troubles with the law in his youth. But that was before my time."

"Do you know what type of troubles?" I asked eagerly.

James shook his head. "Afraid not. As I said, before my time."

"Who might know?" I asked.

"Besides his wife? Everyone." James chuckled. "But they're nae likely to tell you."

I sighed, toying with my glass on the bar. "I thought that might be the case." I wasn't surprised that the locals on a small island were suspicious of outsiders. Especially an outsider who appeared to be involved in a strange occult group. I would have to come up with another way to get information about Michael McCrary's past.

Once I finished my drink, I returned to the cottage, where the smell of freshly baked goods led me to the kitchen and made my mouth water. I poked my head around the corner to find Fiona hard at work cutting some root vegetables, a tray of scones cooling on the counter.

She caught sight of me and looked amused at the hopeful look on my face. "If you wait just a minute, you can have a scone. And some tea."

I thanked her with delight and came into the room, settling myself at the tiny wooden table in the kitchen. Fiona looked momentarily startled, then gave a little shrug and set about pouring me a cup of tea from the pot on the stovetop. She gave me another assessing look, then grabbed a bottle of whiskey from the shelf and added a large dollop to my cup. "You look a bit peaked. A wee dram will do you some good."

I thought about objecting to the alcohol, since I didn't need another drink, but instead studied the cup of tea before me for a long moment before attempting a sip. It was hot, but the scalding sensation was definitely from the alcohol. It felt as though she'd added far more than a "dram," but I thanked Fiona after I finished my coughing fit.

She chuckled. "You'll get used to it if you stay on the island long enough." Fiona went back to what she'd been doing. "The scones need just a minute of cooling yet."

"Thank you; they smell delicious." I paused, then forged ahead. "How did you and Mr. McCrary meet?" I asked.

It was certainly not what Fiona expected me to ask about, and she stopped in her tracks, surprise evident on her face, before wiping her hands on her apron. "We met during a brief period when I lived on the mainland. In Glasgow." Her lips tipped a bit at the edges, and she seemed to think for a moment before pouring her own cup of tea and joining me at the table. I was relieved that my question had apparently been the right approach to opening the woman up.

"I wasnae yet twenty and had taken a job in a shop. I wanted to see what life was like off the island, since I had spent my whole life here. Mr. McCrary came in one day, dressed like a dandy, and asked if he could take me to dinner. I made him ask several times before I agreed."

I smiled at her reminiscences. "Mr. McCrary wasn't from the island."

She shook her head. "I was surprised he agreed to move here with me. But he took to the island life right away. It's nae for everyone, mind. But it suits the two of us."

After hearing about Michael's trouble with the law, I couldn't help but wonder if he'd been running away from something—like the law—and found the island a convenient place to hide, but I held my tongue.

"He had a bit of trouble with the coppers," Fiona said, as though she'd read my mind. "He had the devil in him when he was young. Nothing serious, though," she hurried to say. "Just the foolishness of young men. Driving too fast and drinking too much."

I nodded and smiled, although I was disappointed at the lack of detail in her story. Of course, did I really expect Fiona to tell me that her husband had been a master criminal when he was a young man? It was quite unlikely.

"And here we are." Fiona smiled, but it didn't quite reach her eyes. "Our children are grown and moved away now, so it's nice to have boarders to keep us company."

I wouldn't want a series of strangers in my home, but to each their own, I supposed. Fiona must have caught the look on my face because she chuckled and tipped her head at the ring on my finger, a real smile creasing around her eyes.

"Ach, just wait until you have children and then they grow up and leave. You'll find you miss the noise. Twice-yearly visits just aren't the same."

Children. If I was to be married, I supposed I needed to address the issue of whether or not we were going to have them. It was what was expected, of course. But I was tired of doing what was expected of me—it had never turned out terribly well in the past. Which meant I needed to figure out what I wanted when it came to starting a family, and then discuss it with my fiancé.

It was something that I hadn't really thought about until now, and I felt a little panicky that Redvers and I would come down on opposite sides of this issue. I'd never asked him whether he wanted children, and I wasn't quite sure where I landed either. What if we wanted very different things in life?

But I didn't have time to anguish about it right then, because a cloud passed over Fiona's face, and she changed the subject. "I'm worried about you, lass. I think you should forget this ceremony nonsense and get off of the island, much as I enjoy having you here."

I looked at Fiona in surprise. "Why do you say that?"

She shook her head. "I dinnae want anything to happen to you. Like poor Netta."

I cocked my head. It didn't sound as though Fiona had specific concerns, just general worry. I was about to reassure her that I would be fine right where I was when she abruptly stood and went to her pantry. She returned a moment later with something wrapped in an old piece of black velvet. She placed it on the table with reverence, carefully unwrapping the ends of the fraying cloth to reveal an old deck of cards. They were large, about the size of Fiona's hand, and as she shuffled the deck, images flashing by, I could see that they looked hand-drawn. I didn't think we were about to play a hand of whist, since the drawings I'd caught glimpses of were not what one saw on playing cards.

"I'll just read your cards right quick. But I have a feeling you'll be safer if you go."

CHAPTER TWENTY-TWO

"Mr. McCrary is at the MacDougalls' on the other side of the island, so it's safe to have the tarot cards out," Fiona said matter-of-factly.

So this was a tarot deck. I'd never seen one in person, although I knew that the tarot was something that was included in the Golden Dawn teachings. I was only a neophyte, but I'd heard that, at a few levels higher, initiates were required to memorize the various tarot cards and their meanings. I just hadn't advanced enough—well, at all, really—to see any of the writings on them. If I looked ahead in my manual, would I find explanations for this type of deck?

"Mr. McCrary doesn't know about them?" I already knew the answer to this question, but I still needed to ask.

Fiona looked amused. "Of course not. And he's never gone in the pantry a day in his life, so that's where I keep 'em."

The deck Fiona had unwrapped looked very old, and the drawings were faded, despite being kept so carefully. She finished her shuffling, then set the deck in the middle of the table, placing her hand over them for a long moment before drawing a card from the middle of the stack. She set this one on the table face down. She repeated that action two more times, so there were now three cards in front of me.

"Past, present, and future. Just a simple reading for today." She was about to flip over the first card, but I had another quick question first.

"Who taught you to read the cards? And the leaves?"

Fiona paused with her hand on the card. "My gran. She was a superstitious woman, but both the cards and the leaves spoke to her. She always knew things." The last was said heavy with meaning.

I simply nodded, since I doubted there was anything mystical at work with either medium—it was likely nothing more than intuition that these women were tapping into. But I was curious enough to let Fiona go ahead with her reading.

Fiona flipped over the first card to reveal a drawing that clearly showed death. Fiona paused for a moment, then closed her eyes. "Death set you free. That isn't always the case, but here it is true."

I frowned, since the reading was closer to the truth than I was comfortable with. The death of my first husband had, in fact, set me free. Fiona saw my look and nodded. "Aye," was all she said before flipping over the second card, revealing two people holding hands. Fiona smiled. "The lovers. You're very much in love with your young man."

I smiled back, but I also didn't think this one was too difficult to figure out. I was clearly engaged and not yet married. It didn't take a psychic to guess that I was likely in love—which I was—so this was clearly nothing but Fiona stating what she already knew. My ring glinted in the light as if reassuring me that I was right, and I was back to feeling confident that reading these cards was nothing but a way to tap into a person's intuition. Intuition and a touch of being observant.

Fiona flipped the third card over, revealing a tower with what looked like people falling from it. I stared at it for a moment, curious, but when I looked up at Fiona, I could see that her face had gone white. "What is it?" I asked.

"I was right; this does not bode well. You have to get off the island, Miss Jane, if you know what's good for you."

"What does the card mean?"

"Destruction," Fiona answered simply.

I watched her face, but it remained in deadly earnest. "Surely there could be another meaning."

"Aye, but any way you interpret this particular card . . . nothing good can come of it." Fiona's eyes were concerned, and I knew that she believed what she was saying with all her heart. "You're in danger if you stay here."

I took my leave of Fiona, forgetting to eat one of her fresh scones, and returned to my room upstairs after assuring my hostess that I would consider leaving the island.

There was no way that I would actually leave, but I was deeply unsettled by Fiona's tarot reading. Back in my room, I found my head spinning with images from the cards and her verbal warnings. I picked up my Golden Dawn manual, not intending to study it, but to look and see if there was anything pertaining to tarot readings in it. Surely, there had to be other interpretations for the cards that Fiona had pulled out of the deck, and she was only fixating on the meanings that her subconscious was looking for.

After a moment, I realized that I was taking the reading entirely more seriously than I should, and I put the manual down. There'd been nothing useful in it anyway. I hadn't been given the materials that covered tarot, and at the rate I was studying the manual I had, I would never see anything more advanced than what I held in my hands. Which was fine by me, although it wasn't helpful at the moment.

Fiona's interpretation of the first card had been quite accurate, but how? That was the question I should be asking myself. The second card was easy to explain, and I couldn't speak to the third card, which "showed" the future, so the only card that I couldn't explain away was the first. There was little chance Fiona had any knowledge of my past or my first marriage, so had it simply been a good guess? For most people, death was a negative; losing someone you loved brought only grief and pain. It was unusual for death to be a blessing, as it had been for me. So how had she guessed that?

The strangeness of Fiona's reading had nearly made me forget that I needed to search Giuseppe's room. I left my own room once more and crept down the hall, putting my ear softly to his door. I didn't hear anything, and I stood like that for some time, listening, before rapping gently on the wood. There was no answer, so I turned the knob. It was locked, which was hardly surprising. I went back to my room and fetched the lockpick set that I'd taken to carrying with me on my travels—they'd come in handy more than once. With one ear listening for any feet on the staircase behind me, I set to work on the lock, cursing my lack of skill with the picks. I needed to practice more, but other things always seemed to take priority.

I finally got the door unlocked and, without hesitating, pushed it open. If Giuseppe hadn't come to the door while I was fiddling with the lock, he wasn't in the room.

Which was confirmed for me in one quick look. The room actually looked deserted, except for Netta's pile of luggage next to the door. I did a cursory search, but didn't see Giuseppe's bag that he'd brought with him, or any of his things. Had he taken it with him somewhere? Had he decided to stay somewhere else and I hadn't heard the news?

I went back to my room and continued to mull all of this over until it was time for me to crawl into bed. Perhaps the next day would bring some clarity.

Chapter Twenty-three

Clarity was still nowhere to be found when I opened my eyes the next morning, but at least I hadn't been kept awake by strange dreams. I got myself ready for the day, putting on a green knit dress with a white belt and my wool tights with low-heeled shoes. The bathroom was empty, and as I thought about it, I realized that I still hadn't heard anything from the other end of the hall. I tried the knob to Giuseppe's room, but found that it was now locked. Had Giuseppe returned in the night without my hearing him? Or had Fiona checked on the room and locked the door behind her?

I headed to the breakfast room, where Fiona brought me my coffee. Fiona didn't say anything, but I could tell by the look on her face that she thought I was foolish for not heeding her warning and leaving the island. I would be more than happy to leave, but I had two investigations I had to finish up first—Netta's mysterious death and whether or not Robert Nightingale was fit to work for Redvers' employers. I knew the answer to the second; I just needed to come up with enough evidence to support my conclusions, and evidence was proving difficult to come by. In any case, I couldn't say any of that to my hostess, so I quietly endured her obvious displeasure.

When Fiona brought my plate of food, I pointedly glanced

at the other end of the table, where the other guest usually dined. "Do you know where Mr. Fornario is? I haven't seen him since yesterday, and I didn't hear him leave this morning either."

Fiona pursed her lips. "I havnae seen hide nor hair of the man. If he was leaving, I wish he would have said something." She dropped her voice to a mutter. "And paid us before he left."

"Are his things still in his room?" I asked. I knew perfectly well that they weren't, but perhaps Fiona would know whether he'd taken his bag with him. Or admit to locking his door.

Fiona shrugged as she left the room. "I havnae looked. I thought I would see to the rooms once breakfast was over."

I was tempted to sit and linger over my coffee awhile longer, but the desire to check on Giuseppe's room once more outweighed even coffee. And besides, the pot was nearly empty.

I climbed the stairs, knocking on the door to what was once Netta's room. So much had changed in just a few days, and yet here I was, once again, knocking on this door, looking for a member of the Fornario family. I didn't expect him to answer, but I knocked again with my ear to the wooden door, just to make certain he wasn't sleeping so soundly that he'd missed my earlier knocks. There was no sound from within, so I tried the doorknob. It was still locked.

I frowned in frustration, then went downstairs and stuck my head into the kitchen. "I went to Giuseppe's room. There's no answer," I told her. "Maybe we should look inside and see if everything is okay." I hoped that the woman wouldn't need any further explanation than that—I had no reasonable excuse to be poking around the man's room.

Fiona looked at me for a moment, then nodded her head. "I have a key. Let's take a look and make sure nothing is wrong."

I breathed a quiet sigh of relief that there were no further questions and followed her back up the stairs. Fiona knocked again, calling Giuseppe's name, and when there was still no answer, she put the key in the lock and opened the door. I braced myself for whatever we might find behind it.

But there was no one to be found. Simply an empty room, with Netta's luggage still stacked at one side and nothing else worth noting. "Did he have any luggage?" I asked.

Fiona was about to reply when there was a loud knock at the front door downstairs. When we didn't immediately answer, another knock came rapidly behind the first—it sounded as though someone was using the door knocker with a bit too much enthusiasm and it might come right through the wood. "Who could that be?" Fiona asked, and she bustled back down the stairs.

I took the opportunity to take another quick look around, although nothing had changed from the night before. The bed hadn't been slept in, and there was no additional luggage and no personal effects of Giuseppe's. I'd forgotten to look for Netta's blackened jewelry the night before, so I did a quick sweep of the dresser, looking for the pieces that I'd seen a few days earlier, but there was nothing to be found. Had he put the items back with the rest of her things? Or had he taken them?

But why would Giuseppe leave without the rest of his daughter's effects? Unless he had what he needed once he'd found her will. It was an uncharitable thought, but one that I couldn't keep from crossing my mind. And what significance did the blackened jewelry have if he'd taken that as well?

I considered doing a quick search of Netta's luggage to see if I could find the jewelry, but I heard the murmur of voices downstairs and then two pairs of footsteps coming up the stairs toward me, so I moved back to the doorway and did my best to look nonchalant. Fiona reappeared, followed by a man I didn't recognize. He was of medium height and build and wore a dark pinstripe suit beneath a heavy wool coat that was unbuttoned. He held his hat in one hand, and I was rather surprised that Fiona hadn't asked to take his hat and coat when he came in.

"Miss Jane, this is Detective Inspector Campbell. He's looking for Mr. Fornario." Fiona's expression was unreadable, and I couldn't begin to guess how she felt about the arrival of the police.

It had been several days since Netta's death, and I was truthfully shocked that it had taken so long for the inspector to finally come to the McCrary cottage. I'd heard rumors that the police were looking into things, but I'd seen no evidence of that and had started to assume that they were just that—rumors. Especially once the cause of Netta's death had been declared inconclusive, I'd assumed that the police had no further interest, but with the inspector's arrival, it appeared that I was wrong.

Campbell looked me up and down. "You are?"

"I'm Jane Wunderly."

"That doesna answer my question," he said.

It did, technically, but I decided against arguing the point. "I'm staying here at the cottage." I gestured to my room down the hall from where we stood. "I only knew Netta very briefly, if that's what you're here about." I wondered if Redvers knew this detective inspector and whether it would make a difference in Campbell's attitude if he knew I was working with Redvers. Not that I could say as much in front of Fiona.

Campbell didn't fall into my trap of answering what he was doing at the cottage. Instead, he gave me a steely look. "And what are you doing in this room, exactly?"

I blinked at the near-hostility in his voice and decided that my associations were of no interest to the man, Redvers or otherwise. "I was worried about Mr. Fornario. We haven't seen him since yesterday morning."

"So you thought you'd go through his things, did you?"

I'd been forced to deal with the police more than I would have liked in the past year, and while this was not the first time a police inspector had been hostile, it was surprising all the same. I found my mouth was slightly agape at the question. I snapped it shut and decided not to answer—anything I said wasn't going to be received well, that much was obvious.

"I asked you a question, lass." Campbell looked at me steadily.

I shrugged. "There's nothing to go through, even if I was so inclined."

The inspector glanced around, then gestured at the stack of luggage. "These things belonged to Netta Fornario, then?" This question was directed at Fiona, and I breathed an internal sigh of relief that I was no longer under scrutiny.

"Aye," Fiona said, but she didn't elaborate.

"And did Mr. Fornario have luggage when he arrived?"

Fiona shook her head. "Only a small bag."

Without looking around, the detective asked his next question. "A bag that isn't here now?"

Fiona didn't break eye contact with the man, and I was impressed with her backbone. She clearly wasn't one to stand down, even if I thought it was foolhardy to challenge the Inspector. "No," she said. "If you dinnae see it, I obviously dinnae either."

"So where is Mr. Fornario now?" Campbell asked.

That was my question precisely, not that I would say so out loud.

CHAPTER TWENTY-FOUR

I answered a few more questions about the last time I'd seen Giuseppe, and I was grateful to escape once Campbell dismissed me. I didn't bother to attempt to learn anything in return—this man wasn't giving anything away.

I left the cottage, deciding to make my way to my meeting spot with Redvers. I was early, so I walked slowly, enjoying the rare sunny day while wondering where Giuseppe could have gone to. It wouldn't be too difficult to find out whether he'd left the island—with such a small population, especially this time of year, the ferry operator would no doubt know whether he'd taken Giuseppe back to Mull. Giuseppe had a rather distinctive look about him that made him difficult to forget—or, rather, easy to remember. I would walk down to the ferry dock later and ask the crew if they'd seen him.

As I crested the hill near the fairy circle, I saw two figures in the distance, standing very near where I'd found Netta's body. I paused and squinted, finally determining that I was looking at Dion Fortune and Robert Nightingale. From the distance I stood at I couldn't see their expressions, but I could see that Robert was poking a finger at Dion quite emphatically. I considered going back the way I'd come, but it looked as though Dion had already spotted me. She quickly turned and marched away from Nightingale in the opposite direction of the village. Nightingale stood there for a moment before following her.

What had that been about? And had they recognized me despite the distance? As much as I hoped that they hadn't, I thought it was likely that Dion at least knew exactly who I was.

I continued on my way, my pace quite a bit faster now, and I made it to my meeting place with Redvers well before our appointed time. I walked up and down the small beach for more than half an hour before Redvers finally appeared. He looked dapper in his tweed suit, a plaid scarf wrapped around his neck, and I took a moment to appreciate my fiancé before I described what I had just seen to him.

"Perhaps Nightingale learned that Dion is the one publishing information about their group."

"How would he have learned that?" I asked.

"The same way I did?" Redvers suggested.

"If Nightingale searched Dion's room, it would mean he had reason to be suspicious of her in the first place," I said.

"That's true."

"Hmm," I said, turning over the possibilities in my head.

Redvers took my hand and led me into a cove that was protected from the wind. The skin on my face appreciated it—I could feel the windburn on my cheeks. He set about spreading out the plaid wool blanket that he'd brought along with him, while I paced around him.

"The police were at the McCrary cottage this morning." I told Redvers about the police inspector and his hostility toward me and Fiona.

Redvers' eyebrows went up in surprise. "Last I heard, the police were closing the case and writing it off as natural causes."

"Do you know the inspector?" I asked.

Redvers shook his head. "I'm not familiar with the name. I'll have to do some asking around. Discreetly, of course."

I nodded, then recounted for him everything else that had happened since I'd seen him last with the exception of Fiona's tarot card reading. That I kept to myself, although I couldn't say exactly why. It probably had to do with the fact that Redvers would think it was all foolishness, and I wasn't ready to completely discount what Fiona had "seen" in the cards. I also didn't want to recount her warning to leave simply because I didn't want to heed it yet.

I did recall what the woman had said about children, however, and I studied my fiancé for a moment.

"What is it?" he asked, head cocked to the side.

"Do you want children?"

Redvers blinked a few times. "Where did that come from?"

"Fiona said something," I said vaguely. "And it occurred to me that I have never asked you." I suddenly felt nervous about what the answer might be, but I couldn't even say for certain how I wanted him to answer the question.

Which was just as well, since he didn't. "Do *you* want children?"

"You can't answer a question with a question."

"I believe I just did."

I wrinkled my nose at him. "That's not the point. I meant that you shouldn't." But I paused and thought about my answer. "I suppose I always assumed that I would because that was what was expected of me." But because my first marriage had been so terrible, I'd done everything in my power to keep myself from getting pregnant by Grant. I did not want to bring a child into a home rife with danger, and so I'd managed to get ahold of a diaphragm to prevent just that.

But I'd never really considered whether I wanted children.

"Instead of bowing to what is expected of you, take some time to ask yourself what it is that you want," Redvers said.

I looked at him for a long moment, then gave him a kiss. I very much appreciated that he wanted me to consider my own desires above what was expected of me and perhaps even above what he wanted. But it also hadn't escaped my attention that he hadn't answered the question. I decided to let that lie for the moment and get back to the more pressing issues: Netta's death and her father's abrupt disappearance.

"Do you think he's disappeared?" Redvers asked. "Perhaps he's just lying low."

"Anything is possible. But I would like to know whether he's still on the island," I said. "His bag was gone, and his bed wasn't slept in, so perhaps he simply wanted to relocate. Especially after Michael McCrary gave a competing will to Nightingale. I'd be inclined to clear out if that happened."

Redvers nodded. "I can see how that might inspire someone to stay elsewhere. I'd love to say I'll talk to the ferry operator and find out if he left the island, but there are too many Golden Dawn members out during the day."

"I appreciate that," I said. "It is too bad that you can't take something off of my list of things to look into."

He smiled wryly. "Perhaps you can find something else for me to do."

I grinned. "Well, I wouldn't want you feeling left out of the investigation." It was fun having the shoe on the other foot, and I didn't want to admit how much I was enjoying it.

Of course, Redvers already knew. He kissed the top of my head. "You're enjoying yourself entirely too much at my expense." Then he sobered. "I'm sure Giuseppe is fine, but perhaps you should ask around the village all the same."

I nodded. That had already been my plan.

I spent an hour asking around the village if anyone had seen Giuseppe, but no one would admit that they had, and I wasn't able to find anyone who was letting a room to him either. I also checked at the dock on the off chance I would find the man, but the ferry had already returned to Mull after letting off a passel of people, more than we usually saw arriving on Iona. Many were carrying small bags, and checking my watch, I realized they must be staying since the ferry wouldn't return until the following day. With a frown, I headed back to the McCrary cottage to eat supper and get ready for the equinox ceremony, hoping that I would find Giuseppe had returned and my afternoon had been nothing but wasted effort.

But there was no sign of Giuseppe Fornario.

Fiona shook her head when I asked. "No, I dinnae ken where he is. But this note came for you."

I took the note and thanked her, returning to my room, where I checked to see that it was still sealed. It wasn't that I didn't trust Fiona per se, but I also knew how tempting it was to read someone else's correspondence, especially when there was already so much else afoot. I would have been more than a little tempted if I were in her shoes. And there had been another message from Dion that hadn't made it to me, which was probably why she'd sent a physical note this time.

But the note was still sealed, with no signs of tampering. I broke open the envelope, pulling a plain piece of paper from inside and looking at the signature. It was from Dion.

Jane,

We're meeting at the abbey tonight for the ceremony, but please meet me at my lodgings so that we can walk over together. There's something I want to talk to you about.

Dion

I put the note back in its envelope, considering what the "something" could be. Of all the possibilities, I thought the most likely was that Dion had recognized me that afternoon and wanted to talk about what had happened between her and Robert Nightingale on the fairy hill. Whatever they had been discussing, my guess was that Dion didn't want me to mention it to anyone else, but I hoped she would at least fill me in on what it was.

I passed the time before the ceremony pacing around my room and becoming more anxious as the hours wore on. It finally grew dark, and I donned the white robe I'd been given at my initiation ceremony and headed toward where Dion was staying. She was already waiting at the door for me.

"You got my message," she said in greeting.

"I did." Dion was already moving before I'd finished speaking, and I quickened my pace to match her stride. "What did you want to tell me?"

Dion didn't look at me. "Oh, I don't have anything to tell you. I just thought we should walk over together."

My brows knit together. Her note had been clear that she'd wanted to talk to me about something, so why had she changed her mind between then and now? "But you said—"

Dion cut me off. "Oh, I just wanted to make sure you were prepared for tonight's ceremony." This was an obvious lie, but Dion kept talking. "Lots of new people will be there tonight. They came in on the afternoon ferry after Nightingale sent out the invitation." I was watching her while we walked, and I saw her roll her eyes. "It's very like him to decide at the last minute that we don't have enough people and to invite so many more. They're not all even members of our temple—I think he's trying to poach some from Mina's group."

That wasn't surprising, given the infighting between the two factions. What was surprising was how chatty Dion was, almost as though she were nervous about something and trying to mask it with banal gossip.

"I hope you've read up about tonight's ceremony. It's very powerful, although you won't be able to stay for all of it. The neophytes will have to leave about halfway through."

I nodded and murmured something that I hoped sounded

agreeable, even though I was annoyed at the lost opportunity to discover what she'd been arguing with Nightingale about. I wanted to ask Dion more questions, but we'd already arrived at the abbey, and there were too many people around, with stragglers still arriving out of the darkness. The moon was hidden behind a cloud, and it was difficult to make out faces beneath the sea of hoods, since the only light we had was a lantern on the ground near Nightingale's feet. I thought it would be a miracle if we all left with our ankles intact—it was uneven ground, and it seemed certain that someone would lose their footing in the dark.

"As soon as we have all gathered, we will enter the sacred space," Nightingale's voice commanded. He was now holding the lantern aloft, and his face looked spooky in the light that illuminated the high points of his features, with heavy shadows across the rest. I had a sudden shiver—I didn't have a good feeling about this ceremony, although it was likely just the dark and the robed figures I was surrounded by that were making me uncomfortable. I didn't like not knowing precisely who was here.

We were all quiet for a few beats, the anticipation palpable. "I think this is everyone," Nightingale finally announced when it seemed that no one else would be emerging from the dark to join us. "Follow me." He set off toward the entrance of the abbey, lantern held aloft, a procession of robes in his wake. The farther away he moved, the darker it became, and by the time I was moving into the abbey, I found myself taking my steps slowly so that I didn't lose my footing on the uneven path. No one spoke until we found ourselves inside the medieval church where the altar and ceremonial pieces had been set up. I'd expected there to be more sources of light, perhaps some lit candles scattered about the space, but we still had only Nightingale's lantern and the occasional burst of moonlight through the large arched window over the long stone altar.

The others were moving into place, obviously familiar with where they should be, the Golden Dawn officers in their colored robes taking their places around Nightingale. A line of robed figures had also started to gather near the series of arches to the right of the altar, out of the way, but still close enough to the action to feel a part of things. I assumed that these were members who had no official role in the ceremony, and I positioned myself toward the middle of this group with a stone pillar at my back. I shivered—now that I was no longer moving briskly, the cold was more noticeable, and I wished for my thick wool coat.

All around me were members in various colored robes, but someone in a black robe toward the back of the group edged their way through the crowd and came to stand beside me. I couldn't see the person's face, but I smelled the familiar scent of pine and soap, and I realized that Redvers had used his cloak to join the ceremony. I hid my smile of relief that he'd joined us—I felt better knowing he was here. I bumped my shoulder gently into him, and he found my hand, giving it a squeeze before letting it go again.

Watching the other order members get into place, it occurred to me that if Redvers had snuck into the ceremony, someone else could have as well. It was impossible to tell who anyone was because of the hoods obscuring their faces even more than the darkness.

Nightingale knocked on the altar with his fist, starting the ceremony and interrupting my musings about who else might be present. "Fraters and sorors of all grades in this temple, let us celebrate the festival of the vernal equinox. Let us consecrate, according to ancient custom, the return of the equinox."

In a circle around the room, officers of the order spoke aloud one by one, "Light, darkness, East, West, air, water."

Nightingale spoke again. "I am the reconciler between them."

Everyone waved their arms in the air, making some kind of sign, and I did my best to follow suit, recalling that I'd fallen asleep on that page of the manual. Redvers was also attempting to blend in by making the sign, and I was glad that we were in the back since I didn't think either of us was even close to pulling it off. A glance around showed me that no one was paying us any mind—all eyes were focused on Nightingale in his red robe, standing before the altar.

"I lay down my scepter," Nightingale said. He held a gold-painted scepter in his hands, and he placed it at the foot of the altar, then took a single rose from a small bouquet that had been laid on top of the ancient stone and returned to his place at the altar's side.

The next officer of the order moved forward and said, "I lay down my sword," placing a sword on the ground next to Nightingale's scepter. The man took a cup from the altar and returned to his place. I couldn't tell if anything was actually in the cup, but the man was moving as though he were trying not to spill whatever was in it.

A woman stepped forward next and intoned, "I lay down my lamp and wand." This continued, with officers moving forward and laying down whatever implement they had in their hands and taking something that had been set on top of the altar. When the last officer had stepped forward and completed this part of the ritual, Nightingale raised his hands, clearly about to say something, when suddenly there was a loud clang and the light went out.

CHAPTER TWENTY-FIVE

Everyone was silent for several beats, unmoving in the darkness. It seemed everyone was just as unsure as I was about whether or not this was part of the ceremony. After a few moments, I heard the rustling of robes, and then Nightingale barked, clearly annoyed, "Someone get that light back on."

Not part of the ceremony, then.

There was more rustling of robes and the metal sound of someone fiddling with the lantern. But before it could be relit, Nightingale cried out in pain, and there was a heavy thump. The order members began murmuring and shuffling around in the darkness, panic beginning to spread through the crowd. After a bit more rustling, the lantern finally came back on, and we could see that Nightingale had fallen to the ground, which explained the thump of a moment before. We could also see that he was clutching his leg, which had the ceremonial knife sticking out of it.

"Dear God," someone near me muttered.

"I've been stabbed!" Nightingale shouted. "Where's the doctor?"

A man who had been standing with our group moved forward. "I'm right here." He crossed the room to Nightingale, kneeling beside him and blocking my view of what happened next. My guess was that he pulled the knife from Nightingale's leg, because I heard Nightingale shout again and then groan in pain. "I need some cloth to bind this," the doctor said, which started another flurry of movement.

There was a sudden absence to my right, and a quick look behind my pillar showed that Redvers was slipping out of the abbey into the darkness, as was another member robed in black. She turned back to look at the crowd gathered around Nightingale, and I caught just a glimpse of the woman's face.

It was Mina Mathers.

I'd been correct, then, that someone else had slipped into the ceremony undetected. Once Redvers and Mina were well and truly gone, I joined the others who had gathered around Nightingale. The doctor was just announcing that we needed to get Nightingale back to the hotel so that they could get a better look at the wound in his leg. Several men stepped forward to assist, and they hoisted Robert up between them in a makeshift human chair. Dion grabbed the lantern and indicated that she would walk ahead of them, lighting their path so they could see their footing and make it to the hotel without dropping their charge.

I took the opportunity to look around at the order members, most of whom had tipped their hoods back when they'd seen the knife in Nightingale's leg. I recognized the handful of members who had been here for the past week, but there were quite a few new faces, and everyone around me looked shocked at the turn the evening had taken—it was impossible to tell who might have done the stabbing. Frankly, it could have been anyone once the light had been extinguished, and since it had been a single, clean stab, there was not likely to be much blood on the perpetrator, so it was little use trying to get a look at everyone's hands right now.

Could I determine whether the light was put out on purpose or not? If it was intentional, it had to be one of the officers since they were the only ones close enough to have done it. But if the lantern had been kicked over accidentally, then someone may have simply taken the opportunity to stab Nightingale while it was dark. I wasn't even certain whether this was something I could find out. The perpetrator was unlikely to tell me anything in either scenario, and it was doubtful that anyone had seen what had happened, although someone might be able to tell me who was closest to the lantern, and I could work from there.

Why stab Nightingale in the leg, though? If they'd wanted to kill him, it would have been easy enough to stab the man in the chest. Stabbing him in the leg didn't seem accidental. It was difficult to imagine missing someone's chest and stabbing them in the leg instead. Were they simply sending a message?

Or could Nightingale have done it to himself? It was an uncharitable thought, but not outside the realm of possibility. But to what end? I doubted he wanted to interrupt the equinox ceremony. He'd seemed legitimately enthusiastic about performing the ritual and "forming a link between the order and the equilibrated solar forces," whatever that was supposed to mean. Plus, Nightingale had brought Yeats to the island especially for this ceremony, so why stab himself in the leg and bring the ceremony to an end before they'd barely begun it?

I wasn't ruling out any possibilities just yet, but it seemed more likely that someone else had stabbed Robert Nightingale in the leg. For now, anyway.

Back at the Hotel Argyll, most of the order members who had been present in the abbey were now gathered in the lobby near the fireplace. As I listened to the chatter among them, it seemed everyone was more interested in sticking close to the drama rather than showing up out of concern for Nightingale. I doubted Nightingale was aware of just how little his temple members seemed to care for him. I was certain that, in his mind, their mere presence signaled his own importance.

Just thinking about Nightingale and his self-importance made me roll my eyes, although I immediately felt guilty. The man had just been stabbed, after all, even if the attack was far from fatal.

I sidled up next to Dion, who was standing quietly near the edge of the crowd. Most of the order robes had been taken off and were being carried under an arm, but Dion was still wearing hers. She'd been studying the floor, but she looked up at me.

"I didn't think the ceremonial knives were that sharp," she said.

I paused for only a moment. "Have you ever touched one?"

Dion shook her head. "But it was an unspoken rule, so that no one hurt themselves accidentally during a ritual."

I nodded. "Could someone have swapped in a sharper knife?"

Dion considered that, then shook her head. "It was very distinctive-looking. It would be difficult to replicate."

If that was true, it meant that someone had sharpened the knife ahead of time.

"Who is the member that carries that knife? During the ceremony, that is."

"John Bychowski." Then her eyes narrowed shrewdly. "I know what you're thinking, but I don't think he's the one who stabbed Nightingale. For one thing, Robert insisted on keeping all of the ceremonial implements in his own possession, and he is the one who would bring them to the ceremonies. I think he was afraid someone would lose something or forget to bring it along. We were only allowed to touch them during the ceremony itself."

Which meant that either Nightingale had sharpened the

knife himself or someone had broken into Robert's room and done so.

"Did you see what happened with the lantern?" I asked.

Dion shook her head. "I think someone kicked it over, but I can't say for sure."

Before I could ask her anything else, the doctor appeared at the bottom of the stairs. He paused upon seeing the crowd, but came forward to deliver his report on the patient. "Robert will be just fine. The knife didn't go in very far, and he's been stitched up. He'll recover in no time, although I've advised that he keep to his bed for several days."

There were general nods around the group, but no further questions. The doctor looked around and, with a shrug, went on his way.

"Do you know the doctor?" I asked Dion. She was already moving toward the door, and I took a step in that direction with her.

"He's Nightingale's personal physician," she said. "But that's all I know about him. Good night, Jane. It's late, and I'm going to bed."

I nodded and watched her leave. But I couldn't help but think that it was awfully convenient for Nightingale that his personal doctor had been on hand for his stabbing.

The crowd quickly lost interest after the doctor's report and were drifting off to their various lodgings; it didn't look as though there was much more to be learned tonight. From the bits I'd overheard, it sounded as though members were mostly disappointed that the ceremony hadn't been completed. One or two even suggested going back and finishing without Nightingale, but that idea was quickly scrapped since they didn't have the necessary ritual implements.

I mused that ordinarily the police would already be on hand and investigating this stabbing, but an officer would have to be brought over from Mull, and I assumed that wouldn't occur until the following day. I grimaced a bit at the thought of Detective Inspector Campbell—I hoped he wouldn't be the one investigating, although it was unlikely someone else would be sent since Campbell was already familiar with the players.

I made my way back to the McCrary cottage, letting myself in the front door and locking it behind me. The first floor seemed quiet, but when I stuck my head into the sitting room, I found Michael McCrary dozing in front of the fire. I didn't know where Fiona was, but I left Michael where he was and crept up the stairs to my room. This time, I wasn't surprised when I found Redvers waiting for me.

"How did you manage to get in here without being seen?" I asked, closing the door behind me and tossing my robe onto the chair. "Mr. McCrary is downstairs."

"I used to be quite the tree climber in my youth. Those skills come in handy now and again." Redvers was fully reclined on my bed, and his dark eyes tracked me as I went to the window and looked down at the tree below.

I considered the tree for a moment before joining him on the bed. "I'm glad you decided to come to the ceremony."

"And you wanted me to get rid of my cloak." Redvers grinned.

I rolled my eyes at him. "Did you see Mina Mathers?"

Redvers nodded. "I saw her come out of the abbey behind me and go back toward the village."

"And you followed her," I said.

"Of course, I followed her. She is staying at the same hotel as Nightingale. At least, that's where she went."

I pondered that. "That's a pretty bold move. Staying at the same hotel as your sworn enemy."

Redvers looked amused. "Sworn enemies, eh? That seems a bit dramatic."

I chuckled. "I suppose that's true, although Nightingale is

nothing if not dramatic. And the order did fracture because of the issues between the two of them. If they aren't sworn enemies, at the very least, there isn't any love lost between them."

"Strange that she would show up at his ceremony tonight."

I frowned. "I agree. I assumed that she would be holding a ceremony with the members of her own temple. Why else come to this remote island? I thought the whole point of coming to Iona was that 'the veil is thin here' and good for this particular ritual." I paused. "Unless she knew something about the stabbing ahead of time."

Redvers nodded. "I thought of that too. I don't think she was close enough to have stabbed Nightingale, but it's possible."

"It could have been anyone who was there tonight, really." I told him my thoughts about Nightingale and whether he could have done it to himself.

Redvers mulled that over. "I wouldn't put it past him. It's too bad we weren't able to get a better look at the knife while it was in his leg."

I pursed my lips in disgust. "I'm not sorry about that. I didn't need a better view of it."

"Would have been nice to see the angle it went in at, though."

I nodded and attempted to push the mental picture away. I wasn't entirely successful, but it did remind me of another question I had. "Why stab him in the leg instead of somewhere more vital? Like the chest?"

"A warning?"

"That was my thought."

"You'll have to talk to him tomorrow. In addition to Mina Mathers," Redvers said.

I sighed. Nightingale was likely to be even more insufferable than usual. It was going to be an unpleasant interaction, but I also knew that it had to be done. In the meantime, something else had occurred to me. "Now that Nightingale has been stabbed, it seems less likely that Netta's death was an accident."

Redvers agreed. "It does seem unlikely to be a mere coincidence."

CHAPTER TWENTY-SIX

Redvers was gone when I awoke the following morning, and with a sigh of disappointment, I tended to my morning ablutions and got ready for another cold day, pulling on my union suit and some thick cotton tights beneath a long-sleeved navy dress.

I headed to the breakfast room and was shocked to see Giuseppe sitting at the table and eating his meal as though he hadn't disappeared with his only piece of luggage the day before.

"Good morning, Mr. Fornario," I said as I took my seat. Fiona bustled in with my pot of coffee, and she set it down in front of me, giving Giuseppe a dark look before heading back into the kitchen. I poured some fresh cream into my cup and added the dark brew, taking a deep breath of its delicious smell before sipping at it.

"This woman gives you coffee first thing, but I ask for it, and all I get is this weak liquid. Terrible," Giuseppe said in greeting. He gestured with his cup, nearly spilling liquid over the side, and I flinched for Fiona's white tablecloth, which miraculously came away unscathed.

I decided to ignore his challenge, however. "How did you spend your day yesterday?" I thought this was a better approach than "Where the hell were you yesterday?" which is what I wanted to ask.

"Here and there," Giuseppe said vaguely. "I heard the police were here looking for me." He scraped his plate clean with a piece of toast, popped it into his mouth, and stood to leave. "I do not need to talk with police," Giuseppe said around the bread in his mouth. "Not until they figure out what happened to my Netta." And, with that, he left the room. Moments later, I heard the front door open and close again.

Giuseppe's claim that he wouldn't speak with the police until they determined what happened to his daughter was clearly nonsense. I was left with the distinct feeling that the man was avoiding the police purposely, and that it had nothing to do with his daughter's death and everything to do with Giuseppe himself.

Which reminded me that I still needed to verify whether Netta was, in fact, Giuseppe's daughter. I would take care of that directly after breakfast.

Fiona returned with my plate of food, and once she set it in front of me, she began clearing Giuseppe's place. "He disnae want to talk with the police, but I'll make sure they ken he's back." Fiona's eyes flashed. She didn't care for Giuseppe Fornario, that much was certain. I had to admit that I was in the same boat.

As soon as I finished my breakfast—declining a dram of whiskey for my coffee—I went back upstairs, mentally willing Giuseppe to stay wherever it was that he'd gone. This time, I was in luck and found his room unlocked, which in itself gave me pause. But I forged ahead, scanning the room quickly to locate Giuseppe's bag. It was tucked neatly next to the dresser, and I put it on the bed for a moment while I rifled through the contents.

There were a few necessities but very little clothing, which made me think Giuseppe hadn't planned on staying on Iona for very long. Tucked into a pocket I found a leather billfold, and I pulled it out, feeling triumphant, but when I flipped it open and saw the man's identity card tucked inside, I deflated. His name was, in fact, Giuseppe Fornario, according to this official-looking card, anyway. I hadn't realized until that moment just how convinced I'd been that the man was a phony, but it seemed I'd been mistaken, and Giuseppe really was Netta's father. Or if not her father, then at least a relation with the same last name. I finished my search of the bag and found nothing to contradict that information, so I tidied up and placed the bag back where I'd found it, closing the door behind me and heading downstairs.

I stepped into the brisk Scottish air and set off for the Hotel Argyll, hoping that I might catch Mina Mathers before she disappeared back to her lodgings on Mull. I would take the ferry across in order to speak with her, if necessary, but it would be entirely more convenient if I could talk to her here.

Unfortunately, the front desk didn't have a Mina Mathers registered at the hotel. I sighed, not having the slightest idea what other name the woman might have registered under.

"We do have a Moina Mathers," the young man said. I could feel my face brighten—surely that had to be her. "But she left first thing this morning. Before the sun was even up."

I thanked the clerk for his help. It looked like I would be taking a ferry to Mull after all.

Since I was at the hotel, I decided to stop in and check on Robert Nightingale, even though I would rather put that chat off indefinitely. But the sooner I saw him, the sooner it would be over, so I climbed the stairs to the man's room. I'd expected to have to knock, but the door was already open, and a handful of people were gathered around his bed. I stepped through the doorway and offered him a greeting. "Good morning, Mr. Nightingale. I hope you're feeling better."

"Ah, Miss Wunderly. Thank you for coming to check on me." Nightingale was holding a cup of tea from an otherwise untouched breakfast tray placed on the other side of his bed. His leg was bandaged where he'd been stabbed, and the bright white of the wrapping stood out against his blue silk pajamas. I was a little surprised that Nightingale hadn't bothered to get dressed before receiving all these guests.

"You'll have to excuse my appearance," Nightingale said to me, but also to the room at large. "The doctor has advised that I not move unless it is absolutely necessary."

I resisted the urge to roll my eyes and instead nodded along with the others, several of whom also murmured reassurances to their leader. I noticed that Yeats wasn't present, which wasn't terribly surprising, given his feelings about Nightingale, but I hadn't seen him the night before either. I would have to ask about the poet at the desk downstairs before I left.

"I was just saying that it's difficult to believe one of our own members would attack me so violently. It had to have been someone else, someone who shouldn't have been at the ceremony at all." Nightingale shook his head, and I wondered if he'd seen Mina or Redvers. "Obviously, the police have been notified, but I have decided that I do not want to press charges against whoever did this."

I couldn't help it—my eyebrows shot up into my hairline, but Nightingale wasn't looking at me. His attention was focused on the young woman at the end of his bed. I didn't recognize her—she must have arrived the afternoon before with some of the others who had been summoned for the ceremony.

"Frankly, I think it must have been Netta's father. The man is clearly unwell, what with the death of his child, and then learning that her inheritance is going to the Golden Dawn instead of himself." Nightingale managed to look sad at this pronouncement. "It clearly must have been him, which is what I'll be telling the police. If they ever get here."

It was an interesting theory, and one that I couldn't either prove or disprove. Not since Giuseppe had disappeared and reappeared again, and wouldn't say where he'd been during that missing time. I hadn't seen Giuseppe at the ceremony, but that didn't mean he wasn't there—I hadn't been able to identify many of the people in the abbey. How would he have managed to knock over the lantern, though? No one had rushed forward from the crowd gathered at the side of the room before the light went out. Or had Giuseppe simply waited for an opportunity to present itself?

I excused myself a few minutes later since there was little chance I'd be able to speak to Nightingale on his own. As it was, Robert barely acknowledged my departure; he had plenty of others in attendance and didn't need my attention. I swung past the front desk, where the clerk helpfully told me that Yeats had also checked out and was headed for the ferry, although only within the past hour. I adjusted my cloche and set out into the windy morning.

I arrived at the dock a few minutes later, surprised to see Yeats, but only Yeats, waiting for the arrival of the ferry.

"Good morning," I said. "Have you seen anyone else here this morning?"

Yeats's eyes were cautious behind his wire-rimmed spectacles. "Good morning to you, lass. And no, I haven't. Were you expecting someone?"

I considered him for a moment, then decided there was little harm in telling him. "Mina Mathers, actually."

Yeats frowned. "Why do you think that Mina is on the island?"

"I saw her at the ceremony last night. Were you there? I didn't see you."

Yeats gave his head a little shake. "I was there, but I left before the group went into the abbey. I had a bad feeling about things." He was thoughtful. "I didn't see Mina, though. It's interesting that she showed up."

"I thought so too." I didn't want to discount his "bad feeling," but I was hopeful that he'd had more reason than that for leaving before the ceremony had even begun. I couldn't take a bad feeling to the police. "Was there a reason for your bad feeling?"

"Can't put my finger on it," he said. "I just sensed that it would be best for me to leave. And it turns out that I was right, now."

I looked at the man for a long moment. He'd come an awfully long way to participate in this particular ceremony, only to leave at the last minute based on a gut feeling. I couldn't help but be suspicious. Had he really left? I hadn't seen anyone break away from our group, but it had also been quite dark, and I'd been concentrating on not turning an ankle on the uneven path leading into the abbey. It was entirely possible that when we'd started our procession into the abbey, he'd simply turned and left instead.

Yeats tapped his stick on the ground a few times. "Now that you mention it, I didn't see Mina, but I thought I saw her assistant that night. At the time, I'd thought it was a trick of the light—or rather, the dark."

"Oh, really?" I tried to recall the young woman I'd met in Mina's room, but all I could pull up was a hazy mental picture.

"I thought she looked familiar, but I couldn't place her at the time." Yeats cocked his head. "Yes, I'm nearly certain that it was her." He paused. "There's something not right about that lass."

"What do you mean?"

"Her accent." Yeats shook his head. "It's not quite right. Again, I can't put my finger on it, but something is amiss there."

I thanked him and told him it had been a pleasure to meet

him. I doubted that I would see the man ever again, given that he was leaving the island and heading back to Ireland. He nodded graciously, his gray wool coat blowing around in the wind against his lanky frame, and I took my leave.

I had no real reason to distrust Yeats—he had the least motive to lie to me, so it was likely that he had, in fact, seen Mina's assistant. Yeats had also kept his knowledge about my forged letter to himself instead of telling Nightingale about it, which meant that he was true to his word. So why lie about this?

There was the chance he was mistaken about the young woman's identity, however. I could barely remember what Colleen looked like because I'd only seen her very briefly. Unless Yeats had met her before—or had a fantastic memory for faces—he might be mistaken that it was the same young woman. As far as Colleen's Irish accent went, though, I had no idea what to make of that. I hadn't noticed anything amiss, but I was no expert either. I found both the Irish and Scottish accents difficult to understand at times, so I would have to take Yeats's word that something about her Irish accent wasn't right.

The more pressing question was, if Mina and her assistant had both been on the island the previous night, where were they now?

CHAPTER TWENTY-SEVEN

I took a seat near the fire in the hotel lobby, both to warm up for a moment and for a chance to think about my next move. Was it worth going to Mull this morning if Mina and her assistant were still on the island? I was anxious to speak to both of them, since they were now at the top of my suspect list for Nightingale's stabbing. Although I still questioned why the man was stabbed in the leg instead of somewhere more potentially fatal. Even in the dark, it was a strange error to make unless it was simply a warning.

But where on the island could the women be? If Mina had left the hotel before the sun was up, where would she have gone? The ferry didn't run that early in the morning, so why give up her room with no destination? Unless she'd gone to where Colleen was staying, but I hadn't determined where that might be yet. Perhaps I would grab the next ferry to Mull after all, in the hope that they'd made it back there somehow. Iona was a small island, but it seemed simpler to check Mina's lodgings on Mull rather than try to do a sweep of all the places to stay on Iona.

A draft of cold air from the front door swept Yeats and Detective Inspector Campbell into the hotel lobby. Yeats caught my eye and gave a shrug, heading to the front desk. I could hear him asking for his room back, and I assumed that the inspector had stopped him from boarding the ferry. The inspector headed up the stairs, and I stood and followed him at a discreet distance. The man went straight for Nightingale's room, the door of which was still open, although many of his acolytes had left.

I thought I'd been following at enough of a distance, but Campbell stopped before entering Nightingale's room and shot me a look down the hall. I gave a weak wave, and the man narrowed his eyes at me, but didn't say anything. I scurried back down the stairs, not interested in having another conversation with him. I would try to find out later what Nightingale and Inspector Campbell discussed.

I checked my watch. The ferry shouldn't have left yet, and with the inspector occupied, I hoped I could sneak off to Mull. I hurried out of the hotel and down to the dock.

But that wasn't to be. The ferry operator stopped me before I could even step foot on the vessel. "Can't let anyone cross today."

"Not even if I'm coming right back?"

The man shook his head. "Inspector's orders. I'm not supposed to let anyone off this island, not until he gives me the go-ahead."

"This is the first run, correct? There wouldn't have been one earlier?"

He shook his head. "Not the ferry, no."

Of course, that didn't include the small fishing vessels that went out every morning. Could Mina and Colleen have taken a fishing boat across to Mull? It was possible, and entirely frustrating, since it appeared that I was confined to Iona unless I could find a fishing boat of my own. I would have to put my conversation with Mina on hold until I could either search Iona or find my way to Mull.

Before beginning a sweep of the island, which I knew would take hours, I decided to check the pub first and see if there was anyone there that I needed to speak with. I still had plenty of other questions to answer, about the McCrarys' backgrounds, about whether anyone else had seen strangers during the equinox ritual, and where Giuseppe Fornario had disappeared to for the night.

It was closing in on lunchtime; there weren't many other places to dine on the island other than the two hotels, and I felt that avoiding the Hotel Argyll until the inspector left was a wise course of action. Which meant I was heading to the St. Columba.

I pushed open the hotel's heavy door and moved through the lobby to the pub, where I found a small crowd. This was no surprise, since there had been an influx of Golden Dawn members the day prior and no one was allowed to leave the island at the moment. It made sense that they would gather here since there was only so much to see on Iona.

I found John Bychowski sipping a pint of Scottish heavy near the fire. "Mr. Bychowski," I said, "how are you?"

This clearly wasn't his first pint since his tongue was already loose. "I've been better. I can't believe Nightingale was stabbed with the knife that I carry during rituals. I'm quite nervous that the police are going to suspect me."

"But hadn't you already set it down by the altar and gone back to your station when he was stabbed?" I asked.

He nodded. "But that doesn't mean anything." He rubbed at his short gray beard nervously. "They might still try to pin it on me."

"It means that anyone present could have grabbed the knife, though, since you'd already put it down."

He cocked his head, seeming a little hopeful. "That's true. I just hope the police see it that way."

"You don't have a motive for stabbing Nightingale, do you?" There was probably a more subtle way to ask the question, but I was too frustrated with the morning's events for subtlety.

But Bychowski seemed unbothered. "I do not. Nightingale

wasn't popular among some of the members, but I've never had a problem with him. In fact, he's the one who initiated me into the order."

"Do you know who might have done it? Or who might have turned out the light?"

Bychowski took a sip of his drink. "I've been trying to figure out who kicked over the lantern, but I didn't see anything. My hood was in the way, blocking my view of that part of the church."

I was afraid that would be the case for a lot of the participants that night. When pulled up, the hoods were overlarge and had a tendency to fall far forward, hiding faces, but also obscuring views.

"Was there anyone who had a grudge against him?" I asked.

Bychowski gave a short bark of laughter. "Oh, plenty of folks. Take your pick, really."

"He's that unpopular then?"

"Robert Nightingale has a habit of making enemies." Bychowski shrugged. "I couldn't begin to guess who might have stabbed him."

I sighed. That wasn't helpful, especially since I knew that at least two and probably three people had snuck into the ceremony. Who knew what other enemies of Nightingale might have joined the ritual? It could have been a member of the Golden Dawn or someone else entirely. The only thing I knew for certain was that they were probably still on this island, unless they had their own boat or had bribed a fisherman to take them across.

I glanced toward the bar, where the bartender had been wiping down some glasses, but he'd momentarily disappeared. I excused myself from John and headed in that direction, deciding that a drink was in order—it was early, but I didn't want to be the only one in the pub abstaining. By the time I reached the long wooden bar, James had returned. His eyes searched the room and then fell on me, lighting with recognition. He cocked his head to the left, and I frowned, then moved in that direction. He met me at the end of the bar.

"Follow me," he said.

I was still frowning, not knowing what this could be about, but decided to follow the man since Redvers knew him—I wasn't in the habit of following strange men to other locations otherwise. He led me through the small kitchen in the back to a rear door that was propped open slightly to let some of the heat escape from the room. I looked at the barkeep quizzically, and he jerked his chin toward the door.

"Take a look," he said.

I took a few steps forward and peered through the wide crack. At first, I didn't think there was anything to be seen, but if I moved to the right, I could see two men standing behind the little group of buildings that made up the St. Columba Hotel. I immediately recognized Giuseppe Fornario and Michael McCrary, and they were having what appeared to be quite the argument. Giuseppe's hands were flying about wildly, and he was clearly shouting, while McCrary's face could have been made of stone. I was dearly tempted to step outside so that I could hear what they were saying, but I knew opening the door any farther would give me away immediately.

But perhaps I could hear them if I approached from a different direction. I thanked the bartender and scurried back to the front of the hotel, letting myself out the front door and heading off to the left. I thought that if I worked my way around the long building, I might be able to hear what the two men were arguing about.

But I was already too late. By the time I reached the end of the whitewashed building, Michael McCrary was stalking back toward his cottage. I stood and watched him for a moment, and a few beats later, Giuseppe Fornario came around the corner, carrying his single piece of luggage. He headed straight for the front door of the hotel and, I could only assume, the front desk. What had happened that Giuseppe now appeared to be moving out of the McCrary cottage? He'd had plenty of opportunity to move out since McCrary had turned over the will to Nightingale. Giuseppe had even disappeared for an evening with his luggage, so why return at all? Fiona hadn't been shy about her dislike for the man from the very beginning, but her husband had seemed happy enough to take Giuseppe's money. So what had the men been arguing about?

CHAPTER TWENTY-EIGHT

Instead of going back into the pub for a drink, I decided to set off for my meeting with Redvers. It was the highlight of every day for me, and even though I'd seen him just a few hours before, I was looking forward to seeing him again. I didn't have any answers, only more questions, but I always found it helpful to talk things over with him. It often brought clarity to whatever I was mulling over.

But this was not to be my morning. I was a few minutes early to our meeting spot, so I anticipated having to wait a bit, but as the minutes passed, finally stretching into an hour, I realized that something had held him up and he wasn't coming. I gave it another half hour, but when there was still no sign of my fiancé, I grudgingly started the long trek back to the village, now thoroughly chilled and my mood matching the clouds that darkened the sky. My bad humor compelled my feet to kick a few rocks in the path along the way.

I passed through the village, head down, hands in my pockets. I had plenty of questions to ask, but little desire to hunt down the people I needed to ask them of. Without thinking, I found myself on the other side of the village, well on my way to the abbey. Once I realized the destination my feet had decided upon, I leaned into it, quickening my steps. It was a good idea to revisit the place during the day—perhaps something would reveal itself. Barring that, I could get a better sense of how close everyone had been to Nightingale the night before.

Before entering the chapel, I strolled through the ruins of the attached cloister buildings, admiring the arched colonnade bordering a square of green grass and wondering if this part of the site would ever be restored as the chapel had been. I made my way into the chapel itself, where the roof had been repaired, new wooden beams arching overhead. At night, the abbey had seemed spooky, but during the day, it was obvious how ancient the structure was. The stone walls were broken up by matching pillars supporting peaked arches; looking up, I could see rows of windows near the roof that hadn't been obvious the night before. They cast little light; most of the illumination came from the large arched window behind the altar. I could also now see numerous candles on the large stone holy table and wondered why they hadn't been utilized the night before.

Standing where the ceremony had taken place last night, it suddenly occurred to me how sacrilegious it seemed to have an occult ceremony in what was a Christian church. I was surprised that Nightingale and the group hadn't been stopped before the ceremony could even take place, especially since they hadn't been secretive about their intentions since their arrival on the island. I didn't have long to ponder the implications of this, however, because I turned to see Dion Fortune sitting on a stone tomb at the other end of the room. Her eyes were closed, and she was clearly in the middle of some type of meditation. I considered leaving, but instead took a seat in one of the wooden pews along the wall to wait it out.

It wasn't all that surprising that I kept running into the woman—the island was tiny, and it was starting to look as though Dion was looking into the mystery surrounding her friend's death as well. I wondered whether I should ask her outright, and if I would get an honest answer. It had become obvious over the last week that Dion had plenty of secrets of her own.

Without opening her eyes, Dion addressed me, calling across the space between us. "Jane, what are you doing here?"

I gave a little start, wondering how she had yet again known I was there and who I was without opening her eyes. I rose from my pew and started toward her. "Probably not the same thing you are," I said.

Dion made a strange sign in the air with her hands, then finally opened her eyes. "I was vibrating Netta's name on the astral plane, hoping to get some answers."

I was correct, then, that Dion was looking into things as well. Just not on this "plane." "Did you learn anything?"

She shook her head. "I can't seem to contact her spirit. I thought I might be able to reach her here, but I think I will try again from the fairy circle."

"Why try here? Did Netta have a connection to this abbey?"

"Not necessarily, but I thought perhaps she'd had something to do with Nightingale's stabbing."

"Why would you think that?" I really wanted to ask how a dead woman could be responsible for stabbing a man who was very much alive, but the question seemed too obvious. And in any event, I didn't think I would get a rational explanation.

"Netta could have been working through someone else," Dion said. She was still sitting in the same position, and I wondered how she could sit on the stone for so long without the cold seeping into her bones. Dion seemed perfectly content to remain there, however, much as she had been content to sit on the cold ground for long periods of time.

I tried to think of the best way to formulate my next question, but Dion beat me to the punch. "There are plenty of people who would wish Nightingale harm." Her brows wrinkled into a deep frown. "He has a reputation with young women that is . . . less than savory."

"Was he ever involved with Netta?"

Dion shook her head gently. "I can't say for certain, but I always assumed something happened between them."

I was frustrated that she was only just telling me this now. Hadn't she claimed before that Netta and Nightingale hardly interacted with one another? "Why would she stay in his order, then?"

"I asked her that once, and she couldn't answer. I think she would have been better off staying with Mina, but she didn't."

"Even though Mina attacked both of you?"

Dion looked troubled. "Perhaps if Netta had stayed, the attack never would have happened. And Netta would still be here with us."

The mention of the attack reminded me of something I needed to follow up on. "Speaking of the attack, where did you have the scratches? Just on your arms?"

Dion looked at me for a long moment. "My arms and my legs. Why do you ask?"

Which meant that Dion could easily have given them to herself—I couldn't rule her out as a suspect. "Netta had them all over her body."

The other woman simply shook her head and sighed. "Netta was receiving the worst of the attack, so that doesn't surprise me."

This wasn't useful, so I decided to change tacks. "What was it you wanted to talk to me about last night, before the ceremony?" I had asked this question the night before, and Dion had avoided answering. I was curious what would happen now.

She sighed. "I had a bad feeling about the ceremony." I nearly rolled my eyes—first Yeats and now Dion with their "bad feelings"—but I kept my face still, and Dion continued talking. "But I also wanted to talk to you about what Netta burned before she died."

Now we were getting somewhere. Although I did have to bite my tongue to keep from asking why she didn't just tell me the night before, knowing that I needed to let her talk without interruption.

"I hope you will keep this in the strictest confidence," Dion said. She waited until I agreed before she continued speaking. "I write about the occult under a pen name." She looked at me closely, and I did my best to pretend this was new information. I must have been convincing because she nodded and continued. "I'm afraid that Netta suspected me. She confronted me with something I'd written; she said it had to be me because it was too much like my own voice."

Here she paused long enough that I prompted her. "What happened then?"

"We argued, and she said that if I didn't stop publishing the order's secrets, she would be forced to go to Nightingale."

"Giving you plenty of motive to kill her," I said.

"I didn't have anything to do with her death. But it would be quite inconvenient if the police found out that I had a motive," Dion agreed. "If they investigate and learn about what I've published, they'll surely let Nightingale know what I've been up to."

"And you'll be kicked out of the order."

Dion cocked her head. "It wouldn't be the worst thing that could happen. I would like to start my own group anyway—I think both Mina and Nightingale have strayed too far from what the original purpose of the order was. I would like to go back to the origins and distill things back down to the truth."

I almost asked what that "truth" was, but instead I simply nodded. I didn't have any desire to know what she thought the order should be—it still seemed like a lot of nonsense and had little to no bearing on Netta's death, her will, or Nightingale's stabbing.

I'd already known about Dion's tracts and suspected that Netta knew about them as well, but it didn't seem like enough of a motive for Dion to kill Netta. And if Dion was admitting her writings to me, it made it even more unlikely that she'd harmed Netta, especially if Dion wanted to start her own occult group. It meant it wouldn't be worth killing over if she were asked to leave this one.

"I never would have harmed Netta," Dion said. "She was a delicate soul who needed tending. I admit that I should have been more present for her troubles, but I would never have done anything to harm her on purpose."

I assumed Dion was referring to that last day before her death, when Netta had seemed especially troubled and was trying to flee the island. I felt a twinge of guilt that I hadn't been more helpful to the young woman or gotten up to investigate the noise I'd heard that night. I might have been able to stop her from going out into the cold wearing nothing but a cloak.

I decided to ask Dion about Netta's blackened jewelry. "Some of the bracelets and necklaces Netta wore had turned black. Do you have any idea how that might have happened?"

Dion frowned. "I've heard of that happening before. Something to do with the person's skin and lacking some vitamin. I can't remember which one it is, though."

That set me back a bit. Could the blackened jewelry have been a natural occurrence and nothing nefarious after all? But did it explain the marks on Netta's wrists?

Dion frowned. "Was her talisman one of the items that turned black?"

This was the first I was hearing of this. "What talisman?"

"I suppose you're not there yet in your studies. At a later point, you have to make and consecrate a talisman. It helps to keep you safe and grounded, especially when you're entering the astral plane."

I nodded knowingly, hoping it was convincing. "Of course."

"Netta's talisman was an amethyst wrapped in silver. It would have been on a long necklace." Dion's hand was over a place on her breastbone, and I assumed that her own talisman was hidden there beneath her clothing. "Amethyst is good for shielding against negative energy." Dion's brows were furrowed again. "It looks as though it didn't work. Unless she didn't have it on her that night."

I thought back to Netta and how she'd been entirely nude when I found her. There had been no necklace, and nowhere to hide one, either. "It wasn't on her when she died," I said. I felt strongly that a piece of crystal wouldn't have made the difference that night between life and death, but I kept that to myself.

"I wonder where it went, then. She was almost never without it."

Where could Netta's talisman have gone indeed? The blackened pieces of jewelry seemed to have disappeared as well, but the rest of Netta's jewelry had been packed up, so this piece might have disappeared with the rest. I wasn't sure it was something of importance, but I filed it away all the same. As for whether Dion could have hurt Netta, I truly felt that Dion was telling the truth. Her words rang with sincerity, and I doubted that she would have done anything to harm the other woman.

Although the question remained whether Dion could have done something to harm Robert Nightingale.

Chapter Twenty-nine

D ion left to "vibrate Netta's name" on the fairy circle, and after she left, I took a close look at the chapel. Everything from the ritual the night before had been cleared away, including the knife that Nightingale had been stabbed with. I was a little surprised to see that there was no blood to be found anywhere at the front of the church. Either it had been cleaned up or there hadn't been much in the first place.

That alone was something I found quite interesting. I recalled that the doctor had said the wound wasn't terribly deep, so it made sense that there wasn't any blood left where it had happened, but the doctor had asked for something to bind it with. Would he have done that if there weren't any blood? And the fact that the wound wasn't deep struck me as suspicious by itself. If someone had taken the opportunity to stab Robert Nightingale, it seemed unlikely that they would make only a shallow wound. Of course, that might be explained by the fact that it was done in pitch darkness, and the assailant hadn't gotten good leverage to stab Nightingale harder. They couldn't see, after all. But I couldn't help but think it was exactly how someone might stab themselves— not very hard, just enough for effect.

What motive could Nightingale have for stabbing himself, though? That was what kept me from truly believing this theory. Unless he was trying to frame Giuseppe for something. It was obvious that Nightingale was going to share his theory about Giuseppe with the police, but he'd also said he wasn't going to press charges against his assailant. Why go through all the trouble of setting Giuseppe up for the stabbing but not follow through with it? That didn't make sense either.

There was nothing else to see in the chapel, so I headed outside, wandering through the cloister ruins for a few minutes of quiet thought before heading back toward the village.

Walking often helped me work through thorny issues, clearing my mind and allowing me to sort through complications to see the bigger picture. This time, I kept coming back to the conclusion that, if Nightingale had stabbed himself in the leg, there surely was a reason behind it. And if I could figure out what that reason was, I could wrap up that part of the investigation and stop pretending to study the Golden Dawn's teachings. Because if the man had stabbed himself, it was clearly indicative of larger personal issues, and there was no way the crown could trust the man enough to use him as an agent or even for gathering information on their behalf. It would certainly be enough to convince Redvers' employers of Nightingale's instability. As an added benefit, Redvers wouldn't have to hide on the other side of the island any longer.

It was just a question of how to learn what I needed to about Robert Nightingale.

Once in the village, I paused on the main street, looking around. Visiting Nightingale wouldn't get me anywhere—he was the least likely source for any sort of truth. Dion was the person I trusted the most in the order, but she was keeping all kinds of secrets as well. I might be able to get some information from Mina or her assistant, if I was able to find them, but I sincerely doubted they were still here in the village.

I turned on my heel, heading back the way I'd come toward the cottage, turning the puzzle pieces over and over in my mind and not liking how any of them fit together. Of course, now that Giuseppe had vacated the cottage, I could look through Netta's things again to see if her talisman was there. As long as the luggage was still at the McCrarys'. I rather thought it would be since Giuseppe had only been carrying his small bag when I'd seen him heading for the hotel, and I doubted that the detective inspector had confiscated Netta's things once he'd gone through them. Campbell would have taken anything of interest to the investigation, but I didn't think that a crystal hanging from a chain would have meant anything to either of the two men. If it was among her things, it would most likely still be there.

The cottage was quiet except for the sounds of Fiona working in the kitchen; rather than bother the woman, I went straight upstairs to Netta's room. The door was un-locked, and I pushed it open. Fiona had already been inside and refreshed the bed and everything else in the room—clearly Giuseppe was not coming back, and this time she knew it.

Netta's stack of luggage was still piled near the door, al-though it looked like it had been gone through several times. Which I supposed it had—by myself, Giuseppe, and the po-lice inspector. Possibly by either Fiona or Michael McCrary as well, although it was impossible to determine that.

I started with the luggage containing her clothes, making sure that I searched her pockets this time, in case she'd stowed her talisman—or anything else—in one of them. They were empty. I worked my way systematically through each piece of luggage and was sweating slightly once I'd finished. I hadn't found anything interesting, although I noticed that the Golden Dawn manuals I had seen before were now gone. I wondered if it was Giuseppe or the inspector who had taken those. Everything else appeared to be present, except for the talisman that Dion had described. I'd even found Netta's blackened jewelry neatly packed up and stowed away—I wondered if that had been Fiona's doing—but there had been no amethyst crystal among the other pieces.

Why would someone take Netta's talisman? I tried to put myself in the shoes of a true believer of the occult teachings for a moment in order to figure that out. Dion had said that it was meant to protect its creator, so perhaps whoever took it believed that it would remove Netta's protection. Could that person have thought that stealing it would put Netta in danger or open her up to attack? It seemed plausible—for a true believer, that is. Which meant that the amethyst necklace was most likely taken before Netta's death. Was that part of what had sent the woman into such a spiral?

There was no proof that Netta's death was a murder, or even anything but a tragic accident, but I was leaning more and more toward someone being responsible for her death, whether it was outright murder or not. Despite her secrets and her changing stories, I felt in my gut that I could rule out Dion Fortune as a possibility, which left me two other suspects—the two who had the most to gain in terms of Netta's fortune. Her father, Giuseppe Fornario, and Robert Nightingale.

I didn't hear the footsteps behind me, so when Fiona spoke from the doorway, I nearly jumped out of my shoes. With a hand to my thumping heart, I whirled to face her.

"Didnae mean to scare you!" Fiona said. "I heard you come in earlier."

I nodded, gesturing vaguely at the room. "Giuseppe isn't coming back?"

Fiona folded her arms over her chest. "Thank the stars, he is not. Mr. McCrary finally tossed the man out on his ear."

I cocked my head, but Fiona answered the question before I could ask it. "It took him finding that man looking through our things to do it." She rolled her eyes. "Mr. McCrary doesnae like to part with a single shilling. But he won't stand for a thief."

What had Giuseppe been looking for in the McCrarys' things? Michael had already turned Netta's will over to Nightingale. Whether or not it was valid had yet to be determined, for either of the wills. But what else did Giuseppe think he would find?

"I dinnae ken what to do with that poor girl's things," Fiona said. "That man didnae even want them. Said I could burn them, for all he cared." She shook her head. "A father shouldnae behave in such a way about his child's things."

I was inclined to agree. It was a little disconcerting how cavalier Giuseppe was about Netta's personal effects, but perhaps not everyone was sentimental in that way. Or at all.

Or perhaps he really hadn't cared much about his own daughter beyond her money.

CHAPTER THIRTY

Fiona looked at me shrewdly. "I still think you should have left the island this morning, Miss Jane, but I understand why you didnae. I pulled a card for you this morning after breakfast, and it was justice." She nodded. "You'll be needing to find justice before you can leave the island. I just hope you'll be careful."

I didn't know how to respond to that, but it didn't seem that Fiona needed me to. She simply nodded again and took herself back downstairs, leaving that rather ominous warning ringing in my ears. I still found it unsettling how accurate Fiona's readings were, but again, it had to be the woman's intuition at work. She must have picked up on the fact that I was looking into things surrounding Netta's death and intuited that I wanted to find who or what was responsible.

That said, the justice card still felt very specific.

I gave myself a little shake and went back to my room, half expecting to find Redvers there, and letting out a sigh of disappointment when I found no one. We'd agreed that, instead of meeting on the beach, he would come back to my room, since he'd proven so adept at climbing trees. Looking out the window, I saw that it had started to rain in earnest. Is that what had held the man up?

*   *   *

I didn't find out until later that evening, well past supper. I was thinking about getting ready for bed when I heard a noise at the window. I peered through the glass and saw a large figure in a black cloak climbing the gnarly tree. He was pretty nimble at the climbing, but I stifled a giggle at his ungainly dismount into my room. He landed with a thump on the ground.

"Very elegant," I said.

"Not my best work," he replied with a grin, pushing back the hood of his cloak. We waited quietly for a moment to see if either of the McCrarys had heard that loud landing downstairs, but after a few beats ticked by, I figured we were in the clear. Redvers removed his black cloak, flinging it over the chair, and we took a few moments to reacquaint ourselves before I started grilling him about his whereabouts that afternoon.

"I am sorry to have left you waiting," Redvers said. "But it couldn't be helped."

"What kept you—the rain? Were you afraid you would melt?"

"I was following Mrs. Mathers and the young woman that was with her."

My face lit up. "Are they still on the island, then? I did a half-hearted search this afternoon, but there was too much ground to cover."

Redvers looked amused at my admission of a half-hearted search. "It's a tiny island, Jane. There's not that much ground to cover."

"I suppose not, but I wasn't keen on knocking on the door of every cottage on the island. Especially not in the rain." The rain I'd noticed that afternoon had turned into a full-blown storm, so I'd taken refuge in my room for the remainder of the day instead of wandering about and getting soaked to the skin. Thus the half-hearted nature of my search—once it had started raining, I'd given up on going back out.

"Where are the ladies staying?" I asked.

"They've actually taken refuge at my cottage. They're sharing a room—the one opposite mine—but have very little luggage."

"That's terribly convenient. Why did it take you so long to follow them, then?"

"They inquired at a few other places on the outskirts of the island before making their way to my lodgings." He shrugged. "Seems like most of the places that rent out rooms are full at the moment, and they didn't seem keen on staying anywhere remotely close to Baile Mòr."

"That makes sense. I can see why they would look for somewhere outside of town to stay, not wanting to be seen. And since quite a few Golden Dawn members joined us yesterday, it also makes sense that the lodgings are full. They're not likely to empty out anytime soon either, since no one can leave the island." I cocked my head at him. "How have you explained your presence in the cottage?"

Redvers shrugged. "They haven't asked." Then he smiled. "I'm keeping up with my mysterious reputation."

I didn't bother responding to that and instead told Redvers what the ferry operator had related to me. "The police inspector isn't letting any of us leave, even for a day trip to Mull."

"I suppose that's not surprising, since Nightingale was stabbed. Whoever did it was in that chapel with us."

"Except that Nightingale isn't going to press charges."

Redvers' eyebrows shot up, and I explained to him what Nightingale had said about Giuseppe Fornario and what I'd seen that afternoon between Giuseppe and Michael McCrary. I even remembered to tell Redvers about Netta's missing talisman.

"Well. It seems that quite a bit has happened today," Redvers said.

"But the pieces still aren't fitting together. Perhaps things will start to fall into place once I can talk to Mina Mathers and Colleen again."

"I hope that's the case," Redvers said, then grinned wolfishly. "But that interview can wait until tomorrow."

I smiled. "You have other plans for me right now?"

"I certainly do."

Morning came, but this time Redvers overslept, and I was tasked with distracting Fiona and Michael in the breakfast room while Redvers quietly made his escape out of the cottage—via the front door instead of climbing down the wet tree. I knew we were running quite a risk of being caught, but I did very much enjoy waking up next to my fiancé.

To distract my hosts and keep them busy, I asked question upon question about the island's landscape—something I was already quite familiar with due to my daily treks around Iona. Once I was certain Redvers was safely on his way, I stopped my interrogation and tucked into my coffee, followed quickly by my breakfast plate.

Michael McCrary gestured to his wife for a refill of his cup of tea and sat down in the chair across from me. "If you're interested in the landscape, you should see the marble quarry. It shut down a few years ago, now. The company left their equipment to rot, which is a real shame. But it's worth seeing."

I feigned interest since I'd brought up the topic in the first place.

"I ken you like to do your walks, so it shouldnae be too far for you."

I nodded and listened while McCrary gave me directions to the quarry. Then I finished up my meal and poured myself another cup of coffee. I cursed myself for bringing up this topic since now I felt obligated to actually go look at the quarry, in case McCrary asked me something specific about it later. The detour would add quite a bit of time and distance to my walk this morning, delaying my plans. I had intended to head to the cottage where Redvers was staying first thing this morning so that I could talk to Mina and Colleen.

After consuming every drop of coffee in the pot, I bundled up and headed out. It wasn't raining anymore, but it was blustery and even colder than it had been on the previous days of my stay. The clouds were still hanging dark and low, and I hoped they would hold on to their moisture, for a while longer anyway. I considered going back for an umbrella, but decided against it. With this wind, it was unlikely to be of much use, even if it did start raining; I would just have to hope for the best.

I took my usual path out of town across the green fields, but when I reached the western coast of the island, I went south instead of north. It was a rugged path, little more than a sheep trail in most parts, and I once again cursed my morning's questions, especially as I climbed an especially rocky and rather steep hill. I paused for a moment at the top, taking in the view toward Mull, then continued on my way.

I finally reached the quarry, after first finding Columba's Bay and having to do some backtracking to find the right piece of coastland. It felt like an accomplishment when I finally did reach the old quarry, and I cautiously approached the cliffside. There was a sharp drop-off where I stood, the broken-down remnants of machinery having been left to rust in the elements below the jagged cliffs, just as McCrary had described. Beyond the machinery lay a sea of jagged gray-and-white marble boulders, and I caught sight of something blowing in the wind from the top of one. The boulder in question was far below me, and I didn't want to get much closer to the edge—it felt as though one good gust of wind could push me right over and onto the rocks below—but it definitely looked as though something were lying wedged between two of the boulders.

I crouched down and edged slightly closer, trying to get a look at what was on the rock without tumbling over the edge of the cliff. Another gust of wind blew up from the inlet, and my face felt the cold, salty mist from the ocean. But the wind also billowed up what I could now see was a jacket on the rocks below.

I had a sinking feeling about what would be inside that jacket.

It only took me a quarter of an hour to find the path down from the cliffs, and I picked my way carefully along it, not wanting to slip on the loose gravel beneath my feet. But even in that amount of time, I was cold and shivering from the mist off the ocean and my slower pace. Despite my discomfort, I made my way past the various bits of machinery, one of which was tall and resembled scaffolding, to where the sea of marble began. Luckily, the boulders were midsized, and I was able to easily scale one and move to the next, until I was close enough to tell exactly what it was that I had seen.

A body. It was definitely the body of a man, lying face down among the boulders. I didn't have to get any closer to know that the man was dead; for one thing, there was a knife sticking out of his back.

I had a sneaking suspicion that I knew who this was, but I needed to get closer to confirm it, since the man's face was turned away from where I stood. I scrambled onto another rock and moved around, craning my neck to catch a glimpse of the face. I finally saw the big moustache and unseeing eyes.

It was Giuseppe Fornario.

CHAPTER THIRTY-ONE

I got off the rocks and retraced my path back into the village, my chat with Mina and Colleen on hold for the time being. On the way, I considered the best place to find the inspector, hoping that he was on the island today, and landed on the Hotel Argyll as a likely spot to find him. It was where Nightingale was staying, as well as several of the other members of the Golden Dawn, so I decided to check there first.

Glancing around the lobby told me nothing—it was quiet today, so I headed up to the second floor to Nightingale's quarters. The door to his room was closed, and putting an ear to it told me nothing; all was quiet. I went back downstairs and stopped by the front desk to see if the clerk had seen the detective inspector.

"Aye," the young man said. "The man himself was here this morning, but he left not an hour ago."

"Any idea where he might have gone?"

The clerk shook his head, and I sighed in frustration, then decided that my next stop might as well be the McCrary cottage.

This time, luck was on my side, and I found the inspector seated in an upholstered chair in the McCrarys' sitting room. Michael was seated across from Campbell, with Fiona standing near the doorway of the room, and everyone stopped speaking when I opened the front door, all eyes turning to me as I came into the cottage.

"I apologize for the interruption," I said. "But I'm afraid there's something you need to know, Inspector."

"Aye? And what is that?"

"I've found Giuseppe Fornario's body," I said. Fiona gasped beside me, and Michael muttered something beneath his breath, but I continued on. "I can take you to where I found him."

Campbell narrowed his eyes at me, but nodded. I hated that this most likely meant that I was a suspect in Giuseppe's death, but there was nothing to be done about it. I couldn't let the man lie out there in the hope that someone else would find him, an unlikely scenario that might last for quite some time due to the remoteness of the quarry. Besides, I had an alibi for the night before, which was when I assumed the murder had taken place.

While I waited for the inspector to get his coat on, two things occurred to me. The first was that it was a rather strange coincidence that Michael McCrary had recommended that very spot to me over breakfast. Could he have known what I would find? Did he have a motive to eliminate Giuseppe Fornario and then send me out to the quarry to find the body?

The second was that Giuseppe Fornario was no longer a threat to Robert Nightingale's version of Netta's will.

"What do you know about Mr. Fornario?" Inspector Campbell asked me after we had walked in silence for a quarter of an hour. I was a little surprised at the sudden question and looked at him out of the corner of my eye. He wasn't looking at me, his intense focus alternating between the view and his footing on the uneven path.

"Well, he really was Netta's father," I said. The inspector arched an eyebrow but didn't say anything to this. "And he didn't seem very interested in his daughter," I added slowly. "Except for her money."

This was apparently not news to the inspector. "Yes, I heard that Nightingale and Fornario had competing wills." He speared me with a look. "Which one do you think was real?"

I was surprised that the man was seeking my opinion, but I only had to give it a moment's thought. "I'm not sure either is real."

The inspector didn't reply, moving ahead on a path that had narrowed so that I was behind him, but I knew that he'd heard me. "What do you think?" I asked. The words had popped out before I could consider the wisdom of asking.

For a long moment, I didn't think that he would bother answering, or perhaps he hadn't heard me, my words whipped away on the wind. "I think I'm inclined to agree with you," he finally said, turning his head slightly to toss his comment over his shoulder.

We neared the point where I had first seen the body, and I showed the inspector where I'd been standing. I stayed well back from the edge, but Campbell inched closer and peered over the side, giving a single nod, which led me to believe he'd also seen Giuseppe's coat. I then led him to the path down the cliff, past the rusted machinery, but when we reached the sea of marble rocks, I simply pointed the way. I didn't need to make the climb again, and I let the inspector clamber up alone.

He stopped, obviously having seen the body. "I'll take it from here, Miss Wunderly." I could see he wasn't looking at me, but when I turned to leave, he called again. "I'll be wanting to talk with you later, though."

I supposed that went without saying, much as I wished it weren't the case.

I retraced my steps and headed for the cottage where Redvers and the two women were staying. As I walked, I thought about what we had so far, none of it good. Two dead bodies, two men stabbed, a missing talisman, and a pair of wills that may or may not be valid. And those wills were probably the reason there was now a knife in Giuseppe's back.

I hadn't failed to notice that the knife used to stab Giuseppe looked an awful lot like the ceremonial knife that had been used to stab Robert Nightingale, although I hadn't gotten close enough to say for certain. I would do some asking around to see where that knife had ended up after the ritual, however. It seemed as though the police would have taken it, but if Nightingale wasn't pressing charges, perhaps they hadn't seen the need. In any event, I needed to find out where it had gone after the ritual and who'd had access to it.

I also needed to see if Nightingale was mobile or if he was truly confined to his bed. I couldn't think of anyone with a better motive for killing Giuseppe Fornario than Robert Nightingale. With Giuseppe gone, there was no one to challenge the will that Michael McCrary had turned over to him, and Netta's considerable wealth would come to Nightingale's order without a lengthy court battle.

The only other person who'd had an open disagreement with Giuseppe was Michael McCrary—I hadn't forgotten that they'd been arguing the day before. Based on what Fiona had told me, however, the argument had most likely been because Fornario was caught snooping through the McCrarys' things. I couldn't imagine that would give either McCrary motive to kill the man. Kick him out of the cottage, yes. Stab him? I couldn't see it.

That didn't mean the police would see things the same way, though. And I still hadn't been able to get a read on the inspector, so I had no idea how he would proceed. I could only assume that, right now, we were all under suspicion.

When I reached the door of the cottage where Redvers and the women were staying, I knocked and waited, then knocked

again. After a long moment, the door was finally opened by a
middle-aged woman in a brown wool dress with her graying
brown hair pulled back severely into a bun.

"Good morning," I said, although it was now approaching afternoon. "Is Mina Mathers staying here?"

The woman looked at me suspiciously, narrowing her
eyes. "You seem familiar."

I didn't respond to this, since I hadn't seen this woman before, although I had snuck out of her cottage after spending
time with Redvers. I didn't know how she would recognize
me, though—we'd been careful not to be seen.

The woman finally gave a little shrug and tipped her head
for me to enter. "You can wait in the sitting room. I dinnae
ken if they're about, but I'll check."

The room she showed me into was large, nearly twice the
size of the one at the McCrary cottage, and I once again
shook my head at Redvers' description of this place as a
shed. I sat in the chair closest to the fire, mentally sending up
a prayer that the rickety-looking thing would hold me. It was
surprisingly comfortable, though, and I could see why the
owner hung on to it. I heard some murmured conversation
on the floor above, and after a few long minutes, Mina Mathers appeared in the doorway.

"Jane," she said in surprise. "How did you find me?"

"I'm sorry to tell you that it wasn't terribly hard. This is a
small island." It wasn't an answer to her question, but I
hoped she wouldn't notice since I wasn't about to explain
that Redvers had followed her all over Iona.

Mina gave a small sigh and took a seat across from me. "I
suppose that is true. I was hoping to be more inconspicuous,
though."

"Why are you here in the first place? And where is your
assistant?"

"Colleen? She's lying down. It's been . . . well, it's been a
difficult few days for her."

I looked at Mina, but it appeared that was all she had to say on the matter. I would leave it alone for the moment, but I wouldn't let it go forever. "And why are you here on Iona?"

Mina rubbed her temples. "I followed Colleen here. I've been afraid for some time that she's fallen under Robert's spell." Mina's face darkened. "He's notorious for it."

Numerous people had suggested Nightingale's way with young women, but I hadn't seen any evidence of it in person. That didn't mean I was disbelieving, of course. I was just curious that he actually seemed to be discreet. "Why did she stay with you, then? Instead of defecting to his temple?"

Mina looked sad. "She's still devoted to me."

That didn't make any sense. It seemed to me that it was one or the other—either you were devoted to Mina or you were involved with Robert. It seemed too much at odds to be both simultaneously, especially given the reported tension between the two faction leaders.

"So Colleen came to the island for Nightingale's ceremony and you followed her? What about a ceremony of your own? You didn't have one planned?"

Mina shook her head. "I had already decided to forego the equinox ceremony. It was rather last minute, but I thought it was for the best to cancel. There were too many disturbances on the astral plane."

I recalled what Dion had said about Mina attacking her and Netta on that plane. How best to approach the subject without accusing the woman outright, though? "What kind of disturbance? A conflict of some kind?"

Mina paused, studying me. "How serious are you about your studies?"

Here was where I needed to lie outright and be convincing about it. "Very serious. I came all the way from the States for the equinox ceremony."

She was looking at me closely and finally nodded. "I'm sorry that the ceremony wasn't completed."

It was the closest Mina had come to admitting that she'd been in the abbey that night, since it was unlikely she could know that the ceremony was interrupted unless she'd been present. But I needed to know more about the "conflict" between herself and Dion.

"Dion mentioned that she'd been having some troubles while visiting the astral plane as well."

Mina cocked her head at me and spoke slowly. "I would be less surprised if it had been Netta having the trouble. Dion is usually quite in control of her visions."

That wasn't helpful in the slightest, but accusing the woman outright would shut down this conversation entirely—I knew that in my gut. "Dion also mentioned some trouble with black cats."

Mina nodded. "That can definitely be a sign that a person is under attack. Did she say who she thought it might be?"

I shook my head. "She didn't, but she thought it might have something to do with Netta's death."

Mina looked appropriately sad, but it was impossible to tell whether or not that was put-on. From what I had seen so far, this woman was an experienced actress, changing emotions like a chameleon changed colors. "Poor Netta. She was such a troubled soul."

"Do you have any idea what might have happened to her talisman? It seems to have gone missing."

Mina's hand went to the same place under her dress that Dion's had, her hand pressing somewhere near her heart. It made sense to me that they wore them under their clothing, but I was curious to get a look at someone else's. I didn't think Mina was the person to ask this of, however.

"It's a bad sign that her talisman is missing," Mina said. "It would have opened her up to bad vibrations and possible attack. Unless her father has it?"

I shook my head. "I don't think that he did. And in any case, we can't ask him since he's dead."

Mina looked genuinely shocked at this, what felt like the first real reaction I'd seen from the woman. "Dead?" she repeated.

"I found his body at the quarry this morning."

"Perhaps it was simply an accident," Mina said unconvincingly.

I sat back in my chair. "From the knife in his back, I would say that it was not."

Mina stood, but stayed where she was. "We need to leave the island," she said, although I couldn't tell who the "we" referred to. "It's not safe to stay here. We should go immediately."

I was intrigued by this reaction. "I rather agree with you, but I'm afraid the inspector isn't letting anyone off the island."

Mina sank back into her chair. I wondered that she didn't already know this, since I had assumed it was the reason she and Colleen hadn't left already. But perhaps she'd forgotten that little detail?

I changed directions yet again. "Why has it been such a difficult few days for Colleen?"

Mina was distracted, picking at the collar of her flowing dress, her eyes unfocused. "It's always hard for her to come back home."

My eyes went wide as I processed that information, but Mina didn't notice my reaction, her attention on the wall behind me as she mentally worked out something else.

"Colleen is from here?" I asked. That would explain the trouble Yeats had had with her accent—she wasn't Irish at all, but Scottish. I wondered if "from here" specifically meant Iona or just Scotland in general.

Mina nodded; then her focus snapped back to me. "But that has little to do with anything."

I disagreed, but didn't bother to say this. I was certain my expression said plenty for me.

Mina's eyes narrowed. "Just why are you here anyway? You ask a lot of questions for a neophyte."

Chapter Thirty-two

I'd been wondering when someone would start to question why I was snooping around and asking questions about Netta instead of falling in line like any other member of the group. So I answered as honestly as I was able to. "I feel bad that I didn't do more to help Netta that day. I don't feel responsible," I stressed this part, "but I do feel that I could have done more to help her. She was so troubled leading up to the night that she died."

Mina was quiet for a moment, considering me, but gave a quick nod. "I'm sorry she came to such an end."

"And I'm also questioning whether I chose the correct group. Perhaps I should have joined another group altogether."

Perhaps this was overselling things, but Mina nodded again. "It's wise to question your choices in this matter. It's very important, and Robert Nightingale . . . well, I obviously believe that the Golden Dawn is the only true order, but perhaps you should consider another temple." With that, she stood, obviously finished with our conversation. I was disappointed since I still had plenty of questions, but unsurprised. "This was . . . enlightening," Mina said.

I stood as well. "I hope we get the chance to talk again."

Mina's lips pressed into a tight smile, and she swept from

the room. I sighed. I hadn't gotten much from the conversation—not nearly as much as I'd hoped, anyway, except for the tidbit about Colleen and her origins. Perhaps Redvers would have more luck. I knew he would search the women's room the first chance he got.

I paused before taking my leave, considering whether I should ask to speak with Colleen, but decided this was futile and left. Mina wasn't going to let me speak with the girl, not after our conversation. I thought I'd explained myself reasonably well, but Mina had been suspicious of me—that much was obvious. I would have to do my best to find Colleen on her own if I wanted to talk with her.

In the meantime, I needed to figure out just who Colleen O'Connell really was.

I had a lot to think about on my walk back to the village. Mina and Colleen were still in the running for suspects in Nightingale's stabbing, as far as I was concerned, although I couldn't see that either of them had a motive for stabbing Giuseppe. Of course, we could be looking for two different people, but the coincidence of the same knife being used was one that shouldn't be overlooked. I didn't like coincidences—too often they turned out to be connections instead.

I could think of plenty of reasons why Mina or her assistant might want to stab Robert, especially if there had been a love affair gone wrong between any of the three of them. It was interesting that Robert's reputation with women kept coming up, as well as suspicions about his various love affairs, but I'd seen little proof of any of them. Could he be that circumspect about his love life? I found it unlikely, given what I'd seen of his personality. But if his Casanova reputation wasn't true, then where did all the rumors stem from? Usually, where there was smoke, there was fire.

Unfortunately, there were a lot of other suspects for Nightingale's stabbing besides the two women—Robert hadn't done much to help himself in this regard. According to numerous sources, there were any number of people who might have wanted to take a stab at Nightingale and had the opportunity to do it, given the dark setting that night.

The only thing that seemed certain to me at this point, however, was that Netta's death was no accident. Someone had to have had a hand in it, however that might have been accomplished.

The other issue that my mind couldn't stop tumbling over was whether Colleen was related to someone on this island. Perhaps it didn't matter, but it felt significant that if the young woman had family on Iona, she was choosing not to stay with them. Or perhaps she wasn't welcome to stay with them. I would make some inquiries and see if anyone would admit to knowing the young woman, although it would be difficult without a photograph—she didn't have any truly defining characteristics that I could describe. In fact, one of the most defining things about her might be that she blended in so well.

Looking back on my interactions with Mina, it was clear that the woman was a talented actress, and most of what she said should be taken with a grain of salt. But she'd been distracted when she let it slip that Colleen was from here, and that would have been an extraordinary bit of acting indeed. No, I thought that comment had been genuine, especially since it coincided with what Yeats had said about the young woman's accent being not quite right.

Which brought up yet another question. Colleen O'Connell sounded like a very Irish name, and not one likely to be found on the Scottish isle of Iona. Was that really her name at all?

I was normally an active person, but I wasn't accustomed to this much hiking; the back and forth across the island multiple times a day was finally starting to take its toll. By the time I made it back to the village, I was tempted to head back to the McCrary cottage and take a nap. But, by sheer force of will, I resisted the urge and went to the hotel instead, heading up to the second floor to talk with Robert Nightingale.

For the second time in days, I found the man's door closed, but this time I knocked. When there was no answer, I knocked again, more firmly this time.

"Who is it?" Nightingale's voice came from behind the door, muffled and slightly irritable.

"Jane Wunderly. Might I come in?" I didn't wait for permission, twisting the knob and pushing the door in. I had a moment's panic that I might find him in some state of undress due to my hasty entrance, but I was happy to find him sitting up in bed, leg slightly elevated and fully clothed in his blue silk pajamas.

All the same, he didn't look happy to see me. "Can this wait? I was hoping to get a little sleep. My leg has been keeping me awake at night."

I managed not to roll my eyes. "I thought the doctor gave you some pills to help with sleep."

"He did, but they haven't been strong enough."

I had thoughts about men and their tolerance for pain, but I kept them to myself. "I'm very sorry to hear that. Can I send for him? Perhaps he can give you something stronger."

"Yes, that would be helpful," Nightingale said. "He's most likely in the pub at the Columba."

"I'll be sure to head there next and send him back here," I said. Which I would actually do, but not before I asked some questions. "Have you been able to leave the room?"

Nightingale blinked at me. "Of course not. I'm not able to move with my leg like this. I even need help to get to the . . . well, the facilities. The clerks downstairs have been instructed to check on me periodically and assist when I need it."

I had nothing but sympathy for the hotel staff here, and I

would be sure to ask around to see if that was actually true. "That must be difficult for you. Having to stay here."

He sniffed. "It is, actually. Thank you for your sympathy. Now, if you don't mind . . ."

"Oh, I don't mind at all." I took a seat in the wooden chair that had been placed at the end of his bed, deliberately misunderstanding him. "What do you know about Colleen O'Connell?"

"Who?" The question was asked entirely too innocently to be anything but a cover-up.

"Mina Mathers's assistant. I'm sure you remember her."

"How do you know Mina Mathers?" Nightingale asked.

I made something up on the spot, hoping to keep the conversation going. "She attempted to recruit me for her temple."

Nightingale shook his head. "You seem to have sense, Miss Wunderly, so I hope you know that you made the correct decision in joining our temple. Mina Mathers might have good intentions, but she's quite lost sight of our goals. And she'll never be as powerful as I am. That's why her husband wanted me to take over the temple once he passed away."

I nodded knowingly. "I can see that. But what do you think of her assistant, Colleen?"

"I don't think anything of that girl. She's just as lost as Mina, and best to be avoided." Nightingale gave a flippant wave of his hand.

But he'd reversed himself. He was admitting that he knew exactly who Colleen was. "Have you seen either of them lately?"

He frowned. "Not in recent memory, why do you ask?"

"I just wondered if they might be behind some of the trouble here on the island."

Nightingale shrugged. "It's possible, I suppose. Although if either of them was seen on the island, anyone in our temple would have reported it to me."

That was interesting. It made it seem as though he had order members on the lookout for Mina and Colleen. It was also interesting that no one else had noticed them at the ritual that night. I knew that at least Mina had been present at the ceremony, but had no one else seen her? Or were his members simply not reporting back to Nightingale, as he insisted they should?

"Now, I hate to bring this up, but it does make me slightly concerned," I said. "I heard that perhaps you and Colleen were . . . romantically linked."

A flash of something passed over Nightingale's face, fast enough that it might have been missed if one wasn't watching for it.

"That's preposterous. Now, if you don't mind—"

I cut him off. "I'm glad to hear it. That puts my mind at ease about having joined the one true temple under your powerful leadership." This obscene flattery seemed to work because Nightingale's face and shoulders relaxed once again. He even preened a little bit, but I had learned what I needed to. I thought it was very likely that something had gone on between Robert and Colleen O'Connell.

But how to find out if he knew the woman's real name? I was about to embark on that line of questioning when he interrupted me with a bombshell of his own. "I'm sorry that you were the one who found Giuseppe Fornario."

I wondered who had brought him that bit of news. "Yes, it's quite sad. First Netta and now her father."

"That police inspector is looking for you," Nightingale said casually. "He was here earlier, asking about where I was, but of course I was right here in bed. Couldn't possibly move, you know."

I looked at the man for a long moment. What a convenient alibi. "Of course. Out of curiosity, where was the knife held after the equinox ritual? The one in Giuseppe's back looked like the same knife that was used to stab you."

Nightingale nodded sagely. "The police inspector said that it was the same knife. Unfortunately, it was here in my room." He tipped his head toward a wardrobe against the far wall. "All the ceremonial pieces are in there."

"The inspector didn't confiscate it after you were stabbed?"

"Since I wasn't pressing charges against Giuseppe, there was no need."

I had nearly forgotten Nightingale's firm belief that Giuseppe was responsible for stabbing him. I thought someone else was a more likely culprit, but Nightingale had seemed convinced that it had been Giuseppe. Of course, now that his injury offered him an alibi for the time when Giuseppe was killed, I was more convinced than ever that Nightingale was the best suspect for his own stabbing. I just had no idea how he'd pulled off Giuseppe's murder from his bed.

"How was the knife taken from your room then?"

Nightingale waved a hand. "Oh, anyone could have taken it once I was asleep. The sleeping draught the doctor gave me knocked me out cold."

"I thought you said you were having trouble sleeping because it wasn't strong enough."

Nightingale pierced me with a look. He was not a man who liked being contradicted. "I slept hard for several hours, but it didn't last long enough. I woke up early this morning and couldn't get back to sleep."

"Ah, of course. I see." I stood, my head buzzing with thoughts. "I'll just head to the pub now and see if I can send the doctor your way."

"Thank you, Miss Wunderly." Nightingale had already closed his eyes. It was impossible to tell whether he was actually tired or simply done with our conversation.

Either way, he'd given me a lot to chew over.

CHAPTER THIRTY-THREE

I stopped by the front desk and spoke to the clerk there about Nightingale's arrangement with the staff to check on him periodically and help him to the facilities. It seemed well beyond the purview of what could reasonably be expected of the hotel staff, but I needed to ask the question.

The young man behind the desk wrinkled his nose. "Yes, we're supposed to check on him every two hours. I haven't had to help him with anything; he always seems to have people in his room, and they must be helping him with his . . . needs. I did hear Liam, the chap who worked before me, say that he had to help the man to the facilities this morning, though." He shuddered, and I offered both my sympathies and my thanks for the information.

Perhaps Nightingale really was confined to his bed, then.

I made it to the St. Columba Hotel and through the lobby to where the pub was located, stopping just inside the door. The atmosphere in the hotel pub was strange—both quietly abuzz and apprehensive. It only took me a moment to figure out why. Detective Inspector Campbell was interviewing John Bychowski at a table in the far corner while everyone else was gathered opposite, chattering anxiously among themselves and not so discreetly watching the interview.

I shifted from foot to foot, undecided whether I should

stay or go. I wanted to talk to whoever might be willing to speak with me about Nightingale and the goings-on, but I also wanted to avoid the police inspector. Just as I was about to turn on my heel, the inspector looked up and caught my eye, then pointed one finger down at the ground. It was an unmistakable directive to stay put. With a sigh, I headed toward the bar, ordered myself a gin rickey for fortification, and looked around at the small crowd. I spotted the doctor standing by himself at the other end of the long wooden bar and made my way to him.

"Doctor, I just spoke to Robert Nightingale. He's hoping you might have something stronger for sleeping."

The doctor pressed his lips together. "That man," he muttered. "I doubt anything will be strong enough." Then he appeared to remember I was there and nodded at me. "Thank you, lass. I'll stop by and see him again."

"May I ask who invited you to attend the ceremony? I assume you're a member of the temple."

The doctor looked at me quizzically, but gave a small shrug and took a sip of his drink, a "pint of heavy," as I'd heard the Scots call it. "Nightingale asked if I would attend. Practically insisted on it, really. I had other plans, but I was able to change them and make it here for the ceremony. I always did have an interest in attending an equinox ceremony on Iona, so I was happy to do it."

That seemed to be the general consensus on why people had made the trip to this remote isle—they wanted to attend the ceremony here because of Iona's mystical reputation. I found it more than a little interesting that Nightingale had asked his personal physician to attend, however. Was it because he knew he would need a doctor on hand? Everything I learned only cemented my belief that Nightingale had stabbed himself. But to what end? For an alibi at the time of Giuseppe's death? But who had done the actual killing?

The doctor took a long swig of his drink and put it down on the bar. "I'll see to him now."

I murmured a goodbye and watched the man go. I didn't even have time to take a sip of the drink that the bartender had deposited on the bar for me before there was a tap on my shoulder. I jumped slightly and turned to find the police inspector standing behind me.

"Miss Wunderly, if you would come with me."

The words were ominous, but Campbell simply led me back to the table in the corner where he'd been speaking with John Bychowski. I noticed that Bychowski had left the pub instead of joining his compatriots at the bar, and I wondered why. Probably because he wanted to get as far away from the inspector as he could.

Which was what I was wishing I could also do at the moment. I'd had my share of unpleasant run-ins with the police over the past year, but I'd also had some relatively pleasant ones as well, although they were never under pleasant circumstances. I hoped there would come a day when I would no longer have any run-ins with the police, but today was not to be that day.

I took my seat, and the inspector studied me for a moment before saying anything. "Tell me again how you found the body."

I repeated my story once again to Inspector Campbell, leaving out the part where Michael McCrary had recommended that I go out and see the quarry—had almost insisted on it, really. I knew it wasn't wise to keep that information back from the inspector, but I wanted more time to investigate before I made Michael McCrary the prime suspect in Giuseppe's murder. Which would certainly happen once I related McCrary's insistence that I hike out to the quarry.

Once I'd finished recounting how I'd found Giuseppe, I asked a question of my own. "The knife in his back. Was it the same one that was used to stab Robert Nightingale?"

"What makes you ask that?" The inspector narrowed his eyes.

"I didn't get a very close look at it, but it appeared to be the same knife."

Campbell studied me for a long moment, then nodded his head. "'Tis the same knife."

I cocked my head, wondering why he'd decided to answer my question when he answered that for me. "Your fiancé vouched for ye."

"Ahh, yes. You met Redvers then."

"Aye," Campbell said, but left it at that. I was more than a little curious about how the meeting between Redvers and the inspector had gone, but I would clearly have to wait until I spoke to Redvers to find out. "What can you tell me about Fornario?" Campbell asked.

I checked off the few things I knew about the man on my fingers. "He showed up on the island quite quickly after Netta's death. He conveniently 'found' a copy of her will, leaving all of her money to him, dated only a few days earlier. Giuseppe and Nightingale argued about Netta's will here in the pub, quite loudly. And Giuseppe disappeared for an entire evening with his luggage before reappearing at the Mc-Crarys' the next morning as if nothing had happened."

"Did you see him arguing with anyone else?" The inspector had his notebook open, but was studying me instead of making notes.

I recalled his argument with McCrary. The bartender was likely to report that to the inspector, so there was little point in my trying to hide it, even if I was inclined to protect McCrary. "I saw him talking with Michael McCrary behind the pub."

"Were they talking or arguing?"

"It was hard to tell. McCrary wasn't saying anything, but Fornario appeared to be shouting and waving his hands about. Fornario moved out of the cottage shortly after that, so I assumed it was because he'd been asked to leave."

Campbell nodded.

"I know the results were inconclusive, but do you think someone might have been responsible for Netta's death as well?"

The inspector paused, appearing to consider whether to answer my question. "I don't believe in too many coincidences, Miss Wunderly."

I nodded. We had that in common at least.

Once I was dismissed, I did the same thing that Bychowski had done and left the pub instead of staying to talk with the other order members. I started my walk to the McCrary cottage when I heard a short whistle. I stopped, wondering if the wind was starting to play tricks on my ears, when I heard it again. I looked around me, finally spotting the cloaked figure standing in the shadows of the doorway to St. Oran's Chapel to the side of the path. I gave my head a little shake and hurried up the path, meeting Redvers inside, grateful for the shelter from the wind.

I greeted him with a warm kiss and an embrace. "Thank you for coming to this side of the island. I wasn't looking forward to trekking over to you again today."

"I figured as much, especially after your walk out to the quarry and then out to the cottage. How was your discussion with Mina Mathers?"

"I didn't see you there. You weren't eavesdropping?" I asked playfully.

"Sadly no. I was following Colleen O'Connell onto the moor."

I could feel my eyes light up. "What was she doing out there?"

"Burying something."

I looked at him expectantly. But he was the one enjoying himself now, and I wrinkled my nose at him. "Am I supposed to guess? I'm assuming you dug it up, whatever it was."

Redvers feigned offense. "I can't believe you would think otherwise." He kissed the top of my head, then reached into his pocket and removed a handkerchief that had been folded over itself several times. It was dirty, so clearly whatever Colleen had buried was tucked inside.

I reached out and took it, unfolding the cloth to reveal an amethyst crystal on a long chain that had once been silver, but had now turned black.

CHAPTER THIRTY-FOUR

I looked up at my fiancé. "It's Netta's talisman."
"I thought it might be."

"I never saw it on her, but it matches the description Dion gave me. And the chain has turned black, like the rest of the pieces I saw."

Redvers considered that. "The black chain means that it likely belonged to Netta. But I'm curious, is Dion the only one who described it for you?"

"No," I said after a moment. "Mina Mathers did as well. And since Dion and Mina aren't exactly friendly at the moment, I think it's likely that this is it." I considered the purple crystal. "Why would Colleen have it? And why was she burying it on the moor?" These were rhetorical questions, but Redvers felt the need to answer them.

"It could mean that Colleen was involved in Netta's death."

"Netta died days before Mina and Colleen arrived here, and the ferry wasn't running that day, so it would be difficult for Colleen to have come and left the next day without having lodgings."

"Difficult but not impossible."

"True enough," I said. "But what motive could Colleen have? Mina I can see, but not Colleen."

"That is a trickier question."

I thought about what Dion had said about the attacks on the "astral plane" and how this talisman was supposed to protect Netta from them. I said as much to Redvers, even though I knew precisely what his reaction would be.

"Foolishness," Redvers said, proving me correct. "There's no way that taking this necklace would open up Netta to any sort of harm."

"I agree. But the fact remains that there is an entire group of people who believe that it would."

Redvers sighed. "That is a fair point."

"We have to keep in mind that just because we don't believe things to be true, the people here do." I thought about Fiona's unnervingly accurate tarot readings, but held my tongue. I told myself that they didn't really relate to either of the deaths, and there was no reason to start an argument.

I would examine my reluctance to discuss the readings later.

I had no reluctance, however, to discuss the strange, shared visions I'd experienced in Mina's room, especially since I thought there was likely a reasonable explanation for how Mina had pulled that little trick off. "Any luck on the hypnotism front?" I asked.

Redvers shook his head. "I have someone doing research on the subject for me, but nothing useful yet."

That was disappointing, but not terribly surprising. We were in quite a remote location. "Did you have a chance to search Mina and Colleen's room?" I asked.

"Not yet," Redvers said. "One or both of them have been in there at all times. Almost as though they're taking turns leaving the room."

"Could they have something in there that they're protecting?"

"I'm starting to wonder that myself." Redvers switched gears. "What did you learn from your chat with Mina?"

I filled him in on our conversation, including her reaction to the news about Giuseppe Fornario. "She seemed genuinely shocked. She nearly jumped out of her chair and said it wasn't safe here on the island."

"Hmm. That's a strong reaction," Redvers said.

"I thought the same thing. Which leads me to believe that she didn't have anything to do with his death, although I suppose we still can't rule it out." I then recounted my conversations with Nightingale and the inspector as well. While he mulled it all over, I sighed.

"What is it?" he asked.

"I cannot wait until we can stop this charade and run the investigation together." I was tired of playing catch-up once a day and barely spending any time with my fiancé. Not to mention trekking back and forth across the windswept island, grateful as I was that he'd made the trip today. "When do you think we can make the report on Nightingale and be done with having you hide?" I wasn't about to drop my investigation into what happened to Netta and her father, but I didn't have to explain that to him.

"I already sent in a report on Nightingale, I'm just waiting to hear if they want more, or if what we've provided is sufficient. I'm assuming it will be, since the man is obviously unstable, which is why I risked coming here during the day—it won't be the end of our case if we're seen together at this point." Redvers smiled wryly. "But even when I do officially come out of hiding, I'm afraid no one on the island will let us have a room together, or even in the same cottage, because we aren't married. Maybe at the hotel we could get away with it, but they're fully booked."

I growled a noise of frustration, and Redvers chuckled. "Something to think about, I suppose."

I'd been reluctant to set a wedding date, happy to enjoy a long engagement, but perhaps it was time to rethink that.

*   *   *

On my way back to the cottage, I walked slowly, thinking things over and trying to parse out exactly what information we had so far.

Robert Nightingale was obviously a poor choice for the crown to use as an agent, and I knew that Redvers had reported as much. I still felt as though he had likely stabbed himself in the leg, although I didn't have a good motive as to why; I just felt that the presence of his family doctor was too much of a coincidence. And if he'd been using that as an alibi for the night that Giuseppe was killed, he would have had to know in advance that Giuseppe was in danger. Which meant he was working with someone, but I couldn't begin to decide who that might be since he wasn't terribly well liked, even among members of his own temple. Something didn't add up there.

I hadn't found concrete evidence that Nightingale had been involved with any of the female members of the Golden Dawn either, including Netta. So perhaps there was no motive there, simply a distasteful aspect of the man's personality, or even just rumors. Still, Nightingale had the best motive to kill Fornario because of the competing wills. I just didn't know how he'd managed to pull it off since he was confined to his bed.

Speaking of which, I wondered where the will that Fornario had been flashing around had gone to. If the inspector had it, he wouldn't have mentioned it to me, but I suspected that whoever killed Fornario was now in possession of it. If they hadn't destroyed it by now.

As far as Nightingale's stabbing was concerned, if he hadn't done it himself, the best suspects were either Colleen O'Connell or Giuseppe Fornario. I hadn't seen Giuseppe at the ceremony that night, and even if he had been hooded, I felt as though someone would have noticed him. Mina and Colleen had been interlopers, and they had been spotted by me and Yeats. I thought it unlikely that Fornario could have gone completely undetected, although it was possible.

Colleen O'Connell was a real mystery. Not only was she using a false name, but she was related to someone on the island. Someone she was not staying with at the moment, which in and of itself was strange, especially with rooms so difficult to come by. Then there was the matter of how she'd come to be in possession of Netta's talisman and why she'd tried to bury it on the moor. Perhaps she didn't want to be linked to the woman's death, but how did she get it in the first place? And had Colleen taken it in order to open up Netta to some kind of attack? Why were Colleen and Mina taking turns leaving their room? Did they have something that they were concealing in there? It certainly seemed that way, but I couldn't begin to guess what it might be.

Mina Mathers was also cloaked in mystery, although less so than her assistant. She'd seemed distressed when I'd told her about Giuseppe, but then I had to remember that the woman was an accomplished actress. Of course, this still didn't explain how she'd conducted the group vision exercise. I'd participated myself, and I knew that I'd been seeing the same things in my mind's eye that others were seeing at the same time, and I had no rational explanation for it. Much as I had no rational explanation for Fiona's tarot readings.

Redvers was quick to dismiss it all as nonsense, but I was finding that more difficult to do. I supposed my reluctance to discuss it with him was in part due to the fact that I wanted to figure out my own feelings about it all first.

But that was something that could be determined later. Much more pressing was the question of who Colleen O'Connell really was.

I headed to the hotel, wondering if Robert Nightingale knew anything about the girl. He was rumored to be involved with her, after all, so perhaps he knew her real name. While walking, I thought up and discarded numerous ways that I might ask him the question and hadn't come up with anything good by the time I arrived at the Hotel Argyll. With a shrug, I headed up the stairs. I would direct the conversation that way and present it as rumor, perhaps, in the hope that he would spill something.

But as soon as I reached the top of the stairs, I heard an argument coming from down the hall. The door to Nightingale's room was open, and several members of the temple, including Bychowski, stood in the hallway, clearly not knowing whether they should leave or continue listening in.

"I'm not the slightest bit surprised that you were stabbed," Mina Mathers was shouting. "I'd go so far as to say you had it coming. The way you take advantage of everyone around you and use the temple as a hunting ground for young women."

Nightingale shouted back, equally as loud. "That's outrageous, and you can't prove a word of it. I wouldn't be surprised if you were the one who stabbed me."

"If I had, I would have aimed a lot higher." Mina's voice was vicious and low.

Nightingale gasped. "I'm reporting you to the police inspector."

"For what," Mina shot back, "wishing you dead? You can't be arrested for having good sense."

I had heard enough, so I turned on my heel and went back downstairs. I doubted anything productive or even interesting would come of that interaction and I didn't need to listen to the two of them threaten each other further.

I stood for a moment in the lobby, deciding on my next move, finally heading over to the pub in the St. Columba. I didn't want a drink per se—it was still awfully early—but perhaps the bartender would have an idea of who Colleen O'Connell was.

*   *   *

I made my way through the lobby and into the pub and, with a single glance, took in who was there. Just a couple of locals this time—it seemed most of the Golden Dawn members were in the hallway of the hotel listening to Nightingale and Mina shout at each other.

I took a seat on a scarred wooden stool at the bar, and the burly bartender finished up what he was doing and came over.

"I'm out of gin, I'm afraid. Cider?" he asked.

I paused, looking around. Everyone else was well into their drinks, and I supposed I might as well have a little something. "A half pint, please." I shrugged to myself. Cider was made of apples, after all, and apples were good for you.

When he returned with my drink, I pinned him with a statement. "I'm looking for a young woman in her twenties who was born here on the island."

He stayed where he was and said nothing, looking bemused.

"I know, that's not terribly specific." I paused, thinking about what Colleen looked like. "She has brown hair and blue eyes."

"You're going to need more than that, lass." The bartender's eyes moved to a spot over my shoulder.

"You ask an awful lot of questions, Miss Wunderly."

I turned to find Yeats standing behind me. I didn't say anything, but watched as he took a seat on the stool next to mine, leaning his walking stick against the front of the bar.

"I suspect you have little to no interest in the occult. What are you really doing here now?"

I sized Yeats up while he did the same to me. I was genuinely surprised it had taken this long for someone to notice how many questions I asked and to confront me about it. I supposed I was lucky that it was Yeats since he was one of the only people on the island whom I didn't suspect of being involved in any part of things. Of course, this was mostly based on the fact that the man was relatively famous and had recently started a political career, but I felt certain he wasn't involved—he couldn't afford having his name linked to what was going on here, let alone risk killing someone. I said as much to him.

He gave me a long look, then nodded. "Aye, that's true. It's well known that I'm interested in the occult and the mystical side of the world. But I cannot have my name associated with a murder."

"How do you intend to keep your name out of things?" I was merely curious how he planned to go about it.

His eyes twinkled behind the little glasses. "I have my ways." Then he became serious. "But you haven't answered my question."

I decided to give him a small part of the truth. "Do you remember Mina's assistant, Colleen?" Yeats inclined his head, and I continued. "That's not her real name. I've learned that she was born here on the island, but I cannot figure out who she actually is."

"And this is important for reasons you're clearly not going to share with me."

I nodded.

Yeats thought things over for a moment while the bartender brought him a small glass of what looked like scotch. "This is a small island with a small population."

I nodded. That was stating the obvious, but I didn't point that out.

The poet took a sip. "And we know the general age of the girl."

I cocked my head, then nodded. "She is probably in her early to mid-twenties."

"Then we check the church register."

I found the "we" to be curious, but I also could have smacked myself in the forehead. Why hadn't I thought of that? "Of course," I said, and made to stand, but was waved back onto my seat.

"Let me finish my whisky first, and I'll accompany you."

I looked at him curiously, and he gave a shrug. "I don't know what you're up to, young lady, but it's a damn sight more interesting than anything else on this island right now. Especially since we're trapped here for the foreseeable future."

I nodded. "I'm not sure when Inspector Campbell will let us leave again."

We passed the time while Yeats finished his drink discussing Yeats's family. He had a wife and two small children at home, and I wanted to ask how his wife enjoyed being left home alone with them while he traveled about, but I held my tongue. It did occur to me, however, that I would never be content with that type of setup—staying at home with children while Redvers had the fun of traveling. It was becoming pretty clear to me what way I was leaning on the issue of whether I wanted children.

The man finished his scotch and stood. It was perhaps against my better judgment, but it looked like William Butler Yeats and I were going to investigate at the church together.

On the walk over, I brought up the argument I'd heard between Nightingale and Mina.

Yeats shook his head. "I'm not surprised. Those two always did fight like cats and dogs, even when Samuel Mathers was still alive."

"Do you think something ever went on between the two of them?" I realized that I'd had to ask this question about Robert Nightingale quite a bit—whether he was involved with any given woman in his sphere. But for all the rumors, I hadn't gotten any sort of confirmation.

"It's difficult to say," Yeats said thoughtfully. "I always suspected there might be something, but Samuel insisted that it wasn't the case and that his wife was entirely faithful to him. If there was something, it clearly didn't end well."

I nodded. It surely hadn't, not based on the venom I'd heard in their voices.

I'd walked past this little church plenty of times, but other than admiring the high cross out front, I'd paid the church behind it little mind until now. Yeats and I passed through the metal gate that broke up the stone walls bordering what felt like every path on the island. The church was quite small, built of smooth, square blocks, unlike the ancient abbey with its uneven stone that seemed to have been plucked from the fields. The heavy wooden door was surprisingly unlocked, and we poked our heads inside the little church. It was a more modern building than other religious spaces on Iona, but the church was empty, so we walked fully inside.

"I suppose the island is too small to have its own priest," I said.

Yeats nodded. "Doesn't mean we won't find what we're looking for, though."

I looked at the man in surprise and followed as he moved steadily toward the front of the church. "If we're lucky, we'll find the record just sitting here," Yeats was mumbling as he looked behind the lectern.

I decided that I was in for a penny, in for a pound, so I joined the search of the front of the church. There was a large wooden box off to one side of the altar, and I approached it curiously, flipping open the lid. "I believe this is it," I said.

"See, barely a search at all."

I pulled the heavy book from its resting spot and laid it on the altar. Yeats did some fast math, giving me the range of years we wanted to look at, and I flipped back through the heavy pages to the earliest. The handwriting was difficult to read, a tight script that curled around itself, but I got the hang of it after a few moments. Lots of deaths on the island, but not many births, and the first two we came across were boys. I kept flipping the pages slowly, using my finger to trace down each page, stopping if I found a birth.

And then we found something.

"A girl," I said excitedly.

"Catriona McCrary."

The name stopped me dead as Yeats said it aloud. The Mc-Crarys had only ever mentioned that they had sons.

So who was Catriona McCrary?

CHAPTER THIRTY-FIVE

"What will you do now?" Yeats asked. I'd explained that neither Fiona nor Michael had ever brought up the fact that they had a daughter.

I didn't want to make any rash decisions. "I think we need to check the graveyard," I said slowly. It would take forever to continue combing through this register, but there was probably a McCrary plot. Before I confronted either Mc-Crary about their daughter, I first wanted to ensure that she hadn't passed away. The loss of a child was hard enough without someone digging up the tragedy and throwing it in their faces.

Yeats and I made our way to the graveyard, moving slowly across the uneven ground, although he had the benefit of his walking stick to help keep his balance. The sun was peeking ever so slightly from behind the near-constant cloud cover, and I was grateful for even those brief hints of warmth on my face. Scotland was a beautiful country, but it was awfully gloomy at this time of year.

We found the McCrary plot, a few tombstones scattered in a general area. Yeats and I split up and inspected each one, but found no mention of a Catriona McCrary.

"She's not here," Yeats said.

"She is not," I replied, hands on hips. "Which leads me to believe that she's still alive."

"You think that Colleen O'Connell is Catriona."

I nodded. "It all fits. And as you said, something about her accent was wrong—because she's Scottish, not Irish." I pursed my lips. "I should have noticed."

Yeats looked amused at this. "Lass, I wouldn't hold your own feet to the flames over that. You're not from this part of the world." He paused. "What will you do now?"

"Talk to the McCrarys."

We started walking again. "I'll leave you to that. This has been interesting—the most interesting thing in days—but I'm cold, and there's another glass of scotch waiting for me. Not as good as Irish whiskey, but warms the insides just as well."

I chuckled and thanked the man for his help before we parted ways. As I watched him amble down the lane, I considered what to do with the information we had uncovered. Go directly to the McCrarys and confront them? Or try to speak with Colleen/Catriona and ask why she was using an assumed name? Of course, that was just the first of many questions I wanted to ask Colleen, but I wasn't sure I would be able to get through Mina in order to talk with the girl. And yes, Mina had just been at the hotel, but I'd been snooping around the church long enough that Mina was probably back at her cottage by now, or at least well on her way. There was little chance I could overtake her.

I sighed. This wasn't the first time, nor would it be the last, that I wished Redvers and I weren't separated by geography and the uptight traditions of a small religious island. We were still waiting to hear whether Redvers' employers wanted more evidence against Nightingale, so we couldn't come fully out in the open quite yet. But even barring that, perhaps it was time to set a wedding date. I was tired of subterfuge and wanted to wake up next to my fiancé.

Of course, then I would have to call him my husband. It

had taken some time to get used to the term *fiancé*. Was I ready to have a husband again?

I headed back to the cottage and arrived just as Michael McCrary was leaving. We nodded at one another, and I went inside, pleased that I would get the chance to speak with Fiona alone. I had a sneaking suspicion that Michael was the reason that Catriona hadn't come back to the cottage she'd once called home.

I followed the scent of freshly baked bread into the kitchen, my mouth watering a bit. I poked my head into the kitchen to find Fiona humming to herself and bustling about.

I didn't waste time with small talk today. "Fiona, why don't you talk about your daughter? Catriona?"

Fiona had been kneading bread, but she went absolutely still at the question. "How do you ken about my girl?"

"I know you have the three boys, but what about Catriona?" I asked again.

Fiona turned to look at me over her shoulder, then sighed and went to wash the dough and flour from her hands. She nodded her head at the little table, and I took a seat while Fiona grabbed two teacups, placing them on the table and filling them with tea, then adding a healthy dollop of scotch to each. I needed answers, not scotch, but I didn't argue with the woman.

After Fiona had taken her own seat and a long drink of her doctored tea, she spoke. "My girl Catriona, it's been a couple years now since I've seen her."

"Why is that? She doesn't come home?"

"She isnae allowed to." Fiona sighed, a sad sound. "Her father disowned her once she started spending time with those strange groups."

That gave me a bit of pause. "He'll let them stay here, but he won't speak to his own daughter because of them?"

Fiona's smile twisted into a bitter smile. "Michael Mc-

Crary is always happy to take someone's money. But he has no patience when it comes to much, even his own children. He didnae like that she was interested in strange beliefs. They had a grand row about it, and he told her to leave and not come back."

"I'm sorry. That had to be hard for you." I couldn't imagine not seeing your own child because your husband kicked her out.

"We wrote letters for a time; Michael didnae like it, but he wasnae going to keep me from doing that much." Fiona took another long sip. "It's been some time since I've heard from her now, though. I dinnae ken where she is."

I considered whether or not I should tell Fiona that I thought her daughter was on the island. But I held my tongue, deciding that I wanted the opportunity to talk to Catriona first.

But I should make sure it was the same girl, first. "Do you have any pictures of Catriona?"

Fiona nodded slowly. "Michael took them all down and put them in the attic, but I have one." She stood and walked to the pantry. I heard rustling, and then she returned, holding a small photograph. The girl in the picture was many years younger, but it was still obvious that Catriona and Mina's assistant Colleen were one and the same. I wondered why the girl had felt the need to change her name and nationality, but that was a question to ask Catriona herself.

"She's a pretty girl," I said, passing the photo back to Fiona.

Fiona took it back and smiled with obvious fondness at the image. "Aye, the boys were always chasing her. Not that there are many here on the island, mind."

"Do you think Mr. McCrary will change his mind and let Catriona come home?"

Fiona sighed. "I dinnae ken. But I dinnae see it in the cards."

I assumed she meant her tarot cards. I was tempted to ask, but I was already uncomfortable with what she'd told me about her readings of the cards—I hadn't figured out yet how I felt about the tarot. I knew that I didn't believe what the Golden Dawn was teaching its members—astral planes and strange rituals were still nonsense to me—but the tarot cards had felt different. More specific somehow, or at least Fiona's interpretation of them had been.

Of course, I still couldn't explain how Mina had managed to project a vision to everyone in the room during her demonstration, but I felt there had to be an explanation for even that. Yet I couldn't explain why the tarot readings Fiona had done felt different to me. Perhaps it was because there was no pomp surrounding Fiona and her beliefs; they felt sincere instead of calculated, completely free of artifice.

Fiona stood, clearly done with this conversation and ready to put her photo of her daughter back in the pantry, wherever it had been hidden. My guess was that it was tucked away with the tarot cards that she hid from her husband—it was quite the treasure trove in there. I wondered what Michael would do if he found that his wife had some strange beliefs as well. Would he toss her out as he had his daughter?

I thanked Fiona for her time and the tea, even though I hadn't drunk much of it. I didn't think I would ever acquire a liking for the taste of scotch, but I had acquired the information I was after.

Now it was just a matter of getting close enough to Catriona McCrary to actually talk with her.

Chapter Thirty-six

Much of the day had slipped away from me by the time I started the long trek across the island. A flat surface would have made for a quick trip, but the rocky hills and ever-present wind made the trip longer than it would have been elsewhere. I could have made this trip in twenty minutes or so back in Boston, but it was impossible to do it so quickly here on Iona.

I made the usual turn toward the north, intending to merely pass by the beach where I normally met with Redvers, but I saw Dion Fortune in the distance following the path down to the beach. I wasn't concerned that Dion would find my fiancé since we'd already met that morning, but it was unusual to see her on this side of the island. I approached where Dion stood on the beach, facing the water.

"Dion," I called out when I was a few yards from her. The woman startled and whirled around to face me, hand to her heart.

"With the wind, I didn't hear you coming," Dion called.

I nearly brought up the other times she had seemed to sense me coming without opening her eyes, but decided against it. "What are you doing here?" I simply asked once I reached the woman's side. The sea was stormy today, waves piling over one another with whitecaps frosting each tip.

Dion's long skirt already looked damp from the mist blowing toward us.

"I needed some space to think," Dion said. "It's a small island, and there are too many order members wandering about now, especially since we can't leave. I remembered that you seemed to walk to this side of the island often and decided to do the same."

I felt my eyes narrow slightly. Had she followed me on one of my treks and seen me meet with Redvers? Then I mentally shrugged. Even if she had, I had nothing to hide anymore. Not as far as Redvers was concerned, anyway. I would keep up the Golden Dawn subterfuge for a while longer, but I was done hiding my fiancé if someone happened to come across us together.

"Did you hear about Giuseppe?" I was certain she had—unless she'd been sleeping out on the moor, there was little chance she could have avoided hearing the gossip about Giuseppe Fornario's unfortunate end.

"I did," Dion said. "Convenient for Robert Nightingale. Now that Giuseppe is dead, there is no one to contest that will."

I agreed. "That's true. But Nightingale was stabbed in the leg. It doesn't seem that he can walk, so I don't know how he would have lured Giuseppe all the way out to the quarry to stab him and then push him over the cliff."

Dion studied me. "You seem to have given this quite a bit of thought."

I gave it right back to her. "I could say the same about you."

We had a moment's standoff, neither willing to concede, but finally Dion sighed. "I've been trying to figure out who might have hurt Netta." She gave me a sidelong look. "I suspect you've been doing the same. Of course, I have the advantage of being able to do it on a different plane."

I didn't bother arguing that with her. Again, she clearly believed it to be true, whether or not I believed the same.

"And did you learn anything of interest?" I asked.

She shook her head. "I did not." Then she frowned. "But it's strange; usually I can travel freely on the astral plane, but my movements have been restricted lately. I still believe Mina has something to do with that. I thought she'd given up after Netta died, but apparently not."

This wasn't even remotely useful to me, since, as far as I was concerned, astral arguments weren't real, so I tried to ground our conversation. "You haven't spoken to her recently?"

Dion shook her head. "I heard that she's on Iona, but I haven't spoken with her. Frankly, I would go out of my way not to."

From their argument earlier, I imagined that Nightingale would have liked to avoid Mina as well, but his confinement made that more difficult. "Other than Nightingale, can you think of anyone else who might have wanted to hurt Giuseppe? You seem to know Netta and her family best."

Dion considered that for a moment. "Not really. Not anyone on this island, anyway. From what Netta said, Giuseppe had a tendency to make bad investments and lose whatever money she gave him. I imagine some of the people he was involved with might want to harm him, but they're hardly here on the island, are they?"

She was right. It was unlikely any of Giuseppe's other contacts would be here on the island. His murder had to be directly related to his daughter's death.

"What do you know about Colleen O'Connell, Mina's assistant?" I had nearly called her Catriona since in my head I'd begun calling her by her real name, but I caught myself in time. That was a bit of information I was going to hold very close to the vest.

Dion shrugged. "She seems like a sweet girl, although rather flighty. There were rumors that she was involved with Robert Nightingale, but I never saw them together. That was before the two temples split off from one another. I remember being surprised that she went with Mina instead of Robert, given that rumor, but . . ." She shrugged.

So far, this was confirmation of what I'd already heard, but nothing new, and I felt myself becoming frustrated. Nightingale had been romantically linked with several women, but it was nothing but rumor, as far as I could tell. Perhaps I should consider that his interests didn't lie with women at all.

Dion spoke again, slowly this time. "Of course, Colleen and Netta seemed to have a bit of a rivalry."

My brows knit together. I hadn't heard this before. "Over what?"

"I just recalled it, because it was a while ago, before the temple split. Mina always had a favorite, and for a while that was Netta. Then Mina transferred her attention to Colleen." Dion shrugged. "I felt that it was all very childish, but I remember Netta was quite upset that Mina no longer seemed interested in teaching her. Mina seemed to have decided that Colleen was her new protégé."

It all did seem quite childish, but that didn't mean it wasn't relevant, and I wondered if there had been some sort of confrontation between the two women. "Do you recall when Netta lost her talisman?"

Dion thought about that for a long moment, while the waves crashed on the rocks nearby. The waves were encroaching on the beach, and I wanted to get away from the misty spray soon.

"Maybe? When we were having trouble with the black cats and the astral attacks from Mina, I asked Netta about the protection from her talisman, and she got upset. Netta never did explain to me why."

I thought it was likely that Netta was upset because her talisman had disappeared. Could Colleen have taken Netta's talisman in order to open her up to attack from Mina? It could explain why she decided to bury it on the moor, as

Redvers had seen her do. But, again, this all seemed quite silly. Talismans and attacks on the astral plane—none of it was concrete, tangible, something that could contribute to an actual death.

I left Dion and walked to the cottage where Redvers and the women were staying with renewed vigor. I had a laundry list of questions that I wanted to ask Catriona McCrary, and I hoped I could get some answers before the list became even longer.

I made it to the cottage in record time and knocked on the door, which was once again answered by the woman who owned the place. She gave me one look and nodded her head toward the stairs. "If you're here for the girls—which I assume you are—they're upstairs in their room. I'd call them for you, but I'm in the middle of something in the kitchen."

I thanked the woman and climbed the stairs, grateful that she was in the middle of something and let me go ahead on my own. I knew which room Redvers was staying in from the time I'd visited him here, so I went to the door at the opposite end of the hall and knocked. There was no answer, but I could hear rustling from the other side of the door, so I knocked again.

"Mina? It's Jane," I called.

There was a long pause. "Mina isn't here," Catriona finally replied.

I wondered where Mina had gone, and how she'd left the cottage, since their landlady seemed to think that both women were still upstairs. "That's alright; it's actually you I came to talk to."

"I don't have anything to say."

"But you don't know what I'm going to ask you."

"I'm not supposed to talk to anyone," Catriona said, sounding frustrated.

That was a different story entirely. It had to be Mina instructing her protégé not to talk to anyone while she was squirreled away on the far side of the island, but why would Mina try to keep Catriona from talking? Because Mina knew that Catriona had something to do with Nightingale's stabbing? Or because Catriona had something to do with Netta's death? I had a hard time picturing Catriona harming Netta, but I couldn't rule it out as a possibility, especially since Redvers had seen her burying the talisman.

But this was all exactly what I was here to talk to the girl about. I just had to be smart about how I went about asking my questions so that I didn't shut the girl down further.

I paused for a long moment, my forehead resting on the door while I considered how to proceed. "Catriona, have you told your mother that you're on the island?"

I nearly fell into the room when the door swung open. I hadn't been expecting it, and I made a mental note to stand on my own two feet the next time I questioned someone through a door.

"How do you know my name?" The girl's accent had slipped from its false Irish lilt to her true Scottish brogue.

"I'm staying at your parents' cottage," I said. It was true, although it didn't answer her question. It was enough for Catriona, however, and she dropped her hand from the door and moved into the room, sitting heavily into one of the chairs near the fireplace.

"My da won't let me come home."

"That's what your mother said. She misses you, though."

"I miss her too. I wish she could help me," Catriona said.

I paused, studying the girl's sad face. "You've found yourself some trouble."

She nodded and looked up at me, her eyes shiny with unshed tears. "I dinnae ken how to get out of it either."

"Is that why Mina wants you to stay here and not speak to anyone?"

"She'll be so angry that I spoke to you," Catriona whispered.

I leaned over and patted her shoulder. "Perhaps if you tell me, I can help you."

It was the wrong thing to say. Catriona shrunk away from me, crossing her arms over her chest and saying nothing.

I decided to try a different tact. "Is it because of what happened at the ceremony?"

Catriona's shoulders hunched even more noticeably, and I cursed myself for digging the hole further. But she surprised me by answering. "I dinnae remember."

I frowned. "What do you mean you don't remember?"

Catriona didn't move, but she glanced up at me from beneath her lashes. "I dinnae remember the ceremony. I actually dinnae remember . . . well, a lot of things."

I was quiet, waiting to see if the girl would explain further. "I keep missing time. Where I cannae remember what I'm doing or where I am," Catriona said. "And then I wake up somewhere, and I dinnae ken how I got there."

I blinked a few times. "Has this been happening a lot?" It meant that even if Catriona had been the one to stab Nightingale, she might not remember that she had done it.

"Over the last few weeks, yes."

I thought fast. "When did this start?"

Catriona's arms relaxed a little from their grip on each other while she thought about that. "Maybe a month ago?"

I nodded, although I wasn't sure what significance that held. Not yet, anyway. I needed to piece together a timeline of everything that had happened—sooner rather than later, from the looks of it. Regardless, it was obvious that Catriona was scared and that something strange was happening to her. We needed to get her to a safe place.

"Why don't we go speak to your mother? I know she would love to see you."

Catriona shook her head violently. "I'm not supposed to leave this room. And my da willnae let me in the house."

I pursed my lips. "Let me worry about your father. I can take care of him." I wasn't certain that was true, but it was a problem to be dealt with later if I could convince her to come with me.

Catriona looked uncertain, but I could tell she was considering it. I recalled what Redvers had said about how it seemed as though the women were guarding something in their room. Was that why Catriona was reluctant to leave?

"Is there something here that you need to stay with?"

Catriona looked confused. "What? What would I need to stay with?"

So there was nothing they were guarding; the thing that wasn't supposed to leave the room was Catriona herself, although she'd managed to slip off to the moor to bury the talisman at some point. But why was Mina keeping her hidden away? I wasn't concerned that Catriona was dangerous, although I was becoming worried that she was in danger.

Footsteps coming up the stairs alerted us to the fact that we weren't alone, and we both froze, Catriona's panicked eyes locked on my own.

I sagged with relief a moment later when Redvers stuck his head around the door. I'd been afraid that it was Mina Mathers, and I knew it wouldn't be well-received that I was here asking her assistant questions. Especially now that I knew that Catriona was blacking out and couldn't remember chunks of time, I had a lot of questions about what she could remember.

"I have bad news, I'm afraid," Redvers said. "Michael McCrary has been arrested."

CHAPTER THIRTY-SEVEN

It was easy, after that announcement, to convince Catriona to accompany us back to the McCrary cottage to see Fiona. With her father under arrest, there was no chance the mother-daughter reunion would be stopped, although Catriona was still upset that Michael had been arrested, despite the trouble between the two.

"The inspector is wrong," Catriona said firmly as we walked toward the village. "My father wouldnae kill anyone."

Redvers and I were walking slightly behind and to either side of the girl, as though physically ensuring that she wasn't going to change her mind and bolt back to her room.

"Mostly what the police have is circumstantial evidence. Your father was seen arguing with Giuseppe, and he doesn't have an alibi for the time that Giuseppe was killed," I said.

"But why would he kill the man? He didnae even know him."

"There was some question about the will that your father claimed Netta gave him. Your father turned it over to Robert Nightingale after Netta's death," Redvers told her. What Redvers didn't say was that both the will and the timing were suspect, although I knew we were both thinking it.

I could see the side of Catriona's face, and she frowned, but didn't say anything for a moment. "What are you thinking?" I finally asked.

"I seem to remember hearing something when I was a child. About my da and his past."

Redvers and I looked at each other.

"He and my mam were arguing that he'd had some trouble with the law when he was young. Something about forgery? But I could be remembering that wrong."

On the other hand, if she was remembering things correctly, Inspector Campbell could have a lot more circumstantial evidence against Michael McCrary.

The reunion between Catriona and Fiona was emotional, not just because the women hadn't seen each other in over two years but also because of their mutual worry for Michael McCrary. I suggested to Redvers that we leave the women alone to reacquaint themselves, so we stepped outside to catch up ourselves. We didn't stray far from the house, finding a wooden bench in the small kitchen garden and settling ourselves onto it. Redvers tucked me under his arm, and I was grateful for the additional warmth.

"It doesn't look good for Michael McCrary," I said. "But I don't think he had anything to do with either death."

"I'm afraid that I agree with you," Redvers said.

"But the person I think most likely to have done it has an ironclad alibi."

"Nightingale?"

"Exactly. But how could he have killed Giuseppe with that leg? I think you would need both legs to push a man over the side of that cliff." I frowned and filled in Redvers on what Catriona had told me about her missing time.

Redvers brows pulled into a frown that matched my own. "I don't like the sound of that."

"Nor do I, but I don't know what to make of it. Other than it makes her a suspect in Nightingale's stabbing. I can't see any motive for her to have killed Giuseppe, though."

"Did you ask her if she and Nightingale were ever involved romantically?"

"I didn't get that far." I paused. "It's interesting that there are plenty of rumors of Nightingale dallying with young women, but no real proof. No eyewitnesses and no firsthand accounts, as far as I can tell. And he doesn't seem the type to be discreet."

Redvers agreed. "No. That is not a word I would use to describe the man."

I cocked my head. "Have we heard about whether your employers want more information about Nightingale?"

"I need to check the post office and see if there are any messages for me. I was hoping to hear something today."

I was quiet for a moment, thinking through everything. "Oh! I nearly forgot. When I arrived at the hotel, Mina Mathers and Nightingale were having quite an argument. It was vicious, to say the least."

Redvers tapped his fingers against the top of the bench. "Did a lot of people overhear this?"

I nodded. "Quite a few, actually. I was surprised that it was so public."

"Interesting," Redvers said. It seemed that he was going to say something more, but Catriona and Fiona came into the garden to find us.

Fiona sized us up. "I'm assuming this is your young man, Miss Wunderly."

I smiled sheepishly. "It is. Redvers, this is Mrs. McCrary."

Redvers and Fiona nodded at each other, then Fiona continued on while her daughter stood quietly behind her. "And I'm assuming you're not really here to join this group, Miss Jane."

I wasn't quite ready to concede that point, so I said nothing, gazing steadily at the two women. Fiona wasn't fooled, however. "Aye, keep your secrets, but we need your help."

"Help with what?" I asked, even though I had a good idea about where this was going.

"You have to clear my Michael's name."

"What makes you think I can do that?" I asked.

Fiona nodded. "The justice card. It keeps coming up for you."

I could feel Redvers' inquisitive gaze on me, but I kept my attention fixed on Fiona. I would explain to him what she meant later. On my own terms.

"We'll go talk with him," I assured the McCrary women.

Satisfied, Fiona led her daughter back into the house. I was glad Catriona was going to have some time alone with her mother while Redvers and I talked with Michael McCrary.

Iona was small, so small that there wasn't so much as a police station, let alone a jail, on the island, so Redvers and I headed to the ferry in the hope that the inspector would be taking McCrary over to Mull.

Along the way, Redvers had some questions for me. "What did Fiona mean by the justice card?"

"Tarot cards. Even though Michael McCrary is very much against anything related to the occult, Fiona appears to have some beliefs of her own. She's done some readings for me—only one of which I was present for—and the justice card keeps coming up." I expected him to dismiss this information as more foolishness, but as usual, Redvers was full of surprises.

"That's interesting. And rather accurate." Redvers took a few beats. "How does she keep this from her husband? He clearly feels strongly about it—he banished his own daughter from the house because she joined the Golden Dawn."

"Fiona keeps the cards hidden in the pantry. She said it's the only place she's certain her husband will never go."

Redvers chuckled. "No fool, that woman." He changed tacks entirely. "It appears as though we're not hiding my presence on the island any longer. Have you given any more thought to a wedding date?"

"I haven't, really, although I agree that it's becoming quite inconvenient when we're working together that we can't stay in the same place."

"Are you still thinking that you want a small wedding? Or do you want your family to be there?"

I had already given that a great deal of thought and was able to answer quickly. "The smaller the better, as far as I'm concerned. In fact, if we could get away with just the two of us, that would be best." I'd had a large wedding the first time around, and that marriage had been a disaster from the time we took our vows to Grant's death in the Great War. I also didn't want my Aunt Millie involved—she would insist on a spectacle, which was precisely what I did not want. I'd be sorry if my father wasn't there, or Redvers' aunts Caroline and Marie, but we could always celebrate with them at a later date.

I studied my fiancé. "What are you thinking?"

Redvers smiled and shook his head. "Just gathering information."

I rolled my eyes. "Have you given any more thought to the question of children?" I found myself bracing for his answer. I hadn't realized that I had such strong feelings about the subject, but it turned out that I did, if my gut reaction was any indication.

"I have. If children are important to you, I'm open to the concept." Redvers' brows were furrowed into a frown. "But with the nature of my work, and my own family . . . I had always assumed that I would not have children." He made a huffing noise. "I never expected to get married, to be quite honest."

I pondered that for a moment and realized that Redvers' shoulders had stiffened. It looked like he was waiting for an answer as well. "I've given it quite a bit of thought, and I don't want children either."

Redvers let out a puff of air in obvious relief, and I raised an eyebrow in amusement. "There's our real answer on your feelings."

"I know, I just wanted to give you the option if you felt strongly about having a family."

I shook my head. "Perhaps it's selfish of me, but I don't want to bring children into the world. I think it would be too much to have a daughter and worry constantly that she might go through what I've been through. Or to have a son and watch him go off to war like so many just did."

"A fair point," Redvers said. "I don't think that's selfish at all."

"Not to mention that I couldn't stand the idea of being left behind with children while you are off investigating something."

Redvers chuckled. "Of course, you couldn't."

I smiled at him, but any further conversation on the topic was halted as we neared the ferry dock. The inspector was standing quite close to Michael McCrary, who was leaning against the wooden railings, arms crossed and looking quite cross himself. Understandable, since the man was under arrest, although he wasn't bound in any way. It was undoubtably why Inspector Campbell was hovering so close.

McCrary looked up as we came near, but his grim expression didn't change. I couldn't really blame the man.

"Inspector, might we have a word with Mr. McCrary?" Redvers asked.

"Go right ahead," Campbell said, not moving an inch.

"Alone?" Redvers asked with just a hint of an edge to his voice.

Campbell looked at my fiancé for a long moment before conceding with a slight incline of his head. "Very well. But I'll be right over here." He moved down the dock a bit, blocking the exit toward land as though McCrary might decide to make a break for it, even though there wasn't really anywhere for the man to run to on an island as small as this one.

"Your daughter, Catriona, came home. She's with your wife."

Michael didn't look surprised by this information. "At least she'll have her girl to comfort her."

Further down the dock, I heard the inspector mutter, "My wife's name is Catriona." I looked at the man, and he caught my eye, shrugged and moved further away. Hopefully he was actually out of earshot now.

"I don't actually care if the man hears," McCrary said. "I've done nothing wrong."

"The evidence against you does appear to be largely circumstantial," Redvers said.

"Except for that little business with forgery in your past," I added.

McCrary's expression finally changed from combative to chagrined. "Aye, that was the foolishness of youth. But it doesnae look good for me, I know."

"Was that really Netta's will that you gave to Robert Nightingale?" I asked.

"In a manner of speaking," McCrary said.

CHAPTER THIRTY-EIGHT

Redvers and I both looked at the man expectantly, and he sighed. "I didnae forge that will. But I can't say whether Nightingale did or not. He brought it to me with a large sum of money and suggested that I 'find' it in my cottage after poor Netta passed away." McCrary scratched the side of his face. "I didnae see the harm, not for that sum."

His wife had said that Michael would do nearly anything for the right amount of money. It looked as though she'd been correct.

"And so you turned it over as though Netta had left it with you," I said.

McCrary nodded, looking miserable. "I didnae expect all the trouble with her father. And now it gives me a motive to have killed the man. I'm nae looking for another trip to prison. I did my time and mended my ways."

I thought that was a point that could be argued, but I held my tongue.

"You don't have an alibi for the night Mr. Fornario was killed?"

McCrary shook his head. "I was at the pub for a bit, but then stopped to check on my flock on the way home. I was in the fields later than I should have been, but the sheep willnae be able to testify for me."

It made sense that Campbell had placed the man under arrest. With no alibi, a criminal past, and the best motive to kill Giuseppe—after Robert Nightingale—it was a natural conclusion. It was a little too pat for me, though. I still thought Nightingale had to be behind things. I just couldn't figure out how.

"Will you tell my wife and daughter that I love them?" McCrary blinked rapidly to fight the moisture in his eyes. Redvers and I pretended not to notice. "I shouldnae have sent my girl away. It was pride and stubbornness on my part, and I'm sorry I didnae see that sooner."

We assured McCrary that we would pass along the message and left him standing on the dock, under arrest for a murder he likely hadn't committed. Neither Redvers nor I told him that we would try to clear his name, even though that was what I fully intended to do. I felt strongly that the man was innocent, and I truly hated to see injustice. He'd made mistakes—taking money from Robert Nightingale being chief among them—but I didn't believe for a second that he'd killed either Netta or Giuseppe Fornario.

Everything came back to Robert Nightingale. But his conveniently injured leg made him an unlikely suspect for Giuseppe's death. I was more convinced than ever that he'd stabbed himself—it was the only thing that made sense, especially given what a perfect alibi it gave him. But that meant I didn't know who'd actually stabbed Giuseppe, not to mention why they'd used the same knife that Nightingale had been stabbed with. There were still so many pieces to this puzzle that I could not put together, and I wished for a few moments of peace just so I could fit things together.

As we passed the inspector, Redvers paused, obviously wanting to talk with the man. I looked at him and quickly made a decision. "I'll keep going," I said. The less time spent with the police the better, in my opinion. "I'll meet you at my cottage later."

Redvers smiled and leaned down to give me a quick peck on the lips, and I continued my meandering walk back toward the village. The sun was going down, and the wind had even more of a chill than earlier, so I was shivering lightly by the time I reached the McCrary cottage. I stepped inside, expecting to find Fiona and Catriona at the kitchen table with a pot of tea between them, but Fiona was alone.

"Where's Catriona?" I asked.

Fiona looked vaguely troubled. "She went back to get her things." Fiona turned, her eyes meeting mine. "I dinnae have a good feeling about it."

"Why didn't you go with her?"

"She insisted on going by herself." Fiona wiped her hands on her apron. "Did you talk to my husband?"

I nodded and related the message that Michael had asked us to. Fiona's own eyes filled with tears, and she too blinked them back. "Well," she said in a no-nonsense voice. "That's fine then."

Fiona went back to work, and I wandered back out of the kitchen. I wondered if the woman ever rested, but, on the other hand, keeping busy was probably quite useful for her right now.

Her bad feeling left me troubled, though. If it were anyone else, I would dismiss the idea immediately, but I couldn't so easily discount Fiona's intuition. Perhaps because that intuition had been so accurate up until now.

I went to the front door and stood there for a moment, not relishing the idea of going back out into the cold, but knowing it was necessary. I needed to go back to the other cottage and help Catriona pack up her things. Once she was safely back at her mother's place and out of harm's way, Redvers and I could figure out the rest of this case.

*   *   *

I was halfway there when I nearly rethought what I was doing and turned back, but I forged ahead, doing my best to ignore the wind and the deepening cold.

When I arrived at the cottage, there was no answer at my knock, which I thought was strange. Where had the landlady taken herself off to? But I tried the knob, and it opened easily, so I let myself inside. "Hello?" I called. There was still no answer, so I closed the door behind me and went to the stairs, climbing them slowly. I was starting to feel apprehensive, so I was relieved when I came to the landing and found the door to Mina and Catriona's room open. Catriona was standing near her bed, and it looked as though she was packing.

"Catriona?" I called.

The young woman startled and whirled around. "Oh! You scared me."

"You didn't hear me calling before?" I asked as I came into the room.

She shook her head as I came into the room. "I didn't hear anything."

I thought that was strange since I'd never been accused of having a soft voice, but I let it go. "Your mother said that you were packing up your things." I looked at the small bag she had laid on the bed, not much more than a handbag, really. "I didn't think you had that much to pack."

"I don't," Catriona said, eyes darting about. "But there are one or two things that I can't leave behind."

"I understand," I said. I watched her for a moment, noticing that her movements were almost twitchy and she wasn't making eye contact with me. Something wasn't right here, that was for certain.

"I'm sorry," Catriona said.

"For what?" I asked. And then everything went dark.

*   *   *

I woke up and found myself lying on something hard as stone and very cold. The cold had long since seeped through my clothes and deep into my bones, and I was already shivering before I even opened my eyes. I gave myself a moment, then blinked my eyes open and tried to move, but realized that my hands and feet were bound. My hands were in front of me, a small mercy, but tugging at the bindings was useless—whoever had made the knots knew precisely what they were doing. Glancing down toward my shoulder told me that I'd been laid on one of the stone tombs in the abbey, which explained why my teeth were nearly rattling from cold.

In the dim lantern light, I could see three robed figures, one of whom was standing with the use of a makeshift crutch. Taller than the others, it could only be Robert Nightingale with his injured leg. I should have been surprised he was on his feet, given the fuss he'd made about his leg and the doctor's orders not to move, but truthfully it made perfect sense. What didn't make sense was that I'd believed him to be immobile. It had been the clerk helping Nightingale to the toilet that had truly sold it to me, but that had to have been done for effect. It had worked.

The little trio noticed that I was awake.

"Ah, good. You're with us again. That means we can begin," Robert said.

I didn't know what they intended to start, but I thought it would be best to put it off for as long as possible. "How did I get here?"

"On your own two feet, of course." I couldn't see his face, but I recognized Nightingale's voice. "None of us would have been able to carry you."

That would have been insulting if it weren't for the fact that it was true. The abbey was quite a distance from the cottage where the women had been staying, and the ground between was rocky, hilly terrain. Even with something like a wheelbarrow, it would have been difficult to transport a person here. So how had I gotten here? I tried to figure out what had happened to me, or even what time it was now, but I couldn't recall anything after speaking with Catriona, and I didn't feel any especially sore spots on my head, so I didn't think I'd been struck in any way. So how had they knocked me out? And what did they intend to do with me?

This last question I must have uttered aloud because Nightingale answered it for me. "Sometimes sacrifices have to be made," he said. "We weren't able to harness the power of the equinox, but there are other powers to be harnessed instead. You're going to help us do that."

I was starting to become very nervous, my limbs now shaking from much more than the cold. One of the rumors I'd heard about the Golden Dawn was that they believed in human sacrifice, but it had been thoroughly discounted by all of the members I'd spoken to, members who were much higher up in the order and privy to more secrets than a neophyte was. I said as much to Nightingale.

It was beginning to look like those members were wrong, however, based on the large ceremonial knife that Nightingale held in his hand. It glinted in the lantern light, and I had no doubt that it was sharp enough to get the job done.

Nightingale shrugged. "That depends on who you talk to and how far they've progressed in the order. Only members at the highest echelon learn all the secrets. And, truly, not many are ready for all the power that one can harness at the very highest levels."

I wasn't surprised that Nightingale was behind this, although I was more than a little curious as to who his robed partners were, since he obviously couldn't have done it all by himself. I assumed one was Catriona, but I couldn't be certain since the hoods obscured all their faces. I had no illusions about Nightingale, but I was holding out a small hope that one of the other two might come to their senses and stop whatever was about to happen.

At least I'd been correct in my assumption that Nightingale wasn't to be trusted, and I felt somewhat proud that we'd reported exactly that to Redvers' employers. I might die on this tomb tonight, but at least I'd been right.

It was cold comfort.

"You stabbed yourself in the leg then?" I was both curious about the answer and desperate to stop this little group from beginning whatever ritual ceremony they had planned. They'd done me a favor by failing to gag me when they bound my hands and feet.

I couldn't see more than shadows playing across the very bottom of Nightingale's face, covered as it was by his robe, but he hopped a step closer to me on his crutch, his bad leg elevated off the ground like a flamingo, knife still clutched in his hand. It was intended to be menacing and was somewhat effective. It was even more so when he passed the knife to the robed figure at his right.

Nightingale didn't answer my question, addressing the figure now holding the knife instead. "You'll have to do the honors this time." The figure nodded and also took a step closer to me.

Panic rose in my chest, and I struggled against the bindings on my wrists and ankles. For some reason, I couldn't sit up, and I couldn't figure out why. Then I realized that the ropes binding me stretched to the ground on either side of the tomb and had been anchored to the floor with heavy stones.

I looked to the third figure for help, but whoever it was stood stock still, head lowered. They hadn't moved much at all during all this, and I wondered if they were entirely with us. Whether or not they were, it was clear that help wasn't coming from that quarter.

I heard a faint clacking noise coming from the entryway to the chapel. It was obvious that the others had heard the clacking as well because they stilled, listening. Well, two of them did. The third figure had yet to move at all.

A moment later, a voice from the entryway asked a question of its own. "Well, what have we here now?"

It was Yeats.

I did not breathe a sigh of relief. Unless Yeats had come with a pistol of some sort, it was unlikely that the aged poet was going to be my savior. Instead, it was likely that he was putting himself in as much danger as I was in.

The only positive, as far as I could see, was that the man immediately seemed to have the lay of the land. "Now, Robert, I know we discussed sacrifices once upon a time, but I thought we agreed that they were theoretical and weren't worth the price."

"Since then, I've come across other ancient texts suggesting that true power can be found in the spilling of blood." Nightingale shrugged. "Besides, she knows too much as it is, especially now."

Yeats tsked, still standing just inside the doorway. "Now you know as well as I do that you could just work your magic and that wouldn't be the case."

I opened my mouth to ask what "magic" Yeats was referring to when the robed figure holding the knife moved toward Yeats. I held my breath for a moment, but they merely indicated for Yeats to join us where Robert and the other robed figure stood.

"Mina," Yeats said, "I thought surely you were better than this."

CHAPTER THIRTY-NINE

I believe I actually gasped out loud. Mina Mathers had been the last person I would have expected to be involved in this. But she threw back her hood and gave Yeats a hollow smile, still holding her knife at the ready.

"Love is a powerful drug," Mina said.

For a moment, I was confused. Love? But then Mina and Robert exchanged a private smile, and things began to fall into place.

"Your argument was staged," I said. "And I'm assuming the fracture of the temple was staged as well?"

It was Robert who answered, while Yeats lowered himself to sit on a nearby stone tomb, perching precariously on it. "We had to be sure that Netta would leave one of us her fortune. It was obvious that she'd been growing disenchanted with the order, so we decided it would be best to stage a fracture of the order. That way, I could start a second temple that aligned with what she wanted. Once Netta was out of the way and her fortune secured, Mina and I could reunite."

I thought about the rumors that Robert was involved with numerous young women of the temple, and how I hadn't been able to substantiate any of them. It made perfect sense, however, if he was involved with Mina. And it was also smart to start those rumors to throw suspicion off the pair working together.

"Did Netta even write that will?"

"Of course," Robert said. "Forgery is unfortunately not in my repertoire of skills."

"But how did you get her to do it?"

Here Yeats broke back in. "I would imagine the same way he got her to kill herself."

I craned my head to the side so that I could see the man, but the position was uncomfortable, so I put my head back down and contented myself with only listening to his slow, ponderous words.

"Robert is a gifted hypnotist. So is Mina, for that matter."

In the dim light, I could see Mina smile at the compliment. I closed my eyes for a moment, remembering the "ceremony" that she had performed. I hadn't felt hypnotized, but, of course, one wouldn't. And it was the only thing that could explain how she was able to project a mental vision to all of us at the same time.

But why hadn't Yeats mentioned any of this earlier? He'd been at the ceremony and had clearly been just as hypnotized as I had been. "Why didn't you say something before? Like after the ceremony?" It would have saved both of our lives, frankly, if he had.

"I didn't figure it out until after we visited the church. I was talking with some of the other members and thinking about how the order's vows include the oath to not engage in hypnotism. I realized it had to be how Nightingale and Mina here were doing all this," Yeats said. "I didn't say anything after the ceremony because that vision she shared with us was real."

I didn't bother pointing out how unlikely that was. If Mina and Robert were doing all these other acts with the use of hypnotism, then she had clearly projected the "vision" using the same means. But now was not the time to argue the point with W.B. If we made it out of here alive, I might address the issue later.

I'd been suspicious that hypnotism was at play, but I hadn't considered it as having a role in Netta's death. "How did you get Netta to kill herself?" I asked Robert.

He huffed impatiently, obviously annoyed at the delay we were causing him, but unable to leave the question unanswered because of his pride. "She had a weak mind and was already troubled. It was hardly difficult to hypnotize her and convince her that she needed to do a protection ceremony on the fairy circle in the dead of night."

"Why was she naked?" I asked.

He shrugged. "Clothes would have just slowed down the process. Exposure took care of the rest."

"What about the scratches on her body?"

"What scratches?" Robert looked confused for a brief moment, then straightened. "No, never mind. It's time to get on with our evening."

I still had more questions, though, and a hope that I could continue to delay whatever was about to happen next. "What about Giuseppe? With his version of the will?"

For a moment, I thought I had pushed too far and Robert wouldn't answer. I was relieved to have bought a few more minutes when he did.

"It's perfectly simple. I knew I would be the main suspect if we got rid of that little problem. So I stabbed myself in the leg, giving myself a perfect alibi. I couldn't possibly have done it, because I couldn't walk. Without a connection to me, Mina had no motive, so she lured Giuseppe out to the quarry and took care of matters. She may be little, but she be fierce."

I grimaced at the man quoting Shakespeare, but Mina seemed to find it charming, her face lighting up as she looked at him. Yeats was also making a face indicating distaste, but they weren't paying attention to either of us—they only had eyes for each other. I had to admit, their fake feud had been quite convincing.

I looked at the third robed figure, who hadn't moved once during this entire ordeal. I could only assume that it was Catriona, and given everything we'd just heard from Nightingale and Mina, I thought the girl must be hypnotized. I was guessing it wasn't the first time either—hypnotism would explain the missing time that Catriona had experienced over the last month. Although, from what Nightingale said, it appeared that Catriona wasn't actually involved in any of the murders, and I was glad of that, for her sake. Even if she couldn't remember what she had done during those periods, it would be difficult to live with should she find out.

Assuming any of us lived. I was running out of questions, and we were running out of time.

The last time I'd been in a predicament like this, my Aunt Millie had come to the rescue. But Millie was nowhere near Scotland, and Redvers and I weren't staying together, so there was no reason for him to know that I'd gone missing. It seemed that saving ourselves was down to either me or Yeats, and I was firmly bound to a stone tomb, and Yeats was a man in his sixties who used a walking stick.

How were we going to get out of this?

CHAPTER FORTY

"It's time to begin," Nightingale said. "No more wasting time."

My chest started to tighten with panic, and my breathing became shallow. I knew that I needed to control my breathing, but it was difficult to manage as Robert started chanting. The words sounded familiar, and it seemed as though Nightingale was repeating the ceremony from the night before. But it wasn't long before it took a dark turn.

"By the power to me committed, I pray that from your throne in the West, symbolizing the failing light, will ever remember that the divine darkness is the same as divine glory."

I didn't like the sound of that. Calling to darkness did not sound good.

Mina broke in here. "I claim my sword." She brandished the ceremonial knife that Nightingale had given to her. "Let the power come to the East." Mina moved in that direction. If I'd been able to move, I would have taken the opportunity to make a break for it, but I was firmly secured to the stone beneath me. My fear had now replaced the trembling from the cold. I almost didn't notice it now, but I did reflect how easy it would have been for Netta to succumb to exposure, even in March. Especially naked, as she had been.

Nightingale and Mina continued taking turns calling to

the various elements of the earth. They had begun the ceremony farther apart, but were closing the gap between themselves and us. I couldn't see Yeats without twisting my neck in an impossible direction, so I couldn't make eye contact and try to get a sense of whether he had any sort of plan. All I knew was that Mina Mathers was entirely too close to me with that knife and moving even closer. And I didn't have any way to stop whatever came next.

"Wouldn't it be better for the ceremony if Miss Wunderly were hypnotized herself?" Yeats broke in.

Nightingale stopped the waving of his arms to glare in Yeats's direction. But then he resumed what he was doing, balancing on one leg and his crutch as he did so. I'd have found the sight amusing if I weren't so frightened for my life.

Yeats tried again. "I'm disappointed, Nightingale. I thought you were truly looking for power from the light."

"Why won't you shut up?" Nightingale growled. "I'll take power where I can. Once she's dead," he tipped his head toward me, "no one will be able to challenge me again. I'll be the supreme leader, infused with power of light and dark."

At this, Mina dropped her arms. "I thought we were supposed to lead the new order together?"

"Of course, we are, my dear." Nightingale's voice was soothing, but I wasn't sure Mina was fully buying it.

Yeats had found the crack and was clever enough to realize that it was time to exploit it. "Robert gave himself an alibi for Giuseppe's death and had you commit the murder, Mina. But what if the inspector suspects you?"

Mina kept her eyes on Robert but answered my question, the ceremony forgotten for the moment. "I don't have a motive. And it's been established that Robert and I hate one another. Besides, the inspector has already arrested someone."

"But you were seen on the island, and you were seen at the ceremony. Campbell knows that."

Mina turned her attention to me. "You were the only one who saw me at the ceremony."

I shook my head against my stone pillow. "My fiancé saw you as well. And he's working quite closely with the police." Not entirely true, but not entirely a lie either.

Both Robert and Mina stopped moving, becoming as still as Catriona was. Then Mina's head swiveled toward Robert. "What will I do if they question me? I don't have an alibi like you do."

Robert hopped a step toward her, and Yeats took that moment to strike, sticking his cane out and tripping Robert's crutch. With a shout, the man fell to the ground, his head coming into hard contact with the stone floor. We all watched for a moment, but he didn't move.

"Robert?" Mina said, moving toward him, the knife in her hand momentarily forgotten. She bent down to shake him, but he didn't stir. "Is he breathing? Robert?"

"He was going to turn you in, Mina. To save himself," I said. I had no doubts that I was speaking the truth.

Mina was still bent over the man, gently shaking his shoulder, but she responded. "He wouldn't do that."

"He was using you, just like he used everyone else," Yeats chimed in.

I could see that she didn't want to believe us, but something in the back of her mind couldn't quite discount what we were saying. Yeats was still seated on the edge of his tombstone seat, but I could tell that he was prepared to push up onto his cane at any moment, hopefully ready to grab the knife that Mina had set down on the ground next to Nightingale.

But it turned out that wasn't necessary, because Redvers finally decided to make an appearance.

Chapter Forty-one

When Redvers, Dion, and Inspector Campbell appeared in the doorway, I closed my eyes and blew out a huge sigh of relief. It was only a moment's work for the inspector to separate Mina from the knife on the ground, ensuring she couldn't use it.

"You're under arrest," Campbell said. Mina's shoulders slumped, and she succumbed to the handcuffs without a fuss, which surprised me. I'd taken her for someone who wouldn't go down without a fight, but I'd clearly been mistaken. On the other hand, perhaps it was a relief to finally be finished with the killing and subterfuge. From the relief washing over Mina's face, I guessed that might be the case.

Dion completely ignored Mina, moving to Catriona's side and pulling the hood back from her face. Her head remained bowed, and the blank look in the young woman's eyes said it all—she was still under hypnosis, and I didn't know what would bring her out of it if this chaos hadn't done the trick.

Meanwhile, Redvers rushed over, pulled his own small knife from his pocket, and began cutting at my bindings. "We got here just in time," he said.

"I don't know," I said. "I think we were handling things quite well."

Redvers stopped what he was doing to stare at me incred-

ulously. "You're tied up to a stone tomb." He pointed to
W.B. "And he's elderly."

Yeats huffed in offense. "I'm only in my early sixties; it's
the hair that makes me look old. And I knocked this one out,
you know. Not too old to do that."

"And I'd nearly talked Mina into surrendering," I argued.
I wasn't sure why I was choosing this moment to be contrary,
but I suspected it had to do with the adrenaline coursing
through my system.

Redvers had the grace to look amused as he went back to
cutting me loose and gathered me into his arms. He had to
help support me since my arms and legs had gone numb from
the cold and the bindings. "Very well. You had this under
control," he said. "But let's get you warmed up all the same."

I was happy to accept Redvers' warmth as I curled into his
side on the walk back to the village. Nightingale had eventually come around, and the inspector was walking his two
prisoners ahead of us at gunpoint. Well, one was walking.
The other was awkwardly hopping with his crutch, which
made me feel better since he wasn't putting weight on his injured leg; that much hadn't been faked, at least. Redvers had
his gun at the ready as well, but it didn't seem as though it
was going to be necessary—Mina was unexpectedly docile,
and Nightingale would have a hell of a time getting away on
that leg. He'd brought it upon himself quite literally, which
made me smile.

Catriona had yet to snap out of her spell, and Dion had
taken charge of the young woman, directing her along the
path behind us with a hand on her arm. Nightingale refused
to tell us how to wake her up, as though this would stop him
from being implicated in everything that had gone on in the
last few weeks.

"We would have found you sooner if we'd been staying in
the same place," Redvers said.

"How do you figure?" I'd come to the same conclusion earlier, but I wanted to hear his reasoning.

"It took entirely too much looking around at your cottage and then my cottage before I realized you were missing. I spoke to Mrs. McCrary, and she said you'd gone to fetch Catriona, but neither of you were there. I went back to the McCrarys', and you still hadn't arrived, so I set out to look for you. It's a good thing this island is so small; there weren't many places you could have been."

This sequence of events made sense, but I didn't think he was actually making an argument for his case. He still would have had to search numerous places even if we had been staying in the same room. But I knew what he was getting at beneath his story, and I found that I agreed. I thought it was time to make our union official.

"You're right. Perhaps it's time to set that date."

"It will be easier to keep you out of trouble," he said with a kiss to the top of my head.

"I was going to say the same thing about you."

Redvers laughed.

"That's not precisely how it happened," Dion said from behind us. I paused on the path, holding up our little train, and Redvers urged me forward with a grumble.

"We can discuss that once we're someplace warm," he said.

We headed to the pub in the lobby of the St. Columba, where Yeats and I could huddle in front of the fire. Redvers took up a post behind me, and Dion got Catriona settled into a chair before joining us. The inspector had requisitioned a room to use as a makeshift jail and was pulling guard duty until an officer could be summoned from Mull. The ferry operator had been rousted from his own fire in order to go across the sound to fetch someone. The inspector wasn't taking any chances transporting his two prisoners without a second officer, which I thought was smart, even with Nightingale's injury.

A blanket materialized for me, and I welcomed the additional warmth, although I declined the dram of scotch I was also offered. Yeats pounced on that, however.

"Are you sure, Miss Wunderly?" Yeats asked, sipping at his snifter. "It warms the insides."

I shook my head. "Quite sure." The wind and the scotch were the two things I would never get accustomed to in this country, beautiful though it was.

Yeats shrugged, and I turned to Dion. She was standing near the fire, leaning against the stone. "What did you mean earlier, Dion?" I asked.

Dion cocked an amused eyebrow at Redvers. "He was looking for you; that much is true. But I'm the one who summoned the inspector and told them both where to find you."

Redvers looked annoyed, but he didn't dispute her claim.

"And how did you know where we were? Or that you needed the police?" I suspected I could guess the reason Redvers was so disgruntled about Dion's contributions.

"I was visiting the astral plane, attempting to contact Netta, and I could sense a disturbance. I knew that you were in danger and that I needed to bring help to the abbey."

Redvers was fully frowning now, but still saying nothing. Of course, he didn't have to—I already knew what he was thinking. I glanced at Yeats, who merely looked thoughtful.

I wasn't entirely certain what to say to this. I didn't think the astral plane was real or that Dion could receive messages there from her dead friend. But I was coming to realize that I did believe in intuition, and perhaps some people just needed a different way to explain their own instincts.

"Well, I'm glad you found the inspector and found us."

"Even though you were doing fine without us," Redvers said, the humor back in his voice.

"Despite the fact that we were doing fine without you." I

shot my fiancé a wink before turning to Yeats. Another question had occurred to me. "How did you know where to find me?"

The poet shrugged. "I didn't. I simply couldn't sleep, and I saw a lantern headed for the abbey. I was curious, so I decided to follow."

"I'm grateful that you did," I said. I wasn't sure what would have happened if he hadn't shown up to help me delay the ceremony. I was still quite disconcerted that Nightingale and Mina had seemed determined to draw blood that night— my own—but I was doing my best to push it from my mind.

I frowned. "What about the scratches on Netta's body?" I looked around the room, but no one had an answer for those. Dion gave me a meaningful look—I knew exactly who she believed had caused them, since she'd had similar marks after Mina's "attack." It looked like there were some things I wasn't going to get solid answers for, and this was one of them. I would have to figure out how I felt about that later on; in the meantime, I moved on to more tangible questions.

"I still don't understand what significance Netta's talisman had," I said. "Why did Catriona steal it and later bury it?"

"I didn't steal it," Catriona said. "Mina did."

We all turned in surprise to Catriona, who appeared to be lucid once again, although she was rubbing her temples. "How did I get here?" she asked, clearly bewildered.

Dion gently explained the evening's events, while Catriona's eyes filled with tears. "I would never have done any of that if I'd known what I was doing. I don't remember anything."

My eyes narrowed slightly. "Then why did you tell me you were sorry back at the cottage?" Was it possible she was putting this on?

But her eyes were clear and guileless. "I was telling you that I was sorry that you'd come all that way because Mina was going to help me." Here Catriona frowned. "She said she was glad that I reunited with my mum, and she would help me gather my things. But then Mina heard you at the door and told me not to tell you that she was there."

That explained why she'd looked so furtive when I'd come upstairs. "And then what happened?" I asked.

She shook her head, then moved her fingers back to her temples. "I don't remember anything after that."

Mina had to be a powerful hypnotist indeed. I wasn't entirely certain how she and Robert did it, but whatever their method, it was effective. And obviously well practiced.

My mind went back to the talisman. "Why did you bury it if Mina was the one who stole it?"

"She was my teacher, my mentor. I found it one day in her things, and I knew that it was bad that she had it. It meant that Netta didn't have any protection and was open to attack."

Redvers rolled his eyes here, but I encouraged Catriona to continue.

She shrugged, obviously at the end of her story. "So I buried it. To protect her."

I studied the young woman, unsure how culpable she was in any of what had happened. Clearly, she had been under someone else's influence in more ways than one for the entirety of this case. I simply couldn't say how much blame she should take for anything. Hiding the talisman didn't look good for her, since Catriona must have suspected that Mina had had something to do with Netta's death, and instead of saying something, she buried the evidence, pointing the finger at herself instead.

I sighed. At the end of the day, I wasn't the arbiter of right and wrong nor of anyone's guilt. I would leave that to the inspector.

CHAPTER FORTY-TWO

Michael McCrary was released from the jail on Mull the following morning, and it was a joyful reunion between himself and his wife and a tearful one with his daughter. "I'm sorry I turned you out, lass. It was my own pride, and I hope you can forgive me." She nodded, and the three embraced while I slipped out of the cottage.

I didn't think that Michael was coming around on the occult or his daughter's odd beliefs, but it was a start. I knew Fiona was smart enough to continue to keep her own beliefs—and cards—well hidden.

I'd already settled up with Fiona, who had insisted on my not paying a pound in exchange for bringing her daughter home and keeping her out of trouble. I hadn't argued, but I suspected Michael McCrary was going to have other thoughts about that as well.

Suitcase in hand, I set off for the St. Columba, where I was supposed to meet Redvers. I was relieved that I wouldn't have to make the trek across the island again, even though I did appreciate the rugged beauty of the place. But I'd had enough of the wind and the cold to last me for quite some time, so I was happy to let Redvers make that last trek by himself.

I waited for only a few moments in the lobby before Redvers arrived, and I stood to greet him. He looked me up and down, and I could see the approval in his eyes, which frankly made me blush. I was only wearing a knit sweater with a plaid skirt—appropriate for the location, I thought. The wool tights and practical shoes were entirely necessary for the weather, but Redvers didn't seem to think they were unflattering. Quite the opposite, from the look in his eyes.

He took my hand and led me to the front desk, taking my bag and passing it over to the clerk. "Can you have this put in our room?" he asked.

The young man nodded, tucking the bag out of sight.

I could feel my brows pulling into a furrow. "I thought we were leaving today? Why do we have a room?"

"I think we'll be able to stand just one more night." Redvers pulled me toward the exit, and I resisted.

"I do not need to be outside anymore." It was true. The previous night, it had taken hours before I'd felt completely warm again.

"Trust me," he said. "It will be worth your while."

With a sigh, I let my fiancé lead me back out into the cold, after helping me back on with my wool coat. At least today was a rare sunny day, and I briefly lifted my face up into the sun. "Where are you taking me that is so mysterious?"

"Remember when you said that we should set a date?"

"You do realize that I hate it when you do that, don't you? You're doing it on purpose now," I said.

"Doing what?" His face was as innocent as he could make it.

I swatted his arm. "You know exactly what. Answering a question with a question—it's maddening."

We were approaching the little stone parish church, the sky behind it blue for once, a perfect background for the ancient high cross on the corner. I took a beat to appreciate the warmth of the sun on my face.

"Back to my previous question about a wedding date," Redvers said.

Now I was curious about what he was getting at. "Yes, I remember. And I'm happy to discuss one. Maybe sometime in October? When the leaves are changing?" Fall was my favorite time of year.

"Yes, October is lovely. But I also know that you don't want a big wedding."

I agreed vehemently. "No, I do not." My first wedding had been a grand affair and the marriage after it an absolute nightmare. I was determined to do everything differently this time around.

I'd been alternating my concentration between my footing on the uneven ground, the warm sun on my face, and my fiancé, so I hadn't taken notice of our destination. But now we stopped, and I realized that, instead of heading farther into the village, we had stopped in front of the tiny chapel. I blinked at it for a moment, then blinked up at Redvers.

"Are you suggesting what I think you are?"

For once, Redvers looked uncertain, and his dark eyes searched mine. "I am, but only if you're comfortable with it."

Our time apart had allowed me to think about a lot of things, chief among them that I hated being apart from this man. But he'd also given me space to come to my own decisions about children and keeping my own last name, both unusual choices, and both ones that he supported me in. I felt in my gut that he would always support my decisions, and I knew it was time to trust my own intuition again.

"Let's do it," I said firmly.

His eyes searched mine one last time. "You're sure?"

"I've never been more sure of anything." We took a step toward the chapel, and I glanced at him sidelong. "Besides, I assume you already arranged it with the minister."

Redvers looked a bit chagrined. "I like to be prepared."

I chuckled as I entered the chapel. Redvers had more than prepared; he'd decorated as well. Beautiful bouquets of early spring wildflowers, snowdrops and daffodils, decorated the ends of the wooden pews. Waiting at the front of the little chapel were the minister and W.B. Yeats, leaning against his cane.

Fiona was just on the other side of the doorway, holding another small bouquet of flowers.

"She agreed then, aye?" Fiona said, then gave me a wink.

"We needed witnesses," Redvers whispered to me.

"These are good choices," I whispered back.

Redvers and I looked at each other for a long moment, unsure what we should do next. "Should I go to the front? There's no one to walk you up the aisle." He sounded uncertain again, which I found endearing, especially in that moment.

"I always planned to walk myself this time," I said, which was true. "But I have a better idea. Let's go together."

Redvers' face broke into a smile bright enough to blind. I took his arm, and we walked up the aisle to the altar. Together.

The minister gathered up a long piece of velvet cord from the altar, and I looked at it in mild alarm. Redvers chuckled. "Handfasting. It's an ancient tradition, and no longer done. But I thought it might be a nice touch."

The minister looked to me, and I nodded, clasping Redvers' hand in my own as the minister bound our hands and forearms together. I agreed, it was a nice touch. We were being bound together in more ways than one, and I knew that this time it was going to be fine. Better than fine—it would be grand.

Because we were in it together.

With our hands clasped, we recited the words that legally bound us as well, Yeats and Fiona McCrary standing quietly behind us as witnesses. When we got to the part where Redvers was instructed to kiss the bride, he did so with great enthusiasm, and I was glad there were only three other people there to witness it.

I wiped my eyes as we all signed the marriage license, and I watched the minister write our names in the island register. I liked that we would be part of the history here, recorded with the names of so many before us who had been born, married, and died here.

"We should celebrate," Yeats said as we quietly left the chapel.

Redvers and I exchanged glances. "I think we'll take it from here," Redvers said. Yeats clapped him on the back and shook my hand, then took his leave along with Fiona, who said she needed to get back to her baking.

Our hands were no longer bound together, but they were still clasped as we walked back to the hotel.

"Are you sorry that none of your family was here for it?" Redvers asked. I could tell that he was still slightly worried about the impromptu nature of it all.

I went up on my toes to kiss him soundly. "Not at all. Frankly, it's a relief." We started walking again, then I added, quietly, "I think it was perfect."

"So do I," Redvers said, squeezing my hand.

Then I smiled. "It's a good thing we got a room for to-night, but now I'm thinking."

He quirked one eyebrow. "Thinking what?"

"We're going to need a lot more than one night."

AUTHOR NOTES

Most of this story is made up, because this is fiction. There are quite a few parts that are based on actual people and groups, though.

W.B. Yeats was, in fact, a member of the Golden Dawn, which is why I included him in this story, but he had left the order a few years before this takes place. There was nothing to suggest that he ever came back for another ceremony or was ever on Iona—I just couldn't help but include him, since I found it fascinating that a Nobel Prize–winning poet and Irish senator was involved in this type of group at all. He did maintain his interest in all things occult until his death.

Dion Fortune was also a historical figure who was involved with the Golden Dawn. Dion really did claim that Mina Mathers had attacked her on the astral plane—and sent black cats to torment her—but she wasn't present on the island when Netta died. As far as I could tell, Netta was on the island alone; no other members of the order were with her. Dion did write under the name Violet Firth, which was actually her birth name, and people really were displeased that she was sharing information in her writings.

Netta's death was mysterious, and there is a lot of misinformation about what actually happened. I used some artistic license with the circumstances surrounding her death, obviously, but quite a bit of it is accurate to real events. It's true that they were never sure what Netta's cause of death actually was, although I think it was likely that the girl died of exposure after suffering some sort of mental break. She seemed mentally unwell in the days leading up to her death. It was true that Netta was wealthy, however, and her father was known to ask his daughter for money.

Robert Nightingale was very loosely based on the historical figure Alistair Crowley, who was a member of this order for a time. Very loosely, though. I didn't want to stir up that pot.

Mina Mathers is another historical figure. She and her husband did start the Order of the Golden Dawn, although, again, there was nothing to indicate she was involved with Netta's death or was anywhere near Iona when it happened.

Parts of the ceremonies in the novel were taken directly from manuals outlining real rituals that the Golden Dawn held. I used some of the language, but didn't use all of it— they got pretty wordy, so I picked and chose what I included, trying to make them interesting without dragging things on for too long. I also was inspired by actual members and events, but I took a lot of liberties with who they were and the disagreements between the factions.

ACKNOWLEDGMENTS

Huge thanks to John Scognamiglio, my editor extraordinaire, as well as to Larissa Ackerman and Jesse Cruz, my outstanding publicists. Thank you to Robin Cook, Lauren Jernigan, and Sarah Gibb. Further thanks to the rest of the Kensington team who work so hard to get books into your hands.

Thank you and big love to Ann Collette. I wouldn't be here without you. I'm so grateful for our continued friendship—You bring me joy.

Much love and thanks to Zoe Quinton King, my dearest of friends and editor. I'm so lucky to have you on my team in both my life and my career.

Big love and thanks to Jessie Lourey, Lori Rader-Day, Susie Calkins, and Shannon Baker, my midwest ride or die squad.

Special thanks to Catriona McPherson for making sure I didn't screw up her homeland too badly.

Immeasurable thanks for the friendship, love, and support to Tasha Alexander, Ed Aymar, Gretchen Beetner, Lou Berney, Mike Blanchard, Keith Brubacher, Kate Conrad, Hilary Davidson, Dan Distler, Steph Gayle, Daniel Goldin, Juliet Grames, Andrew Grant, Glen Erik Hamilton, Carrie Hennessy, Tim Hennessy, Chris Holm, Katrina Niidas Holm, Megan Kantara, Steph Kilen, Elizabeth Little, Jenny Lohr, Erin MacMillan, Joel MacMillan, Dan Malmon, Kate Malmon, Marjorie McCown, Mike McCrary, Catriona McPherson, Katie Meyer, Trevor Meyer, Lauren O'Brien, Roxanne Patruznick, Margret Petrie, Nick Petrie, Bryan Pryor, Andy

Rash, Jane Rheineck, Kyle Jo Schmidt, Dan Schwalbach, Marie Schwalbach, Johnny Shaw, Jay Shepherd, Becky Tesch, Tess Tyrrell, Bryan Van Meter, and Tim Ward.

Thank you to the amazing booksellers and librarians who've supported this book and especially to the folks who hosted me for a real-life tour. Special shout-outs to Daniel, Chris, and Rachel at Boswell Books; Barbara and Patrick at the Poisoned Pen; John and Kaeleigh at Murder by the Book; Devin at Once Upon a Crime; and Jane and Joanne at Mystery to Me.

Thank you and big love to my amazing family, Rachel and AJ Neubauer, Dorothy Neubauer, Sandra Olsen, Susan Catral, Sara Kierzek, Jeff and Annie Kierzek, Justin and Christine Kierzek, Josh Kierzek, Ignacio Catral, Sam and Ariana Catral, Mandi Neumann, Andie, and Alex and Angel Neumann.

Love and thanks to John and Gayle McIntyre.

Special thanks and love to my dear friend Gunther Neumann, who is truly a rock.

So much love, gratitude, and thanks to Mike Blanchard for being the amazing person that he is. To the bones, babe.

And all the love and thanks to Beth McIntyre. Always.